A SMALL-TOWN WESTERN FAKE-DATING ROMANCE

Greta Rose West

COPYRIGHT

PRESS

ALSO BY GRETA ROSE WEST

Wild Heart: Welcome to Wisper

Subscribe to the newsletter for this short introduction into the Cade Ranch world and for extra goodies and scenes. Sign up at gretarosewest.com.

THE CADE RANCH SERIES IN ORDER

BURNED

BROKEN

BUSTED

BRAVED

BLINDED

THE WISPER DREAMS SERIES IN ORDER

RIVERS BETWEEN US

STORMS INSIDE US

MOUNTAINS DIVIDE US

LIGHT BETRAYS US

MIDNIGHT SURROUNDS US

ROADS BEHIND US

WYOMING LOVE EBOOK BOXSETS

LOVE AT CADE RANCH (Cade Ranch Books 1 - 3)

CADE RANCH IN LOVE (Cade Ranch Books 4 & 5)

LOVE IN WISPER, WYOMING (Wisper Dreams Books 1 - 3)

ACKNOWLEDGMENTS

Saying thank you doesn't quite cut it, but I'm gonna try to tell all the people who supported, helped, and guided me during the writing of this book… THANK YOU!

Sean, Wyatt, Hannah and Westie: I love you. Thanks for bringing me to the mountains and thanks for giving me a grandkid. I didn't know I wanted one so bad. And Hannah, Crumbl is alllll on you. Don't you even try to pin it on me.

Peter Senftleben: Ten books and three short stories. Here's to another 50! Thanks for saying you're proud of me. It means the world.

MJ, Laura, Julie, M, Geri, and Barbara, you're the best BETA readers, and I love you for your uninhibited (and sometimes unhinged) opinions and margin comments. This book is so much better for them. When I can make MJ jump on her bed, it's a good day.

Tracy, you're on my mind every day. I love you.

Miss Jeanie, all the credit goes to you because you begged me to write an older FMC. Well, here you go. I hope I did ya proud.

To Shelby the painter, who didn't know he'd inspired a character's name when I met him and his romance-reading wife, Janice, in Milwaukee. Thanks! See y'all in Deadwood!

ARC readers, you complete me. Thanks once again for hyping my books and for loving Rye Graves before you even got to know him. Seriously, I appreciate every post and story share and every single review.

Naming the musicians who inspired me in my book acknowledgements is kind of a tradition now, so I'll start with Gregory Alan Isakov, your music will have my heart until my dying day. Seriously, if my family doesn't play a GAI montage at my funeral, I'm coming back to haunt their punk asses. Bon Iver, Shane Smith & the Saints, Chris Stapleton, Jonah Kagen, Postie, Nathaniel Rateliff & The Night Sweats, Noah Kahan, Kelsea Ballerini, The Head And The Heart, and the good ol' Queen of Country, miss Dolly Parton. And Zach Bryan, man, I know you'll never read this but "November Air" FUELED me while I wrote this story. You're an amazing storyteller, and you make it easy for me to imagine sweeping country landscapes and real people who live at the edges of town.

Thank you.

To my fellow women of a certain age:
Ride the 'stache, baby. You know you want to.

TRIGGER WARNING

The heroine in this book is a cancer Survivor. Three years prior to the story, she had her uterus removed due to stage one uterine cancer. The illness and procedure are mentioned briefly, but not in detail. Aubrey is also a military widow, so if these issues trigger you, please read with caution. There is a happy ever after. A big one! But if getting there might effect your mental health, you can email me directly or DM me on Instagram for more details before you read. Or just skip this one.

Email: greta@gretarosewest.com
IG: @gretarosewest

xoxo

Greta

PROLOGUE
RYE

Eight Months Ago

AUBREY GEORGE WAS an angel on Earth, destined to walk among us mere mortals, disguised as an ordinary, middle-aged woman.

She was anything but ordinary.

It was always how I'd seen her, even when I was a kid, although, she'd gone by Aubrey Abbott then. Maybe it was because she was sweet to me, but back then, she was the beautiful angel in love with my brother's best friend.

And then she married him. She became Aubrey George, had Tommy George's kids, and everybody grew up.

I grew up, and since probably the age of fifteen, when I learned what it meant to *really* want someone, I'd looked for ways to thank her for her kindnesses to me when I was small and overlooked by a family too busy to notice me, but it had always been clear that she was unavailable. First because I was too young and she was married, and then because she wasn't anymore and that fact seemed to have defeated her.

But she wasn't off limits now.

Tommy had been gone almost ten years, lost tragically in a military training exercise gone wrong overseas, and I'd watched from the background, catching heartbreaking glimpses of her when I came to town, as she and her boys navigated that loss. But she had come through it gracefully and strong, like the resolute battler I'd always known she was.

Her boys… not so much. Benji and Micah George were known in my neck of the woods as infamous troublemakers. Nothing too serious. Just your normal teenage antics, but they hadn't been smart about it and got caught way too often, drinking when they were underage, pranking their classmates, or starting forest fires. They'd probably forgotten, but I'd found them both puking behind a bar over in Pinedale when they were seventeen. They were shitfaced, couldn't drive, and wanted their mommy. I drove them home, dropped them off a block away, and then sat in my truck when they fell in a pile at their front door and Aubrey came running out of the house to take care of them.

Now, standing across the street from Your Local Bookie, Aubrey's small bookstore in downtown Wisper, Wyoming, I watched her through her big front window as she chatted with a customer.

I'd planned to talk to her, just to check in, see how she was. Actually, what I wanted to do was ask her out. Our short conversations now and again over the years had barely been enough to sustain me, but I'd always felt like an intruder in her life. Just a kid from her younger years. An acquaintance.

But to me, she was a hell of a lot more than that. She had no way of knowing she was the end goal for me. When I made a big decision, I thought about what she'd think. When I went on a date or hooked up with a woman, Aubrey was there.

It had always been her face I saw.

It was stupid. I knew that, but I couldn't help it. The sound of her warm voice and her goodness had been etched onto my heart with a permanent marker at a young age when I fell off my horse and she was there to pick me up. She'd smiled at me and swiped the dirt from my face with a soft brush of her fingers, and nothing I'd done since had made her golden ink fade.

I never fell off a horse again. It became my mission in this life to never look weak in front of Aubrey. Not that she would have noticed if I did.

Her hair was all long, billowy waves, not blond exactly, but more a true strawberry blond. In the shade, the color looked ordinary but in the sun was like a Georgia peach, tinged with pink.

Those lustrous locks had been the stars of my dreams lately. My visits to Wisper had lessened over the years as I got older and work at my family's ranch got busier, and it had probably been a good thing so I could let this stupid obsession go.

But I couldn't.

And now that I was back in town to help my uncle at his Main Street store a block away from Aubrey's, my fascination bloomed back to life.

She seemed different now. Something had changed for her.

Her husband's last name had always been like a dark cloud around her that obscured the moon and snuffed out her light, but today as I watched her, I realized it had disappeared.

She was the bright, wild, happy woman I'd had stars in my eyes for half my life.

Across the street, she laughed at something her customer

said, tipped her head back, and her hair fell in loose waves down her back.

God, she was beautiful. And now I needed to know why she looked different, why she seemed lighter and happier.

I needed to know like I needed oxygen in my lungs. They seized in my chest when she collected herself and looked out her window.

Right at me.

She cocked her head, probably silently questioning why I was standing outside her world, looking in, and I held my breath.

I pressed my hand to my chest, trying to restart my heart. Maybe she could, 'cause when she looked at me, it felt like the muscle had short circuited.

Don't be a baby. Man up and go get your girl.

Aubrey's customer said her goodbyes and waved as she left Your Local Bookie, and I jogged across Main Street. I nodded to the woman leaving, took off my hat, and grabbed the door before it slapped shut.

"Hey there, Aubrey."

She heard my voice and spun to face me. "Ryder." She touched her hand to her stomach, below her breasts. "You scared me. I didn't hear you come in. How are you? How's your family?"

"Apologies, ma'am," I said with a smirk. "Family's fine. All's well. I'm here in town helpin' at my uncle's store. Devo Mescal's stuck workin' there this week and—"

"Yeah, I know all about it. She and your uncle can't seem to coexist, so some judge made them trade places."

"Right," I said. "Anyway, I thought while I'm here, maybe I could take you out for some caffeine."

She laughed, but when the expression on my face didn't budge, she pressed her lips together. She took in my appearance: my worn jeans, black T-shirt with my uncle's store's logo on the front, and my messy hat hair. "Uh, no, thank you."

Whoa. Really?

"Just like that? You ain't even gonna consider me?"

"Rye, I'm not goin' on a date with you. That's what you're askin', right? You're too young for me. Isn't there a pretty cowgirl or some young woman home from college you can take out?"

"Just how old do you think I am?"

She shrugged.

"I'm thirty-four, not twenty-four. I got no interest in college kids."

She scoffed and set her hands on her hips, but I didn't miss the way her eyes scanned Main Street. Was she scared of what people might say?

"Well, in a month, I'll be forty-seven. So you see, too old for you."

I shook my head. "You're wrong about that."

"Whether I'm right or wrong, I'm still sayin' no."

"Okay, that's fair. I respect your answer. But when I leave here, don't you go kickin' yourself in the ass." I looked at her hand still on her hip, trying to see behind it to her lush backside.

"Rye!"

"What? I can't appreciate a beautiful woman?"

She blushed, and her eyes dipped down to my jeans too. I knew what she was looking for. I had to resist the urge to turn so she could catch a gander.

I smiled. Actually, it was more a grin, because that little slip of her gaze was a sure sign that, even though she was telling me no, she'd be thinking about my ass long after I left. It wasn't the first time I'd caught her daydreaming about it.

She snapped her eyes to mine. "Why would I kick my own ass?"

"For lettin' me walk away, even though I know you like to watch me go."

Her mouth popped open and she gasped. "You got some nerve, kid."

You got no idea, woman.

"'Kid'?" I chuckled and set my hat back on my head, and Aubrey bit the inside of her cheek. Her pink lips pursed, and she narrowed her eyes. So at least she was *beginning* to consider me. "Seriously, don't beat yourself up too much."

"And *why* would I do that?"

I tipped my hat in her direction and winked. "'Cause I'm unforgettable."

When I turned to leave, I heard her breathy huff of indignation, but I didn't need eyes in the back of my head to know there was a twinkle in her eye now and that *both* her eyes were glued to the seat of my jeans.

Now, I just needed to let her stew in the idea of me and her awhile. I'd be back. No way would I give up on Aubrey. I'd waited a lifetime already; a few more months wouldn't deter me.

But first, I needed to have something to offer her. Problem was, I didn't have shit.

Squat, zilch, nada.

But that was about to change.

CHAPTER ONE

RYE

COULD you really claim you had a legacy if someone else owned the land, if it was their name on the deed, not yours? If all a man did was work for his daddy, could he even really say he had a job? Or was he just his dad's bitch?

And was he even a man? By most Wyoming standards, that would be a hard no. By my own standards, it was a big, fat *fucking* no.

"Dammit, Ryder," my dad complained. "The west fence is still down. Didn't you do *anything* yesterday?"

Focusing on the sunrise behind him, I thought: *Yeah. Dug holes for a mile of new fenceposts. Managed thousands of cattle. Thought about Aubrey George. Patched up the hole in the east barn wall where a raccoon ripped through it to make a nest. Fed and watered horses. Thought about Aubrey again. Jacked off to thoughts of Aubrey on my lunch break. Exercised the horses. Fed and watered yet again.*

"That goddamn fence is the most important task I gave you. Get to it, now."

"Yes, sir."

My old daddy didn't trust but a handful of people, which

meant many of the jobs that should've been done by ranch hands landed in my lap every day.

Dropping his head to stare at the clipboard he kept clutched close to his heart, he continued to peruse the paper proof of all the money he'd made on our latest cattle sale. They'd just been picked up to be transported to slaughter.

He mumbled, "Lazin' about all damn day when there's work to be done."

"'*Lazin'*? Old man, I work my ass off for you and this ranch, but—"

He speared me with a look, peering over the rims of his glasses. In the shade of his hat, they darkened like sunglasses.

He shook his head. "Don't, Ryder. Don't start. I don't need to hear about regenerative agriculture one more time. I've heard it all. You never shut up about it. Just get to work."

Presley pounded me hard on the back, his not-so-gentle way of telling me to move on. To shut my mouth and get to work. He knew when my dad's patience had worn thin. He'd worked for us long enough to know when to change the subject. It still made me laugh that his mama named him Elvis. I didn't think anybody even knew his last name was actually Decker.

The problem was, if I shut up about all my ideas for our ranch, there wouldn't be much left of it when, eventually, it became mine.

My two older brothers wanted nothing to do with the family business, which was probably smart on their parts. Sure, our cattle were fat, but the soil was dead. The only thing that grew in abundance on our land was misery and weeds, so the money my dad liked so much was spent feeding the cattle.

If he would just listen to what I had to say, we could change the direction of G&S Cattle. We could alter Graves & Sons' carbon footprint on the world, could lessen it by a goddamn mile, which would only make us more money. It might be hard work in the beginning, but didn't we work our asses off every day anyway?

"Give it up," Presley whispered.

He yanked his head toward the west fence my dad hadn't stopped grumbling about since yesterday morning even though there wasn't a cow anywhere near the breach.

Of course, before we could mount our horses and head out, my dad had to get in one last dig. "You don't fix that fence, genius, ain't gonna be no cows left for you to sustainably farm when I kick the bucket." As he turned to walk away, he added under his breath, "That's the only way you'll get your mitts on my ranch."

Fucker.

"Grady's in a fine mood today," Presley said when my dad was out of earshot. "What did you do? Or what *didn't* you do?"

"The fence. He pays no mind to all the other shit I got done yesterday," I said, turning to tighten my cinch. I patted my horse's shoulder and felt energy buzzing in the muscle. Blue was ready to ride.

"No, it's more than that." Presley stepped into his stirrup and pushed up into his saddle. His fifteen-year-old bay mare didn't bat an eye. She was too busy sniffing the dirt, searching for grass that didn't grow anymore by the barns. "He don't talk about dyin' unless you've really pissed him off."

"I tried talkin' to him again about changin' up the way we do shit here." I sighed, but as I mounted Blue, I winced and then admitted, "And I might've, sorta, contacted one of those farms I told you about up in Oregon. The owner called him yesterday to try to talk to him about regenerative farming and all its benefits. You shoulda seen his face. I thought his eyeballs were gonna pop out of his skull. But in my defense, that guy took it upon himself. I didn't ask him to call."

Presley laughed. "Oh, Rye. When you gonna learn? Your dad has no plans to change this ranch. You know that. Why won't you give it up?"

Blue stomped his hooves into the dirt. If the horse could talk, he'd say, "Let's fuckin' go!"

"The old man likes money, right?"

"Yeah," Presley agreed, "he sure does, but he makes plenty the way things are now."

"I'm tellin' you, Pres, if we made some changes, there's a whole world of customers out there who'd pay double what we charge now. Everything's changin'. People wanna feel good about what they eat. They wanna know their food ain't killin' the planet. *We* should want to know that. We should be able to look out at this land every mornin' and be proud that we're protectin' it and the animals and that we're doin' more good than harm."

I shrugged. "Ain't like it's hard. It's the way things used to be done, before crop yield and numbers became more important than the food we put in our mouths or the air we breathe. I mean, yeah, we'd need to hire more cowboys, and we'd work harder for a few years than we probably ever have, but then it'd pay off. He's just stubborn, and he don't wanna pay out the initial investment. He's bein' bullheaded."

"Yeah," Presley said, laughing, "and he's got his horns aimed right at your ass this mornin'. C'mon, let's get to that fence. No sense in makin' the man irate before the weekend. He'll stew the next couple days and just be a bigger asshole come Monday."

"Ain't that the truth," I agreed, and I clicked my tongue twice, nudging Blue with my boots into a trot.

My horse knew it was almost the weekend too. He

protested the slow pace with a kick of his hind legs and a bratty whinny, but then he switched into high gear, pushed into a run, and we raced west, with the Wyoming Range in front of us calling us forward and the rising sun at our backs.

AFTER WORK, I headed to my little house half a mile behind my parents'.

I needed a break from my dad's attitude. He'd been at it all day, and I could only take it so long.

It had been a couple weeks since I'd driven the fifty miles up to Wisper to visit my uncle and see my friends, so that was my plan for the next couple days. If I didn't get off this ranch and away from the disappointment I knew my parents had in me, I'd lose my shit.

The only thing I'd ever done wrong was being the last son born to a successful first-generation cattle rancher. Apparently, it was a sin I'd never escape. Everyone knew the high accolades and honors went to the firstborn.

I grabbed a shower, pulled on a fresh pair of skivvies and jeans, and as I grabbed my hat from the hook by my front door, someone knocked on it.

Having my own place was the key to being able to work alongside my dad every day. It wasn't much, just a small living room, an even smaller kitchen, a tiny bathroom with a standing shower, and my bedroom. No damn closet. But it was all mine. That I'd built it with my own two hands and Presley's and some of the summer cowboys' help made it even sweeter.

"Ryder?" my mama said through the door, though I knew she was itching to barge in. "You in there?"

We'd had to have several conversations about boundaries

and privacy when she walked in on me drinking beer and watching Rodeo championships on TV in my underwear, but another one couldn't hurt.

"Yes, ma'am. Comin'."

When I opened the door, she pushed right into my sacred space, holding a metal Thermos and a brown paper bag. She set them on the end table next to my couch, then straightened with her hands on her hips.

"Why do you antagonize your daddy? You know how he is."

"Antagonize *him*?" I said, trying not to show her just how much her lack of trust in me hurt.

She was as supportive of my ideas as my dad was. If either of them had a rational reason for dismissing what I'd proposed, I could understand. But they disagreed because it was *me* proposing a new idea. Grady and Calla Graves's baby boy couldn't possibly have an intelligent thought in his head. No way. His brothers, they were the geniuses of the family. Too bad they'd both ditched their family just as soon as they could have after they graduated from school.

I was the one who stuck around. It was me busting my ass on a daily basis, trying to keep the cash my dad liked so much flowing in on the regular, fixing shit when it broke, caring for the animals. But in my parents' eyes, I was just the muscle. Another employee.

I could've gone off to school like my brothers. The opportunity had been there, but I chose not to. Ranching was my life. I learned it from my dad, lived it with him. I didn't need a college degree or some professor in a classroom to tell me how to know if an animal was sick or the land was. That shit came naturally to me. It always had. Just 'cause my idea was a little progressive—it wasn't like I was some environmentalist douche going around spouting off all the ways the world should work but never giving real-life solutions.

Now, the business stuff, that was another matter entirely. But I'd been reading up on it.

It seemed funny to me that my parents looked down their noses at my brothers for leaving, but they looked down on me 'cause I hadn't.

How did that make a lick of fucking sense?

If I didn't stand to inherit the whole outfit, minus the shares I'd give my brothers unless my dad really had written me out of his will, I probably would've escaped this place too. But was running Graves & Sons enough anymore? My sanity and autonomy kept telling me no.

My loyal heart said otherwise.

"Yes, antagonize," Mama said. She sighed and dropped her hands, then lifted one to press a wrinkle out of my shirt. "Oh, honey, you know he's stuck in his ways. But it might go a long way to gettin' him to listen to you if you grew up a little."

"'Grew up'?"

Her eyes rose to meet mine, and the smile and pity on her face made me want to scream.

"Your daddy wants to know you're headed in the right direction before he gives you more responsibility. A woman in your life would be a good start."

Here we go again.

"Mama, we've been through this," I said, barely disguising the frustration in my voice. "How the hell would havin' a girlfriend make a difference to Dad? Besides, you won't like any woman I bring home. You never have. The last one was too immature. You didn't like the clothes she wore or the way she did her hair, and you insinuated she wouldn't be a good mother to our nonexistent children when she accidentally stepped on the barn cat's tail."

Never mind that she wasn't wrong. And never mind the fact that I'd told my mama over and over I didn't want kids. Never had. My passion was agriculture, and if I was lucky enough to find the woman to do me in, I wanted to spend the rest of my days working my land and loving her, making her laugh long into the night.

What was so wrong with that? It sounded like a good life to me.

Mama didn't respond. She rolled her eyes and bent to grab the stuff she'd just set down.

"Here." She pressed the Thermos to my chest, and I took it from her hands and took the bag she held out. "I know you're leavin' again, so take some sandwiches for the road. It's beyond me why you like spendin' time with your uncle Red, but he's family, so I s'pose it's fine. Just don't stay gone too long. You know how mad that'll make your daddy."

She wasn't wrong about that either. Thank the good Lord for Presley. If he hadn't been here the last twenty years to keep the place running and bear the weight of my dad's ire when I took one foot off the ranch, I'd be miserable. Somebody would've wrapped me in a straitjacket by now. Besides, Presley was a better cowboy than I'd ever be and he loved the overtime.

"Yes, ma'am," I said, and I leaned down to kiss her cheek.

She smiled up at me. "Good boy."

It was habit to hold in the groan threatening to rip from my mouth. Boy?

I'm almost thirty-five fuckin' years old!

CHAPTER TWO

AUBREY

THE MIRROR HANGING on the wall in my storeroom was a lying bitch.

I should've taken it down years ago, or covered the damn thing, like people do with furniture when they leave their East Coast mansions after the summer season, but I had this maddening need to check my face every ten minutes.

Was I really that old? Inside, I felt twenty-six. Outside, I felt like Blanche from the *Golden Girls*, just with longer hair and less sex.

Fuck. Is that a chin hair?

First hot flashes and now whiskers? And why did they have to be so dark! The rest of my hair was graying; why couldn't my whiskers get lighter too?

Just great. Add onto that a failing business and the fact that I hadn't had a good orgasm in more years than I dared admit, even to myself—oh, and don't forget my twenty-three-year-old twins who wouldn't know the meaning of the word responsibility if it slapped them across their faces—and you could say life wasn't going exactly as planned.

Since they'd moved out of the house and gone off to

school at Montana State in Bozeman, where they subsequently failed and quit, Micah and Benji called or texted for money about once every two weeks. Pizza delivery didn't afford them much past rent and their phone bill. Benji was usually the sacrificial lamb because Micah was too much of a mama's boy, but the result was the same. I paid their damn bills, and then I had to live off of generic microwaveable oatmeal for the rest of the month.

The death benefits from Tommy's service in the military hadn't gone as far as one might think. At least the boys' college and the house was paid off. Maybe I should've been thinking about selling it. The twins and I could've certainly used the money, but I'd been impatiently waiting for them to get their shit in gear. If they ever grew up and took life seriously, maybe I wouldn't feel utter panic at the thought of handing them a big wad of cash that they'd probably use to invest in beer and video games.

If wishes were fishes. If wishes were fishes, I could eat something other than oatmeal for a change.

My small, woman-owned business was just *booming* in little Wisper, Wyoming.

Yeah, right.

Most of the other businesses in town were having way better luck, but in the last week, I'd sold three books. Three! And not even hardbacks. I really needed to dip my toe in that whole foil-embossed/sprayed-edges trend. But jeez. They were so expensive! I'd have to front the cost to order them, but if they didn't sell, I'd take another loss. Sure, there were some customers I might be able to entice into buying them, but not that many, and probably mostly the ladies from book club at the library. Then what the hell would I do with the rest?

There were a few bookstores in the city. Jackson offered a

lot more to draw tourists than Wisper did. I needed to figure out how to get those customers to our little town, but I had no idea how to tie my store or its location to tourism. Why would a customer drive forty minutes to my store, just to see the same books they could find closer to their hotel?

An online shop might be the way to go. Maybe it could be popular on social media if I could figure out how to bully a blogger or two to share the store and hype it up. We could get eyes on Your Local Bookie outside of Wisper. But then I'd have to master social media and learn how to make a website. Who has time for that crap? And there was no way I could afford to hire someone.

It all came down to taxes. I hadn't paid mine in two years. It was only a matter of time until the IRS came knocking on my door. I had four weeks to come up with nearly ten-thousand dollars, and if I didn't, well then, I'd be screwed, and not in the good way. The five grand I'd miraculously managed to stash away in a savings account would only pay it down by half.

After giving up trying to untangle my frizzy mop of hair in the mirror, I plucked the midnight-black whisker using the tweezers I'd never again leave home without and heard voices outside my shop.

When I peeked around the corner and looked out the front window, past the display of mystery classics that hadn't sold for shit, I saw Devo Mescal, my friend Abey's fiancée, and Rye Graves walking past the store on Main Street.

Sneaking closer, I was hoping for a better look at Rye in his jeans, just as long as no one *noticed* me looking. Especially not Rye. I was still blushing from the time he asked me out, eight months ago!

But good God that ass.

I tried to duck and hide behind a shelving unit stacked full of cookbooks, but when he halted on the sidewalk out front, I stopped dead in my tracks in the middle of the store and stood up straight, completely conspicuous and frozen like Frosty.

Rye looked in at me.

I looked out at him.

My heart rate doubled, my palms began to sweat, and when he tipped his tan cowboy hat at me and flashed me a stupidly sexy grin, a hot flash hotter than the infernos of Hell took over my entire body.

They kept walking, and I was left hyperventilating.

Jesus. That man.

But compared to me, Rye was just a boy. Tommy's best friend's little brother. He may've been in his mid-thirties, but I was… twenty-nine. If anyone asked, that was my answer. My auntie always said to "leave them guessin'." And no way would I admit to anyone I had reached well into my forties.

Aw damn. Who was I kidding? Three years away from fifty was a far cry from twenty-nine.

Somebody should probably come and put me out to pasture, which was exactly what would happen if Ryder Graves got his way.

All his nods and tips of his hat couldn't make me forget about my chin hairs, the ever-expanding menopausal spare tire beginning to encircle my midsection, or the fact that my neck was getting shorter and my jowls longer by the hour. I kept getting a pain in my big toe and was convinced I'd inherited arthritis from my dad and it had set in, and soon the whole house of cards would collapse around me. I wouldn't be able to walk anymore and my boys would have to put me in an old folks home I couldn't afford.

And those tight jeans Rye wore—Every. Goddamn. Day? Yeah, they couldn't make me orgasm any more than I could do it myself. I hadn't had one in, *oh, let me think…* five years.

Give or take five. Okay, so that was a bit of an exaggeration. I'd had what one would technically call an "orgasm," when I spent the hour it took for me to work myself up to it, but I wouldn't call them *orgasms.* Not the mind-bending, "exploding all over some guy's cock" kind of orgasm. The kind of orgasm that made a woman scream and mewl and beg.

Who didn't want one of those? Or ten.

After their father died overseas and I'd been left alone to raise two thirteen-year-old boys, it felt weird having "sexy me time" with them in the house, so it wasn't like toys had been an option. Those sneaky little shits went through everything. Nothing was sacred to them, certainly not dildos, and then when Benji and Micah moved out, I'd gotten out of the habit.

Oh sure, there'd been a few men since then, but one of them was ten years older than me and couldn't get it up, which caused all kinds of self-doubt. It lingered still so that every time I looked in the mirror, all I saw was an unattractive oaf with a graying frizz ball on the top of her head. Actually, that wasn't entirely true. I did have good hair, even with the grays peeking through. It was one thing peri- and now full-on-menopause hadn't stolen from me. Yet.

The second guy was younger than me, and he came so fast, he probably could've medaled in the Olympics, which made me think he hadn't really wanted to have sex with me. He'd probably been thinking of some young woman he'd met at a concert festival, but I was there and would do for five minutes. And the last guy had just gotten divorced when we went out, and he cried through the entire sexual debacle.

So, yeah, you might say I'd gotten over the whole thing. And it was fine. I was fine on my own. Sexless. Husbandless. And about to be businessless and possibly homeless.

At least I had my books. And when the IRS came to take my store and my house away, I could use them to build my funeral pyre.

Ugh, Aubrey. Get out of your head!

Fine. Grabbing my cell from the checkout counter behind me, I tapped on the screen till I saw my best friend's face, then clicked Call.

"Aubs? Everything okay?" my soul sister, Roxanne, asked. Thank God she'd taken the open deputy job with our local sheriff's department because, since she'd shown up in town eight months ago, it felt like we'd never been apart. Our standing Thursday lunch dates and the romance book club we'd both joined were the only things getting me through some weeks. "I thought you were meetin' me at the library?"

"You're not on duty today, right?"

"No, I'm off. Dan and Frank have the station covered."

"Good. Screw book club. Come pick my ass up. Let's go eat fries and get sauced at Manny's Bar."

"What about the store? You don't usually close for lunch this early."

I groaned into my phone. "Who gives a crap? I haven't sold a book in three days. I'll just put up the 'Pop a squat, I'll be right back' sign. No one will care."

"Aubrey—"

"Please, Roxi," I whined. "I need a drink."

"Okay, bestie. Be right there."

"WHAT THE HELL IS THAT?" I asked, pointing to the two six-packs of hard lemonade sitting on the front seat of Roxi's truck when she picked me up half an hour later.

She lifted one and reached behind her to set it on the

back seat. "You said you needed a drink, but, girl, it ain't even noon. So I compromised. You get your drink, but we're *goin'* to book club. If you're havin' a bad day, you need the whole group. Not just me. We've all got your back."

Grabbing the second six-pack, I plonked my butt in the seat and set it in my lap. "Fine."

As I clicked my seatbelt into place, Roxi hit the gas. "What's got your nipples in a twist today? The twins gettin' in trouble again?"

"No. Well, probably, but if they are, I don't wanna know about it."

"So what then?" Roxi flipped her newly highlighted waves over her shoulder and wiped a finger under her lined lip.

She was on the hunt for a man, so she never left her house without a full face of makeup and her hair teased and twisted into soft, beachy waves. Too bad there wasn't a beach in sight or an eligible guy over the age of thirty for fifty miles in any direction. Wisper, Wyoming was the small-town equivalent of a cellular dead zone—*nobody* got a signal—but at least with Roxi around, I didn't have to endure my forties and fast-approaching fifties alone.

"It's nothin'. I'm just… God! I'm sick of myself. I'm sick of my life, and I'm sick of complainin' about it."

"So, do somethin' different. Take a chance." She peeked over at me. "I saw Rye Graves this mornin'."

Rubbing at a dirty spot on my jeans, I licked my thumb and tried to scrub it out. "Oh, yeah?" Fuck, was that oatmeal? It was dried and crusty and looked like baby puke.

She scoffed. "I know you saw him too. I was catchin' up with Abey at the station before you called. We saw him and Devo go for coffee at the café, and then they walked right by your shop on their way back. He came to town to see his uncle again. That's why you called me, right?"

"What? Why are you and the sheriff spyin' on Rye Graves? And no, that's *not* why I called."

The knowing smirk on her face made me want to stick out my tongue at her. "Sure about that? Listen, we're officers of the law. We have to keep ourselves apprised on the people of Wisper. You can't be mad at us about that."

"Sure I can," I said under my breath. "My bad mood has nothin' to do with that *kid*, who by the way, doesn't live in Wisper, so I dunno what you're apprisin' yourselves of. But it doesn't matter. I don't give Rye freakin' Graves a second thought."

Roxi rolled her eyes. I hadn't fooled her, and even I could hear how testy I sounded. *The lady doth protest too much, methinks.*

"Kid? He's in his thirties. And maybe not him, but I bet his ass in those jeans gets lots of your thoughts."

"No, it doesn't," I argued. "And he's a hell of a lot younger than me, so he's a kid. He's Tommy's best friend's little brother. I'll always see him as a kid."

"Yeah, well that *kid* has a hard-on the size of Wyoming for you, and you know it. I'm not tryin' to be a bitch, but Tommy's gone. It's been a long time, Aubs. And Rye's brother may've been Tommy's friend, but he doesn't even live around here. Who cares?" She shook her head, and her hair tumbled over her shoulder again. She tucked it behind her ear. "I'm bustin' my ass here, lookin' for any man I can find with a job and a half-decent personality, and you've got the perfect specimen breathin' down your neck. I don't get it."

When she parked in front of the library, she shut off the truck. "Seriously, why won't you give him a chance?"

Because! Because he's a baby compared to me. And because people would talk. I've had enough gossip in my life. I was the focus of the town gossip before Tommy died because I was a doormat to him, and after, everybody talked because I didn't grieve him the way people thought I should. And the twins never help the situation with all the trouble they get into.

And because I'm scared.

I'm terrified to let someone into my life who sees me as a woman. Not a mom. Not a widow. Not an old woman.

Just a woman.

Because then maybe they'd see that I'm not. If you don't have a uterus, if your body quits doing all the things that made you a woman in the first place, are you one, really?

And besides, my boys would probably sacrifice me at their father's alter if I dated some young cowboy. They'd never be okay with it.

"Dammit, Roxi, because… because technically, he hasn't said a word to me in months, and I— You know what? Because I said so. That's why."

Roxi laughed. "You are such a mom." But then she speared me with a look so full of disapproval, I felt it in my Keds. "And we are *not* done with this conversation."

CHAPTER THREE

RYE

"RYDER, WHAT'S GOIN' on with you?" my uncle Red asked. "You've been here two days. I know my little brother has his hands full this spring at the ranch, so I can't imagine he's happy you're here."

He stared me down as I sat on the stool behind his checkout counter in his outdoor adventure store, The Red Wild Outdoors, in the middle of downtown Wisper.

As soon as I'd been old enough to drive, working weekends at my uncle's store was my escape from the ranch, and now, being surrounded by hunting rifles and bear-proof food storage felt like home.

I loved my job. Even as a kid, Graves & Sons Ranch provided new and exciting things for me to learn on a daily basis, but the older I got and the more capable, the more my dad made me feel like his employee and not his son.

My parents never really understood why I liked being around Red, but my uncle, even though he could be gruff, always looked out for me. He listened when I talked, and I was betting having me around sometimes eased the hole in his heart he'd caused when he pushed his son out of his life.

He regretted it deeply. I'd always known that, and I was glad he'd finally begun trying to make amends to my cousin, though it didn't seem like those amends were getting him anywhere.

"Don't get me wrong," he said. "I love havin' you at my house, and I'll never turn down your help here at the store, but aren't you needed elsewhere?"

Red's guest room was an absolute treat because it wasn't a guest room at all but an extra place to store unwanted stock and was the size of a broom closet. The man never got rid of anything. I barely fit in there, and the "bed" was an old couch that smelled like mildew, which I *definitely* didn't fit on. My feet hung over the arm every night.

"Presley has it handled, and as long as the work's gettin' done, my dad don't care where I'm at."

"I doubt that."

Flipping through an old *Field & Stream* magazine next to the cash register, I muttered, "Uncle Red, you can doubt it till the cows come home, but don't hold your breath, and maybe grab a snack so you don't starve while you wait."

"Well, I am hungry." Red turned to his shop manager. "Oscar, hold down the fort while we hit the diner?"

"'Course," Oscar said as he rearranged a reusable water bottle display.

I still felt a little proud of the changes I'd helped Red make to his store last year. My friend Devo kind of forced him into his new personality, but "nice guy and friendly small-town business owner" suited him, as opposed to the curmudgeon he used to be. Devo's mama had a little something to do with it too. Red and Liluye were still in the honeymoon phase of their love story, and she'd promised to overhaul Red's guest room for when I came to stay, but they hadn't gotten around to it yet.

"Can I bring you anything back?" Red asked Oscar.

"Sure. A BLT, please, but ask José for turkey bacon."

I shuddered. *Turkey is not bacon! Why the hell am I busting my ass farming cows if everyone wants to replace real meat with tasteless substitutes? Turkey bacon, Impossible beef, which is impossibly* not *beef, and fucking Tofurky? What's next, vegetarian brisket? Shit, somebody probably already thought of that. But I bet if the beef was responsibly farmed, more people would eat it again.*

"You got it, kid," Red said with a smile.

"Thanks."

"C'mon, Rye. Let's get our feed bags on."

Uncle Red opened both front doors wide and left them open since the day was sunny and warm. Letting the magazine flop down onto the counter, I followed on his heels, sulking.

He was right. I couldn't hide out in Wisper much longer. But when I was here, I felt hopeful. I watched as so many people lived their dreams in this town. They took chances. They fell in love. They lived good lives. Wisper's residents might not have been the richest or the most successful, but they seemed happy.

The community center was booming. The new bakery at the far end of Main Street was killing it with the best French pastries I'd ever tasted. Even my friend Bax was starting up a new venture on his sheep farm that he'd recently decided to turn into a rustic-rental-cabin getaway. So many people seemed to thrive in the small, mountain-town setting.

And that right there was the real reason I came to Wisper so often.

Aubrey George.

Except her bookshop didn't seem to be thriving like all the rest.

I knew because every time I walked or drove by, I looked in the windows. And every single time, I saw Aubrey looking defeated and alone. Not a customer in sight.

The few times I'd gone in to see her after I asked her out and she shot me down, I'd asked her to order some books about modern agriculture that the local librarian had offered to procure for me so I could check them out, but if I bought them from Aubrey, I supported her business, *and* I got to see her twice—once when I put in the order and then when I picked up the books. She knew what I was doing, knew I was making excuses to visit her store, but she kept things professional. I had begun to think that maybe my goal of getting her to say yes to a date with me was hopeless.

But I'd known Aubrey since I was ten years old, so I also knew she was stubborn, and if Your Local Bookie was struggling, she wouldn't ask anyone for help.

Which gave me an idea.

What if the help was offered freely? And from someone she wouldn't have to worry about paying back or that it might offend her pride. Plus, it would get me alone with her.

Oh the things I wanted to do to her alone in the dark.

***

"SERIOUSLY, KID," Uncle Red pressed when we grabbed a booth at José's Diner and the server had brought our waters. "What's goin' on with you? I've never seen you this down."

The place was packed for lunch, but we'd nabbed the last open booth before a loud group of tourists crowded into the diner and stood watching us while they waited. Setting my hat on the bench next to me, I dragged a hand through my hair, listening to the happy chatter from the other diners and the clinking of their silverware against their plates.

"Dad and I just don't agree a lot these days. And..." Sighing heavily, I said, "And I guess, lately I've been thinkin' about the future."

"What about it?"

"I dunno. Maybe I'm on the wrong path."

Red stretched his arm over the back of the booth bench. "I thought you loved workin' the ranch. You'd mastered your horse and could rassle cows to the ground by the time you were twelve. You got stars in your eyes before the cattle drives every year."

"I love it," I admitted, "that freedom I feel out on the range, and the knowledge that what I'm doin' helps people. Feeds people. Doesn't get much better than that. But I got ideas, Red, and it just so happens that my ideas piss Dad off.

"I don't get him. Junior and Shelby are off livin' their lives. They want nothin' to do with the ranch. I'm the one who's been here the whole time. I'm the one gettin' up before the crack of dawn to do the old man's biddin'. I do the work without complaint every day. So why won't he listen to me? I know that land better than anyone. Maybe even him."

"Ryder, your dad has always been set in his ways, but I know he loves and values you. Have you ever thought that maybe he's just scared to try somethin' new? We Graves men grow more stubborn the older we get. I got lucky and had my incompetencies pointed out to me, and then I made changes in my life, but not everyone is so lucky to have friends like I do."

Red sighed, and a sad, faraway look settled on his face. "I tell you what, though, if your cousin would return my phone calls, I'd listen to anything he has to say. So you're frustrated with your dad, but I know he loves you, and I know he appreciates you."

It had been something like twenty years since Red and my

cousin RJ had spoken. Red had tried to reach out many times recently, but maybe the damage had been done and RJ would never call his dad back. I wished he would, though. He'd be surprised at what he'd find if he did.

Shaking my head, I fiddled with the bundle of silverware wrapped in a napkin on the table in front of me. "I wish I believed that."

"What about your mama? What's she say?"

"She says nothin'. Ever. At least not anything positive to Dad about me. And to me, she says she wants me settled down. She wants more grandbabies. She can't understand why I 'can't keep a woman.'"

"Yeah, what's up with that?"

I laughed at my uncle talking like a college kid. "Really, Red? 'What's up with that?'"

"Well, what about that pretty brunette you were seein'? The one you brought to Red Wild? She seemed nice."

"That was almost two years ago. Her name was Vivian, and she dumped me at the fall brandin' barbecue. She was pissed I'd been gone ten days on the drive, and she still hadn't gotten over the fact that I could never take her dancin' 'cause I have to get up so early for work, but she wanted to party till the wee hours in Jackson.

"She was always mad about somethin', and then to prove it, she smashed a paper plate full of potato salad to my face in front of everyone. I'm still livin' that shit down with the ranch hands."

Holding in his laughter, Red unrolled his silverware, looking hard at the old resin tabletop.

"Yeah, yeah, laugh it up," I said, and my uncle let out a little snicker. "It was for the best anyway. She wasn't the one. Not even close."

I hadn't realized I'd done it, but I found myself gazing out the diner window, wondering where Aubrey was. Maybe she'd walk by after her book club and I'd get a glimpse of her infectious smile, her amber eyes, and the way her hips always swayed seductively when she walked.

You ain't that lucky, dumbass. Besides, she'd probably dump a plate full of Jello salad or somethin' over your head if she knew you memorized her schedule, down to what time she gets done at book club.

I kept coming up to Wisper, hoping for... I wasn't sure. An opportunity? A chance encounter? I had no idea. Aubrey George had never given me the time of day. I was just some kid in the background of her younger memories. Why would she? We barely even spoke.

But then, there were plenty of looks.

I hadn't missed how her lips would part when she watched me. I caught her in the mirror at the new hat and boot shop in town a couple months ago. And sometimes, when I walked by her store, she'd actually smile at me. Not every time, but still, it proved she had considered me. The day I asked her out, I'd forced her to see me as something other than her dead husband's friend's little brother.

But maybe she needed a little *more* convincing.

When I turned back to him, Red was staring at me with a dubious look in his eye. "What aren't you tellin' me, Rye?"

"Nothin'. It's nothin' at all."

As our waitress approached, pen and pad in hand, ready to take our order, he said, "Well, kid, when you're ready to talk, I'm here. You hear me?"

"Yes, sir. I hear ya."

CHAPTER FOUR

AUBREY

THE ROAR in the library's back room sounded garbled to my slightly inebriated ears. *In the middle of a workday? Nice, Aubrey.*

I chugged a second hard lemonade and sat back while my book-club friends all talked about my life like I wasn't even there. Nobody else had touched the stuff, so not only was I drinking before noon, but I was also doing it alone.

"If she needs a break," Carly said, "I could work part time at the shop, as long as I can bring baby Donnie with me and Buckey doesn't mind watchin' our older kids."

Right, like hiring an employee would solve my financial woes. Pretty sure that was the opposite of saving money.

"And," our local librarian, Sam, added, "if they really liked a book, I could push library patrons to Your Local Bookie to buy the pretty editions. I mean, I guess I kind of do that already." She winced.

I rolled my eyes. "Guys."

"I don't know why she didn't ask me to make her an online store," Billie chimed in. "She does know that's like cake for me, right? E-commerce is my bitch. And I can hack all the good plug-ins. She wouldn't even have to pay."

What the hell's a plug-in?

I tried again. "Guys."

"Let's get a meal train goin'," Philomena Beasley said. As the mother hen of our group, Phil looked determined to solve my problems. "I call Saturdays and Tuesdays. Then at least we'll know she's not existin' on oatmeal."

Shit. I shouldn't have mentioned how tired I was of oatmeal.

I stood up. "Ladies! I love you but shut *up!*"

The room went silent, and ten heads turned in my direction.

I sat slowly and set my almost empty can on the floor by my feet. "Thank you. I know you're all tryin' to help, but I was just bitchin' to bitch. There's nothin' any of you can do. Billie, I've already thought about an online shop. If and when I'm ready, you'll be my only call. But it wouldn't do me any good right now, and *right now* is the problem. I will figure it out. And Phil, I'll never say no to your pies, but y'all don't have to feed me. I was bein' dramatic. I have food."

"You know," Daisy said, smirking, "I've heard that if you're stuck in life, it's good to get out of your comfort zone. It opens up unused parts of your brain and then ideas flow like waterfalls." She was grinning now, but I knew exactly where she was headed with the bohemian life advice.

I knew what every single woman in the room was thinking. No one had mentioned him yet, but it was only a matter of time before someone said the name of the man-child they all wanted me to ask on a date. All because he'd smiled at me at the town dance last fall. They all swooned and giggled and demanded that I hook up with the guy. Probably so they could live vicariously through my sexual exploits.

I had neglected to mention how Rye had come into the store a week before that and asked me to coffee. Telling them that juicy little nugget of information would've been like dressing myself inside a bloody elk carcass in the middle of a hungry pack of wolves and then standing there while they devoured it, hoping not to get bitten or clawed.

Finally, none other than the deputy sheriff of Wisper, Abey Lee, spoke up. "Devo says Rye asks about you all the time. They talk on the phone like two teenage girls before prom."

And there it was.

Forget "protect and serve." Abey was just as big a gossip as the rest of them. Her style was understated, but she could gab with the best of them.

"Don't," I warned and glared at her.

"Oh my God," Roxi squealed. "Did y'all see him in town today? That ass." With her hands up in front of her chest, she flexed her fingers like she was getting ready to grab two handfuls of said ass or maybe testing the density of a couple oversized dinner rolls. "I swear to all that's holy, the man must need Crisco to get his jeans up those thick thighs." She purred like a horny cheetah, and I clasped my hands and locked my fingers together so I wouldn't smack her.

"He does have a nice butt," Cal said.

Great. Even Miss Priss herself was trying to push me into something I had no intention of getting into. Or under. Whatever!

"How exactly would screwin' that cowboy solve my immediate problems?"

"Um," Billie's best friend, Aislinn, hedged, "no one said anything about sex, Aubrey."

Eyebrows popped all around the room; I could almost hear them pinging like in a cartoon.

"Mm-hm," Juneau, our resident romance author, hummed. "This is the start to a romance book. You need something, and he's got something. Pretty soon he'll corner you somewhere discreet and offer himself up for the taking."

Scoffing, I said, "My life is not one of your books. What's Rye Graves got that I need?"

"Well," she said, trying to hold in a laugh. "A big dick. You need some stress release, and those jeans leave *nothin'* to the imagination."

"Ooo, girl," Carly squawked, "go on!"

They high fived, and I rolled my eyes. Again.

Stomping my foot, I growled, "*No.* I don't need some man tellin' me what to do or how to run my life. I've already been there and done that."

"You shouldn't talk ill of the dead," Cal said, disapproval ringing in her tone.

"Cal, Tommy was *my* husband and the father of my children. I will never talk badly about his service to his country or his sacrifice, but you weren't there in our marriage. You don't know the sacrifices *I* made or the pain my boys and I have gone through since Tommy's death. Respectfully, back off."

"O-o-okay," she said, palms and pristinely painted fingernails raised in front of her.

None of them knew. I'd given Tommy my whole heart, and when the boys were born, I thought we were happy. But things changed.

When my body morphed back into fighting shape, Tommy became more and more possessive. The other moms used to gush over the fact that he bought my clothes. "How thoughtful," they'd said. Except I hadn't told them that the reason Tommy shopped for my clothes was because he didn't trust me. I would rather have died than cheat on my husband, but my bigger breasts and wider hips had him convinced otherwise.

Now, I knew it was Tommy's own insecurities that made him act that way, and because he was gone, I tried to have some grace about it. It used to be a daily exercise, trying to make myself forgive him for treating me like a hunk of ham instead of his wife and for showing the boys that women weren't useful for much besides making dinner and cleaning up after it.

But the last thing I needed now in the middle of my life was another man with any power over me, real or perceived.

No thank you.

MY BUZZ HAD MOSTLY WORN off by the time Roxi dropped me back at the shop.

The coffee she'd forced down my throat from Coffee Shot down the street helped. And really, it wasn't like I was operating a two-ton forklift. Drunk bookselling could totally be the new thing.

Unfortunately, the weak-ass hard lemonade hadn't helped me forget about all the stuff I'd been worrying about before drunk book club, which could also be a thing. In fact, maybe I should put it to a vote.

I flipped the sign on the front door back to "Come on in, it's nice in here," and then my phone rang. My mom's face popped onto my screen.

"Hey, Mama. How are you?"

"Hi, sweetheart. Dad and I are okay. How are you and the boys?"

"Oh, well, we're… Yeah, we're okay."

"Aubrey Louise, don't you lie to your mama. What's wrong? Are you sick?"

The fact that I had survived stage one uterine cancer three years ago still made her freak out anytime she heard hesitation in my voice.

Luckily, I had zero plans to procreate again, and the cancer had been contained inside my uterus, so the surgery to remove it was the cure. But I still had two ovaries, a cervix, and lots of lymph nodes left, so the now-bi-yearly doctor appointments to check for other cancers had her in a tizzy every time her phone rang.

The thought had crossed my mind that maybe the surgery or menopause, or both, was the cause of my often disappointing and ineffectual "sexy me time" sessions, but I was way too embarrassed to ask my *male* gynecologist.

"No, Mama. I'm not sick. Promise. And the boys are the same as they always are, aimless and blissfully unaware of the world around them."

"Good. That settles my nerves a bit, but don't talk about my grandsons like that. Micah and Benji are just young. They'll come around. You'll see."

"Sure," I agreed, just to change the subject, but I still had my doubts. Nightmares of the two of them lounging on my couch when they were my age, watching anime reruns, woke me up in sweats at night.

"Have you seen your aunties or your cousin lately?"

"Uh, I haven't seen auntie Mabel in a few weeks, but I saw Maxie earlier today. He picked Juneau up after book club. He said auntie Darla's fine. She's still datin' the butcher."

"My sister, the hussy."

"Mama! Aunt Darla is not a hussy just because she's datin' someone. You know Jerry Fletcher is a nice man. You don't want her to be lonely, do you?"

"Well, now, of course I don't. It's just a little soon, don't you think?"

"Uncle Lou's been gone seven years."

Jeez. What would she say if *I* dated someone? And if that someone was the little brother of my dead husband's best friend? Even after ten years without Tommy, my mother would have a conniption fit.

Subject change number two: "How's Dad's arthritis treatin' him?"

"Oh, you know him." She sighed. "He's in pain, but he won't take so much as an aspirin, and he never complains. God bless him."

"Tell him I said hi. I miss you guys. Maybe I can come for supper soon."

"Well, that's why I'm callin', honey. Daddy went and booked us a Caribbean cruise. We're headed to the Cayman Islands in two weeks! Isn't that romantic? I can't wait."

I tried to hold back a groan, but damn. Even my seventy-year-old parents were getting some?

"So romantic," I said as the jingle bell on the front door tinkled. "You can tell me all about it over your famous meat-loaf soon, but I gotta go, Mama. Someone just popped into the store."

"Okay. Call before you come, though. I've been wearin' my bathin' suit around the house to get used to it. Don't wanna walk in on that, do ya?"

"No, ma'am." I laughed. "I sure don't. I'll call. Love you."

"Love you too. Talk later."

When I hung up, I gave my usual greeting and spiel. "Welcome to Your Local Bookie. What kinda fictional trouble can I help you get into today?"

A low, gravelly male voice answered, "The dirty kind."

I whipped around like my pants had caught fire, and there, standing not ten feet away, was Ryder Graves, looking devilishly handsome.

Roxi was right. His strong thighs in his jeans were downright sinful, and I could count his abs underneath his thin, gray T-shirt. *Jesus.*

Lack of sex in combination with those thighs, abs, and his ass made my mouth water.

I swallowed my drool and demanded, maybe a little too forcefully, "What're you doin' here?"

The ladies' voices still lingered in my head, urging me to bag this cowboy, and I knew if I did, they'd be supportive, but they were the only people in my life I could count on not to judge me for sleeping with a man thirteen years my junior. I pictured Micah and Benji's faces and the disgust and disapproval it would cause. And I could already hear my mother screaming from Jamaica or wherever she'd said they were going on their cruise. I'd already forgotten, because when Rye walked through my door, all coherent thought went out the window.

Removing his hat, he held it in one hand next to one of his extremely solid thighs, and he clicked his tongue, which of course made me imagine that tongue in places only my GYNO had seen in a very long time.

"I was hopin' to talk to you."

"About?"

"Um, you know. How you doin'?"

"I'm fine, Ryder. How are you?"

"Good, yeah." He pursed his lips. "I'm good." The motion had my eyes zeroing in on his mustache.

I didn't love a mustache on every man, but on Rye Graves, damn, it looked *fine*, and now I couldn't help but imagine how those bristled hairs might feel against my skin in areas I definitely should not have been imagining them touching. And his beard was the perfect length—just long enough for a woman to drag her fingers through.

Not me, obviously, so why were my damn hands twitching?

"How's your family?" God, how awkward was that? Next I'd be asking him about the weather. Wait, wasn't this the exact conversation he and I'd had eight months ago, when he told me I'd be sorry for denying him.

I would *never* admit to him that he'd been right, and that I thought long and hard about him every night in my bed for months.

"Everybody's fine," he said. "Junior's up in Seattle, still workin' at that brokerage firm, and Shelby and his wife, Sorelle, are over in Wisconsin. Parents are fine. Your parents?"

I laughed under my breath. See? Roxi was wrong. This was not a conversation between two people who wanted to dirty up some sheets.

"My parents are fine," I said. "They're goin' on a cruise. Was there somethin' else you needed? I've gotta get back to work." *Right. Like there's any "work" to do besides count all the books I'm not selling.*

He took a couple steps forward, his electric blue eyes flashing and freezing me in place. "Yeah, actually. I've got a proposition for you."

"Excuse me?"

He smirked. "A proposition... or an offer."

Juneau was right! Here was the "offer" of whatever it was he thought I needed. Although, I really had no clue what it could be.

"Ryder Graves, there's nothin' you got that I need."

"You sure about that?" he asked, his voice lowering to a feral kind of hum, but I was already turning, preparing to walk away. "I heard you need money."

CHAPTER FIVE

AUBREY

I STOPPED SO FAST my shoes squeaked on the floor.

But I wasn't going to face Rye now. No way would I let him know just how desperate I was to save my bookstore. Who the hell blabbed? Roxi would be lucky if I let her live out the day.

"Rye, I don't want your—"

"Hear me out," he said, and I heard his big boots on the tile when he moved closer. "What if we came to an arrangement? What if I pay your back taxes?"

That had me spinning in a second. "How do you kn—"

He shrugged indifferently. "Just ran into your friend Roxanne down Main Street. She seemed a little flustered when I asked her about you. She kinda gave up the goods. Plus, it's goin' around that your shop may not be… viable. Small town and all that."

I screeched, "You don't even live here!"

He took one more step closer. "Aubrey, we've known each other a long time. Let me help you. Let me take—"

"Stop. You stop right there. What gave you the impression I need a man to swoop in and solve all my problems? Lemme just get somethin' straight right now. I do not."

"That's not what I was gonna say."

"Oh no?" I countered. "You weren't about to say 'let me take *care of you*'?"

He shook his head. "No, I wasn't. You got me all wrong. All I wanted to say was let me take some of your stress away. And if you'd just listen, you can help me too. We can help each other, and if things get a little… heated, well then, I figure it's fate."

Barking a laugh in his face, I said, "Fate? You're out of your mind."

But my condescension didn't stop him. "Yeah, fate."

He fixed his hat back on his head and took the last two steps in my direction, which put him one foot away from me.

Looking up into his eyes, I had to focus extremely hard not to be charmed by the way his sun-bronzed curls peeked out beneath his hat. They twisted and flicked around his ears, and all of a sudden I had an urge to reach up and coil one around my finger.

Visions of a country love story swirled in my head. Me in some dusty blue-and-white gingham dress and Rye in his jeans and hat, lifting me into his arms and swirling me around, with the high, arid desert surrounding us, mountains behind us, and horses running free in the distance.

Who cared if I was older? In Rye Graves's eyes, it was plain to see that the rumors were true: he really did want me.

What would be so wrong with giving in?

Would anybody really care? Who would even know?

Didn't I deserve some satisfaction? After giving my entire adult life to a marriage that should've ended in divorce instead of death and to raising two barely behaved boys, I sure as hell did. Why was I denying myself?

"Fine. I'll hear you out."

I could see no harm in listening to the sound of his voice a few minutes longer. Then, after I denied him again because the words coming out of his mouth were cuckoo, maybe later I could imagine him ravaging my body while I tried my luck at "sexy me time" again.

"Look," he said, "my old man is stubborn as fuck. I've been tryin' to prove to him I've got what it takes to run G&S, but he ain't buyin' it. He's got my mama in his ear, tellin' him I can't hack it because I'm failin' at life. All 'cause I don't have a woman. It's bullshit."

That really was bullshit. It was the same as if someone told me I couldn't run my own store because I didn't have a husband to support me. I hadn't been out to G&S Ranch in years, but I knew it was thriving. I'd heard Abey talk about Rye and how hard he worked for his dad.

I felt sad for him that he had such unsupportive parents, but I wanted the upper hand in whatever negotiation was happening here, so I tapped the nonexistent watch on my wrist, cocked my head, and narrowed my eyes.

Rye smiled, his lips curving wickedly. "So, date me. Fake date me for a month. I'll parade you around my folks. They'll shut the hell up about my love life, and you'll get your back taxes paid off. I'll pay 'em today."

I rolled my eyes. *Oh yeah, like it's that easy.*

"It *is* that easy," he said, reading my mind and the doubt on my face.

He pulled his phone from his back pocket, where the rectangular shape had left a permanent fade in every pair of jeans he owned. I knew because I'd stared at his ass long enough to commit everything about it to memory.

"Here," he said, and he clicked a few times. When he

turned his screen so I could see it, he shoved proof of his overflowing bank account in my face.

I saw enough zeros on his phone to make me dizzy. "Holy shit, Rye! How do you have that kind of money?"

He shrugged. "My dad may be a dick, but he pays well. I get a percentage of every sale we make plus a salaried wage, and what do I need to buy? I bought my truck, this Stetson"—he ran two fingers along the edge of his hat's brim—"and a few pairs of Wranglers, but then I saved the rest." He had to be feeling smug if the grin on his face was anything to go by.

He'd shocked me, and he knew it.

"That's just my checkin' account. You'd probably faint if you saw my savings."

It's too good to be true, Aubrey. Stop thinking about it!

And it was wrong. I couldn't take his money. Money he'd earned through grit and determination.

In my forty-seven years, the one true thing I'd learned was the value of hard work. I had to give Rye at least that. I'd busted my ass trying to make Your Local Bookie successful, but Rye had worked just as hard, if not harder. Probably harder. He did work on a cattle ranch.

Suddenly, as I gazed up at the sexy cowboy begging me to fake date him, an idea struck me like lightning:

Bag a Cowboy.

I could order tote bags with a cute cowboy logo, and then do a monthly promotion. For every fifty bucks a customer spent on books, they could be entered into a drawing for a date with a local cowboy or cowgirl. It might get customers who'd switched to ordering their books online coming in. At the very least, it'd get people talking about Your Local Bookie again. But who in the world would agree to be put up for auction?

Rye's blue eyes flashed while he watched me thinking,

and they brought me right out of my head. The temptation to take him up on his offer was there. It was so strong that my mouth opened of its own accord to accept.

Instead, what I said was, "How do I know you'll keep your word?"

"You don't trust me?" He rolled his eyes. "You got a link?"

"Huh?"

"A link or an email or somethin' that'll take me to the website where I can make the payment."

"But what if I don't live up to *my* part of the bargain?"

He clicked off his phone and slid it back into his pocket, then grabbed both my hands. "Spitfire, if all I get out of this deal is the satisfaction of helpin' you, I'm okay with that. I'd do anything for you."

Spitfire? Oh, so now we had pet names for each other? His would probably be Playboy Asshat. I'd seen the young women he'd paraded around the entire western US. Although, I hadn't seen him with anyone lately.

"Why?"

It made no sense. Why me?

He chuckled softly. "You remember that dress you used to wear, when you and Tommy would hang out with Junior? Before y'all got married and he went off to the Army?"

"Dress?"

"Yeah, it was pink. It cinched under your breasts, flowed down over your cowgirl boots, and in the sun, the color made your hair shimmer like rose gold."

"No. I-I don't remember that."

"Well, I do. I still dream about you in that dress. More than I probably should admit."

I was speechless. I'd lied; I did remember. I still owned that dress. I used to love that dress. My mom had bought it for me at a boutique down near Salt Lake City when I gradu-ated business college.

I'd worn it for Tommy, but he told me he didn't like it, that it was too immodest. The thing went down to my ankles, but the square neckline accentuated my chest. I thought I looked beautiful, but all Tommy had seen was something other men might covet, so it made him mad.

"Th-that was over twenty years ago."

One nod of Rye's head and the unflinching look in his eyes told me he knew exactly how many years it had been.

He'd been pining for me for twenty years?

Me? He could have literally any woman he wanted.

Reading me again, he said softly, "You got married. I was too young. Life went on."

His name came out of my mouth in a whisper, "Ryder."

It was the sweetest thing anyone had ever said to me.

He squeezed my hands softly. "Make this deal with me. Spend time with me. God, I'd love to take you out. Shit, I'd take you to Paris if it's what you want."

"I don't want Paris. I just wanna save my store."

"So is that a deal?"

Catching my bottom lip between my teeth, I sucked in a breath to say yes, but then I felt a boldness overtake me. It felt dangerous, but it felt like the old me, before I became the mother of two delinquents and the wife to a man who saw me as nothing more than his property.

The me who'd worn that sexy dress.

"Beg me," I breathed, and I pointed to the floor with one unbending finger. I could worry about the impropriety and all the gossip people would be spreading later.

Instantly, Rye dropped to his knees. He looked up at me, and there was so much vulnerability in his eyes that he took my breath away. Vulnerability that said that this man would give me anything I wanted.

Was five-thousand dollars going too far? It was. I knew it, but I could pay him back.

And seeing him like that, down on his knees for me, did something to my body. Nerve endings fired in the most inappropriate places, and for the first time in more than ten years, mind-bending orgasms didn't seem so far off.

Girl, you really need to quit with the dark romance books.

Lifting his hands to my hips, he squeezed and slid one slowly down my leg and back up the inside until he was a hair's breadth away from where I knew he could do some real damage. "*Please*, Aubrey. Let me give you what you need."

Breath hitched in my throat at his double entendre. Oh, who was I kidding? I wanted this man. What was the point in denying it any longer? Maybe he *could* give me what I needed. And even if he couldn't, I'd get to keep my store.

But I kept coming back to my original question. Why me?

"Rye, I'm withered and scarred. Compared to you, I'm an old lady, for Christ's sake. What could you possibly want with me?"

He growled, "You are fuckin' beautiful. Don't you ever let me hear you say different."

Heat rushed through my body, from my toes to the ends of my hair. Another hot flash? Now? Or was it a reaction to the words coming out of his gorgeous mouth? The wetness growing between my legs, heating his hands waiting inches away, told me it was the latter.

Fuck it.

Taking the hat off his head, I fixed it on my own, cocked to the side to emphasize my new, bold mood, and arched an eyebrow.

"Deal."

CHAPTER SIX

RYE

SHE SAID YES.

Holy shit. Didn't see that one comin'.

What the fuck was I even doing? What now? I hadn't thought that far ahead. Well, that was a lie. I'd dreamed up a whole life for Aubrey and me, but that was all it had ever been for me: a dream.

But who was doing the faking in this scenario? Not me. Nothing about the way I wanted her was fake, but it was all fake for Aubrey. So technically, I was fake fake-dating her… kind of?

Whatever. I saw the way she looked at my body longingly, and damn if I hadn't felt her get a little wet through her jeans when I got down on my knees for her.

That alone was enough to make me forget about the whys and hows of the situation.

I transferred money to Aubrey's bank account so she could pay her tax bill before I left the store, though she wouldn't let me pay the whole thing. She kept telling me she'd pay me back, even though I'd insisted she didn't have to, that her help with my parents was all the payback I wanted.

I'd known her pride would bite at her, and I was right about that, but she also proved me right that she was a determined fighter. I had no doubt that as soon as she could afford it, the five grand would show back up in my account or a check would arrive in the mail. Not because of stubbornness, although she was definitely stubborn, but because Aubrey would always do what she thought was right, no matter the detriment to her reputation *or* her bank account.

But if she did back out on our deal, at least I'd helped her. Just having that knowledge filled me with a sense of gratification so intense, I felt almost euphoric. All those times I'd seen her looking defeated and frustrated with life, and I was the guy who helped take that away?

Damn. I hadn't thought it would feel this good. She was right about one thing though. I did want to take care of her. Not because I thought she couldn't take care of herself, but because taking care of her would mean I'd get to be near her. I'd get to soak up her determinedness, get to hear her laugh, not just watch it through a dusty store window, and I'd finally get to *know* her.

I knew she wouldn't back out though. She had always been someone who lived up to her word, was honest, maybe to a fault in some people's view, and she had integrity.

She'd agreed to go to dinner with me so we could hash out the specifics of our little arrangement, but beyond that, I had no clue what to do.

I needed advice, so I called the only person I knew who'd understand, or at least wouldn't think I'd gone *completely* mental.

"What's up, dumbass?" Devo said when she answered my call. How I'd managed to become friends with a four-foot-eleven lesbian activist still baffled me, but she was the most honest person in my life.

"Not much. What's new with you, carpet muncher?"

"I did munch some carpet this mornin', and I licked it and sucked it, and it was delicious."

"Oh God. Stop. Why do you do this to me? You know listenin' to you talk about your sex life activates my childhood trauma, and it doesn't help that the person you have sex with is my oldest friend's little sister and the freakin' town sheriff."

"And I don't feel bad about it," Devo said, chuckling.

"You good though?"

"Yeah. I'm on my way home from the community center. Abey wants to work on the garden today, so I took the afternoon off."

Devo had reminded me that I needed to call Abey's brother, Bax. He'd left me a voicemail last week, but my head had been in the clouds, and I kept forgetting to call back.

"Nice. How's the house comin'?"

"Oh, it's so cool! They just poured the foundation. We may be jumpin' the gun, but we've already started pickin' out furniture and paint colors. I seriously can't wait for all that domestic stuff, you know?"

"Yeah," I said, thinking I agreed and trying to imagine it for myself.

Devo cut into my daydream. "I heard a rumor about you today."

"You did? What'd you hear?"

"Roxi told Abey and Abey told me that Roxi talked you into goin' to see Aubrey, and that you were plannin' to ask her out."

"Truth," I said.

"So did you?"

"Did I what?"

"Did you ask her out? What'd she say?"

"In a roundabout way, I did. And she said yes. That's why I'm callin'. We're havin' dinner tonight. What should I wear? And where should I take her?"

"Pause," Devo said. "Back up. What does 'in a round-about way' mean?"

Oh yeah. I'd forgotten that part.

"Have you heard about Aubrey's financial troubles?"

"Kinda. Abey tells me everything, but not specifics. Why?"

"Aubrey owed some back taxes, so I paid 'em."

"Rye! You did not."

"Yeah, I did. What's wrong with that?"

"I mean, nothin' if she's your friend and you wanna help her, but if you're lookin' for sex in return, it's kinda… prostitution."

"Shut up. It is not. Besides, no one said shit about sex." Well no one *said* anything, not out loud, but… "And anyway, I'm gettin' somethin' out of this deal, too, so it's a fair trade. I have the money. She needs it. What's the big deal?"

"Okay, I'll bite. What can Aubrey do for you that's worth thousands of dollars?"

"Devo Mescal, I hereby swear you to secrecy. You may not share this information with anyone, not even Abey."

"Okay…?"

"Do you swear?"

"Yes," she said, and I knew I could trust her.

"Aubrey and I are gonna pretend to date."

There. I'd said it, and honestly, the satisfaction of saying Aubrey's name and the word "date" in the same sentence made me feel like a king. How long had I waited for this?

Too long.

"Uhh."

"What? What does 'uhh' mean?"

"I don't have words."

"C'mon, Devo. I already feel like I'm in some kinda twilight zone 'cause she finally said yes. I need you to talk me down off a ledge here."

She sighed loudly into her phone. "Okay, fine. First, fake datin'? I thought you really liked Aubrey."

"I do. I've wanted her since I knew how to want."

"Okay, so then, why this arrangement? Why not just walk up to her and say, 'Hey, you wanna go out with me?'"

"She would've said no."

"You don't know that."

"I *do* know that."

"Why would she say no?" Devo asked. "I've seen complete strangers throw themselves at you. Why wouldn't Aubrey wanna jump on the Rye train?"

"Because she's older than me by more than a few years. And because she already said no once, probably 'cause I'm the annoyin' little brother of her dead husband's best friend."

"Oh shit. You never told me that."

"Yeah, my oldest brother, Grady Jr., and Aubrey's husband, Tommy, were thick as thieves their whole lives. Then Aubrey and Tommy started goin' out when they were in high school.

"I was just a scrawny kid who followed them everywhere they went. But I got older, and I saw the way they were together, and I hated him for it. He treated her like she was somethin' to stick on a shelf, not a woman. And then they got married, popped out two kids, and I knew my shot with her was gone. I never really had a shot, to be fair. Tommy was it for her back then."

Slumping back against the seat in my truck, I sighed and

tossed my hat next to me, staring across the street at Red's *actual* red house.

"I gave up, you know? What choice did I have? I was too young, and she was married. But Tommy passed overseas ten years ago, and then last year, when I came to help you at Uncle Red's store, well, things looked different. *Aubrey* looked different, and I thought, or maybe I hoped, I might finally get a chance with her. Of course, then she shot me down.

"But I dunno, Devo. There's just somethin' about that woman. I feel like I can't breathe when she's near."

"Wow, Rye. You got it bad."

"Ain't that the fuckin' truth."

"But why do you think you have to bribe her to get her attention? Doesn't that demean you both?"

"I wasn't tryin' to demean anybody, but I got this money, you know? It's just sittin' in my account, and I see the way Aubrey has been lately, like the world has her by the throat. She's stressed out. I just wanted to help her."

"That's chivalrous."

"Maybe it's stupid. Maybe I am."

"Rye, you are not stupid. Don't you listen to your dad."

"Yeah, well, that's what I asked her to do for me. I asked her to date me so I could stuff it in my parents' faces, so maybe they'd see me as somethin' other than the baby. So maybe my dad could see that he can trust me to run the ranch. Aubrey's older. She's got her own business, and she was married to someone they held in high regard.

"Besides Aubrey, runnin' my family's ranch is all I've ever wanted. But me and Dad? All we do is butt heads. He don't trust me at all, and he sure as shit won't listen to anything I've got to say about raisin' cattle."

"Damn," Devo said.

"What?"

"It still surprises me how rigid these old cowboys can be. I didn't grow up in that kind of environment, so I don't really get it."

"Growin' up in it doesn't make me understand it any better than you."

"Alright, well, where are you takin' her for dinner?"

"No clue. The only places I ever eat when I'm in Wisper are the coffee shop or the diner."

Devo scoffed. "Absolutely not."

"Okay, well what other options do I have? Aubrey never really liked big crowds or busy places, so a restaurant in Jackson is out. Maybe she's different now, but she's still quiet."

"Ooo. That gives me an idea," Devo said in her plotting-trouble, masked-marauder's voice. "I'll call you back. I need to do some recon, which just means I'm gonna make my fiancée tell me everything she knows about Aubrey."

"Okay, but Devo—" Annnd she hung up on me.

THREE HOURS LATER, when I pulled up in front of the little, beige, one-story house Aubrey lived in on Valley Drive, the porch light was off.

She was expecting me, so maybe she'd just forgotten to turn it on?

I stumbled over some cracked cement on the sidewalk outside her yard. Thankfully, her curtains were drawn, so hopefully she hadn't seen me almost kiss the ground. I caught myself and checked my breath, and I made sure my shirt was still tucked in before I knocked twice on her front door.

When she opened it three seconds later, I was speechless.

I couldn't seem to draw enough air into my lungs to tell her how beautiful she looked.

She'd pulled her hair up into an elegant bun at the nape of her neck, but just as I'd requested when I called her two hours ago, she had dressed in jeans and a pretty pink shirt with frilly edges, with a little leather purse that crossed her chest but hung low by her hip. In case it got cold tonight, she had a hooded sweatshirt in her hand, and I'd brought blankets.

She looked me up and down. "I thought you said to dress casually?"

I looked at her legs in her jeans. So sexy with the bottoms cuffed short and those cute little slip-on shoes she liked to wear. The ones she had on tonight had blue and green books all over them.

"I did say that, and you did that."

She scoffed and cocked her head to the side, her eyes sliding down my body again slowly. "*You* don't look so casual."

"What?" I said, looking down at my denim shirt, jeans, and boots. "Yeah I do. I wore jeans too."

"Yeah, but you're *you*, and you wore a nice shirt. Even tucked it in. I feel underdressed. Hold on, I'll go change."

What the hell does "you're you" mean? But before she could run away, I grabbed her hand and pulled her through the door, then shut it behind us and heard the automatic lock click into place.

Her irritation and the feel of her skin on mine made me feel at ease, so finally, I told her, "You look lovely," as I led her around my truck parked by the curb in front of her house. "And what you're wearin' is perfect for what I've got planned. If it'll make you feel more comfortable, I'll untuck my shirt. I can even take it off. I've got a T-shirt underneath."

She shrugged, but the apprehensive look on her face made

my decision for me. Letting go of her hand, I untucked my button-down, unbuttoned it, and took it off, then untucked my T-shirt, and finally dragged my fingers through my hair to mess it up a bit. So much for fashion advice from Devo. Next time, I'd just listen to my own damn instincts. Aubrey wasn't about fancy things. She never had been.

"There. Better?"

She nodded but she didn't say anything, probably because she hadn't yet looked away from my bicep. She seemed fixated on my tattoo peeking out beneath my sleeve.

I laughed under my breath but cleared my throat to hide it as I walked around to open her door, and she followed slowly.

"Hop in, milady."

"Thanks," she said as she stepped onto the running board, and I watched the way her ass filled out her jeans and imagined taking them off and finding home between her supple thighs, but then she slid into my front seat carefully, and my view was obscured.

Walking back around to my side, I had a hard time hiding my smile. She had no idea how many times I'd imagined her in my truck. And she looked good in it, too, like she belonged next to me.

Once my ass was firmly planted in the driver's seat, she narrowed her eyes at me. "What? Why're you smilin' like that?"

"I'm happy you said yes."

Sighing heavily, she said, "Thank you for the loan, Ryder, but I *will* pay you back. And I don't know what you think pretendin' to date me will do for you, but maybe this is a mistake."

"Oh, ho," I laughed. "Don't you go thinkin' you're gettin' out of this, Spitfire. You said yes. I paid your bill, and now you're gonna help me too. I've got it all planned out. We're gonna go for a drive, eat, and then I'll lay it all out for you. By the end of the night, if you still think it can't work, then you'll be free to say so, but until then, relax. Sit back and tell me what you wanna listen to."

I fumbled with the dash screen until I found a Zach Bryan song and turned it up a tic. She didn't protest, so I left it on.

Out of the corner of my eye, I noticed her leg next to my hat on the console between us. She fiddled with her shirt, the dainty gold necklace around her neck, and then she released her hair from its bun. When thick, strawberry-blond waves cascaded over her shoulders, I held my breath. If I got any more turned on at this point in our date, she wouldn't take me seriously.

But then she lifted my hat and laid it in her lap, and I had to bite back a moan.

It was the second time in one day she'd touched my hat. Maybe it was only silly cowboy folklore, but a man's hat was an extension of his body, and when she touched it, it was like the gentlest caress over my skin. Goosebumps rose on the back of my neck, and as she ran one finger lightly over the brim, I swore I could've come right then and there 'cause all I could picture was her soft fingertip doing that to the head of my dick.

In the circles I usually ran, if a woman touched a man's hat, held it, wore it, she'd claimed that man.

Damn, what I wouldn't do to be claimed by Aubrey.

When she asked, "So what's this big plan of yours? Where are we goin'?" I resisted the urge to rearrange the baseball bat in my jeans. Putting my hand anywhere near it would definitely draw her attention.

"I'm takin' you somewhere we can talk."

"Okay…?"

Nodding to the back seat, I said, "We're goin' on a picnic."

She twisted to see the basket of food sitting there next to my discarded shirt, and the cooler I'd brought with white wine and a couple beers, in case she was in the mood for that.

"Rye, it's seven at night."

"Yeah, so?"

"Little late for a picnic, don't you think?"

"Nope," I said, "not the way I planned it. Relax and don't you worry 'bout a thing. You will be fed and satisfied before the night is through."

CHAPTER SEVEN

AUBREY

A COWBOY? *Really, Aubrey?*

And young.

What the hell was I doing? Oh, right. I was taking a chance and trying to save my business just like everyone kept telling me to. Although, *Pretty Woman* probably wasn't what my friends had envisioned when they'd told me to "go get some."

And how exactly did Ryder Graves think he was going to "satisfy" me?

When we parked in the middle of nowhere, on a roadside lookout off Highway 10, I stared at him, waiting for an explanation. Pulling off on the side of some lonely mountain road was *not* my idea of a "date."

Actually, maybe it was. There were no tourists or crowds here. Highway 10 was usually deserted this time of night.

Rye reached for my hand still sliding smoothly over the top of his hat, which was some kind of nervous reaction I seemed to be having. When he lifted it to his mouth and kissed the tip of my finger, I couldn't breathe. All the dirty, improper things he'd done to me in my imagination made him touching me now feel downright forbidden.

It was ridiculous considering the times we lived in, but a small part of me felt like Hester Prynne from *The Scarlet Letter*. Where was my big, fat, red A, which now in my mind stood for Aubrey, the floozy?

"C'mon, darlin'," he said, "this don't have to be the big thing you're makin' it out to be in your mind," and when he reached over to swipe my hair away from my face, my heart began to race.

He was talking about the favor—the money he'd loaned me—but that wasn't where my thoughts had gone. I was thinking about sex with Rye Graves. About how it would be beyond the pale, and how, right now, I didn't care.

Was I really back here again? Letting myself get seduced so easily by any man who paid me the smallest bit of attention?

I shook my head, and Rye frowned.

"Get out of your head," he said, touching the rough pad of his finger lightly between my eyebrows. "You spend entirely too much time up there."

He wasn't wrong. Some days it felt like I lived my whole life in my mind. I had so many plans and ideas—and dreams—running like a river up there, but in my head was where they stayed.

Certain things were expected of a woman my age. Screwing someone more than a decade younger was not one of those things. What would my boys say? Ryder was only twelve or thirteen years older than Benji and Micah.

Oh God. I had to work out the math in my head. Was I old enough to be Rye's mother? *Ugh. Wait, okay, so forty-seven minus thirty-four...* The relief I felt when I came to the conclusion that no, in fact, I couldn't be his mom, unless

I'd had a baby at thirteen, was so strong that I felt kind of dizzy.

"Wait here for just a minute," he said.

He got out of the truck, grabbed the picnic basket from his back seat, and disappeared. I didn't want to turn blatantly to see what he was doing. His ego was already bloated. He didn't need me gawking at him to make it bigger, but I couldn't really see him in my side mirror, so I sat there chewing on the inside of my bottom lip and silently arguing with myself about whether I should make a mad dash down the highway.

The whole thing made me nervous. It seemed like this man might do anything to impress me, and I'd go along with his plan if it saved Your Local Bookie and got the IRS off my back, but would he take it too far? We'd passed Cade Ranch on our way up. If I showed up there out of breath, I was betting they'd take me in. I was seventy percent sure. Aislinn lived there, and if Billie happened to be there, I'd be golden!

But I didn't run. I waited, and when he finished his mysterious preparations, he caught my eye through my open window and smiled. "Come eat."

He opened my door for me and took my hand to guide me around to the bed of his truck, which had been lined and lit up with twinkle lights.

Soft-looking flannel blankets had been strewn haphazardly over the bed, and oversized, fluffy pillows lined the bulkhead. He'd set the picnic basket off to one side by the wheel well, and next to it was a small cooler, on top of which sat a wooden tray with empty wine glasses, two cold cans of beer dripping with condensation, and two bottles of water.

I planted my feet in the dirt to stop him from pulling me further towards this disaster in the making. "What is this?"

"What's it look like?"

"A *way* too romantic picnic."

"Naw, Goldilocks," he drawled, "it's just the right amount of romantic."

"Rye, look—"

"Please, Aubrey? I finally got you here. Would you just hear me out? I'll beg again if you want."

He smirked, and I had to work hard not to blush while I imagined him down on his knees for me again.

"Ryder Graves, we do not need fairy lights and pillows in order for me to hear you. I am *not* havin' sex with you tonight. Understand?"

His face fell, and he backed up a step and kicked at the rocks in the dirt. "That ain't what I... I just wanted to do somethin' nice for you. That's all. I figure you deserve it. Things've been hard for you lately, and—"

Oh man. And now I was officially the biggest bitch on the planet.

I took a deep breath, released it, and apologized. "I'm sorry. Thank you for doin' a nice thing for me. It's sweet, really. But I guess I'm just afraid this all means somethin' different to you. I don't wanna hurt you, Rye. I just want to save my store."

"I know. I get it," he said, sliding his hands in his front pockets and looking at his boots.

"Aw, hell, Rye. You look like I just kicked your puppy."

He raised his eyes to mine at that. There was a newfound resolve in them that had me backing up too.

"Maybe I haven't made it clear, Aubrey, and maybe you don't wanna hear it. I'm fully aware that it's not why we're here, but just 'cause the reasons you agreed to my plan are serious, it don't mean we can't have some fun. Back in the day, I knew I had no shot. I knew where your heart lay. I was too young for you, and there was Tommy."

The mention of my husband made something pinch inside my chest. Rye had no idea, no one did, really, that my marriage was a regret I'd held onto for far too long.

"It seemed like you didn't wanna let him go after he passed. Or maybe it was *you* you couldn't let go—the you you'd been with him—but for so many years, it was like you were wearin' one of those dark widows' things. You know, the see-through hat things?"

"A black veil?"

"Yeah, that's it. It was like when I looked at you, your face was hidden behind a veil, but then I came back to Wisper last year and, I dunno, you looked different to my eyes. And I would know 'cause I've been lookin' at you since I met you."

Lifting a hand to my chest, I tried to hide the sob that wanted to escape. He'd noticed that? I thought no one had.

And he was right. I couldn't explain why at the time, but last summer, I'd finally let Tommy go. For good.

I still remembered the night it happened. I'd sat outside, in my back yard on the twins' old broken-down swing set alone in the dark, dangling my bare feet over my overgrown grass and releasing all the complicated love I'd had for Thomas George back into the universe. There was a time I never could've imagined doing it, but for some reason, that night, the night a bright shooting star zipped across the midnight sky, dreams felt possible again.

And then a meteor came crashing down on me. My business took a nosedive, and it was my own fault. I'd been so scared to move for so long that I guess life just went on without me.

But Rye had seen everything I'd tried to hide from my family and friends. He'd respected boundaries I hadn't even known I'd put up, and now, here he was, doing this amazing thing for me and politely asking me to take those boundaries down to help him.

And to help myself. I needed to remember that I was the one truly benefiting from his kindness and this whacked-out idea of his. I couldn't even describe how relieved having the IRS weight lifted off my back made me feel.

When I reached for his hand and pulled him closer, the surprise on his face was adorable, and I realized then how handsome he really was.

Yeah, sure, his ass was a thing of horny dreams the world over, but now I knew it was the kind look in his eyes that made him beautiful, the optimistic view he had of the world, and the teasing smile I thought I might commit a crime to see again.

Pushing up on my tiptoes, I kissed him. I closed my eyes and let myself *really* kiss him, and he wrapped his well-worked hands around my ribcage and squeezed.

I pressed my whole body against his and felt just *how* much he wanted me, and in that moment, dreams felt real once again.

Everything felt real, like I'd just woken up from a long nap I hadn't even known I needed and found myself in the middle of the most vibrant story. Definitely the sexiest.

Against my lips, he said, "I have wanted you for so long," and he deepened the kiss, tilting his head and seeking entrance inside me with his tongue. I opened for him, and he moaned into my mouth.

I breathed, "Rye."

"Mm?" One of his hands worked its way up my spine and the other headed in the opposite direction.

So much for "Oh yeah, I totally know this is about us helpin' each other."

"You have to stop this," I said, clutching at his shoulders

with greedy hands, pulling him even closer. "I can't. It's been so long, and you feel like heaven."

That just made him kiss me harder.

Crushing his lips against mine, his tongue did wicked things to my mouth. He had me imagining that tongue in other places again, and suddenly, I couldn't breathe. Like, not a sexy breathlessness, but a panting, messy, "Shit, I'm about to hyperventilate" kind of breathless.

"Aubrey? What's wrong?"

It amazed me how quickly such a simple act had turned into a *burning* need.

My hands had been snaking beneath his T-shirt—sweet Jesus, his body was hard and hot—but now I dropped them and stepped away. I bent at the waist, trying to force oxygen to my brain so I could figure out what the hell I'd just done.

"I-I'm sorry."

"You okay?" he asked as I struggled to catch my breath, and he tried to pull me back into his arms. "Was that not—"

"No," I said, holding my hand up between us to stop him. "It's my fault. I started it."

He dropped his arms. "Ain't nobody's fault. It's what you needed. It's definitely what I needed."

"No. You don't get it. I don't *need* a man." I shook my head and finally stood up straight. "Yeah, there are things you can give me that some might argue I lack." I rolled my eyes when Roxi's and Juneau's faces popped into my head. "But I've spent too much of my life givin' all the good things I had inside me to someone who didn't appreciate them. I can't do that again. I won't."

Disregarding the space I'd put between us, he stepped forward and gripped my hips, and my fingers dug into his shoulders again as I squeaked my surprise and he lifted me onto a fleece blanket spread across his open tailgate.

He plopped me down and lowered his face to mine so we were eye to eye. He was so big, he took up all the air around us. I couldn't even see the road behind him.

"You listen here, woman. I watched you do that. I saw how he wore you down and treated you like he owned you instead of loved you." He moved between my legs, widening them until they were practically wrapped around him. "I grieved for you then because I *knew* what that meant for you, even when I was a teenager. I've waited all these years just to see the spark back in your eyes. Now it's there again?

"You best believe I'm gonna be front row for that."

CHAPTER EIGHT

RYE

DAMN. She'd felt good in my arms, and that kiss? Fucking epic. I literally took her breath away.

And now I had her comfy and cozy in the bed of my truck. It's where I'd always wanted her, though, in my imagination, she was sprawled out beneath me, naked under the starlit sky, moaning my name and arching to my touch.

But now that we were here, the walls surrounding her heart had only cracked open the tiniest bit.

It was a start. A slow, small start, but I'd take it any day of the week.

"Wine or beer?" I asked as she sat across from me on the truck bed and crisscrossed her legs like a little girl.

"Water," she said with finality.

"As you wish."

"What I'm wishin' for, Rye, is for you to tell me this plan of yours. What the hell can I do for you that's worth five grand?"

I smiled. Anything she did for me was worth a hell of a lot more than that. I kept having to remind myself why she'd said yes and why we were really here.

But I couldn't stop from teasing her a little. "I want you…"

Her eyebrow twitched and her eyes narrowed when I didn't finish my sentence, but then I grinned, and she rolled those beautiful browns.

"I want you to help me convince my parents I'm capable of runnin' my family's ranch."

"Yeah, you mentioned that, but how exactly do you see me doin' that?"

"Well, you're a business owner, a valued member of the community. My parents respect my Uncle Red a lot, and he respects you. It's been a while, but they always loved havin' you over, you know, back when you and Tommy—"

Some kind of regret flashed in her eyes and she interrupted me. "I remember."

"And, I dunno. Maybe you could talk me up a bit. Maybe then my parents wouldn't doubt everything I do. God, you can't know how ridiculous I feel even sayin' that at my age."

Aubrey laughed quietly, but she said, "Rye, I think you might be overestimatin' the power of my influence."

I studied the curve of her face, wanting to reach over and feel its softness and thinking she had no idea how she'd influenced me over the years. She'd kissed me tonight, but that had been about me seeing her, the real her.

It was a gratitude kiss. Nothing more. At least not to her.

"I'll be plain, Spitfire. My mama won't see me as a man until there's a steady woman in my life. It's sexist and stupid, but that's how she views the world. And my dad won't let me have any control until my mama tells him I'm ready. So I need you."

And I want you. I wanna bury my body inside yours until my truck bounces to the rhythm of your pleasure, and when I make you come, I want you to scream my name while you dig your nails into my shoulders and draw blood.

Aubrey cleared her throat. "My eyes are up here, Ryder."

"Huh?" I said, dragging my attention away from the open space between her legs. I could imagine how warm she was there and how good she'd taste.

"You're droolin'," she said sarcastically, but she couldn't hide the smile curving the corners of her mouth.

As much as she wanted me to think she didn't care about my attraction to her, I could see by the light in her eyes it excited her. And when she stared at my biceps or my lips or at the way my hungry gaze caressed every inch of her body, it was easy to see I wasn't the only one feeling... *something*.

If we'd been here a year ago, things would've been a lot different. She still would've been closed off and mourning a love that was so much less than she deserved.

But it wasn't a year ago. The time was now. Tonight, and she was opening up right in front of me. The realization that I might have a little something to do with that made me happier than I'd felt in a long time. It also made my dick so hard, it throbbed.

"So you think if you take me home and show me off, your parents will magically change their minds about you? I think that plan is a little flawed."

"Why?" I asked as I handed her a tin plate from the camping pack I kept in my truck's crossover box.

Against Devo's advice, I'd picked up a special meal from José's Diner made just for Aubrey and me. José whipped up something he'd called a "mini charcuterie board" himself when I asked what to feed a woman on a date in the back of my truck in the middle of nowhere, with fancy wheat crackers, purple grapes, soppressata, sharp cheddar, and smoked Gouda. He'd offered to make a quick quiche, but Aubrey didn't like eggs. At least, she didn't used to. I still remembered how she'd slipped the scrambled eggs my mama had tried to force her to eat to my old German shepherd, Mikey.

Man, I miss that dog.

Aubrey took the plate from my hand along with a napkin and bit into a cracker with a little cut of Gouda on top as I set a bottle of water next to her leg.

"Thank you," she said carefully, chewing and blushing a little because I couldn't take my eyes away from her mouth. "This is good. I haven't eaten much today."

Dang it. I should've taken her somewhere for a steak.

She probably had no memory of it, but once upon a time, my mama had gotten it in her head that she wanted to open up a cheese section in the little store we ran on the ranch to sell our beef to our direct customers. Most of G&S' product went to be processed and sent around the world to supermarkets, but we still sold to locals who wanted a side of beef to keep in their deep freezers for the winter.

But back then, Mama had spent months perfecting her cheese recipes, and then she'd called all us kids, the cowboys working the ranch, and my dad inside the house to taste test. She'd bought ten different cheeses from a little international cheese shop in Jackson, and then we had to try her versions and compare them to the store versions.

When Aubrey had bitten into the store-bought Gouda, she'd closed her eyes and smiled. My mama's Gouda was disgusting, still to this day, but I remembered just how much that creamy bite had lit up young Aubrey's face, so that was why I picked it when José told me the options earlier tonight.

"Your plan is flawed because it was Tommy your parents loved, not me. Back then, I was just 'the girlfriend.'"

"You're wrong. My mama still asks about you."

"Really?"

I nodded.

Furrowing her eyebrows, she asked, "Why?"

I tossed some soppressata in my mouth with a hunk of cheddar, then wiped my lips with my napkin. "If you want my opinion, I think it's 'cause she saw some of herself in you. She gave her whole life to my dad, and while I know she doesn't regret her decision, maybe there's a little bit of herself she wishes she could've kept separate from my brothers, my dad, and me.

"I think she sees you as someone who did what she couldn't. Now, don't get me wrong, she bosses my dad around like nobody's business. She's one hundred percent in charge at the ranch. My dad would disagree behind her back, but inside he knows it's true. But the ranch has always been my dad's dream, and she followed because she loves him. In her mind, that's what women do, but I think she wishes she could've followed a dream or two of her own, like you did with your bookstore."

"Wow. That's…"

"What?"

"I'm not sure." She shrugged. "Flatterin'? But it surprises me. I wouldn't have thought your mama would even remember me."

I laughed. "You kiddin'? You spent whole summers down at our place. Why wouldn't she remember you? Where else would I have fallen so—"

"Rye."

"Yeah, I know. I'm gettin' ahead of myself," I said and felt my cheeks heat with embarrassment.

I couldn't remember the last time I'd blushed for any reason, but tonight, Aubrey was heating up the blood in my veins at every turn and making me say things I swore I never would.

"Listen, in a few weeks, we're goin' on our big spring drive. I don't know if you remember, but we have a cookout so all the cowboys head out to drive the cattle to range with full bellies. I'd love it if you'd come and see me off."

"That's it?" she said. "That's all you want me to do? And that's worth a five-thousand-dollar loan to you?"

"You don't have to pay me back, Aubrey. I'm happy to help you."

"Oh yes, I do," she said. Then under her breath she muttered, "Or else this whole *transaction* might be illegal."

Pretending I hadn't heard that, I said, "Yeah, it's worth it. I mean, I hoped we'd go out beforehand, get to know each other again so it looks more natural when people see us together."

She hesitated for a moment, looking down at her still-full plate. "I'm gonna ask you somethin', Rye, and I want you to be honest with me."

I promised, "Always."

"Did you pay five-thousand dollars just so you'd have an excuse to date me? Trust me. I know how ridiculous that sounds, and I'm not tryin' to be conceited, but—"

"Aubrey, if I thought money's what you wanted out of life, I would've offered it up months ago. I know how independent you are." I winked at her when she looked up, and she tried not to smile. "And how stubborn. But I also know you've been strugglin'. So have I. I thought I might be able to help you, and you might help me.

"And if that puts me in your crosshairs in *other* ways, I'll always be waitin' for that, but if you don't want me, then I won't push." *I might nudge a little.*

"When'd you get so grown up?" she asked, her eyes steady on mine.

I shrugged. "Dunno. Sometimes I'm not sure I did, but I

think I have an old soul. It's just that nobody can see it 'cause I've always been Grady Graves's baby boy. I've got all these ideas about how to make the ranch better, more efficient, and more profitable, but nobody listens to me."

"I'm sorry," she said. "That's gotta be frustratin'."

"You ain't kiddin'."

She took another bite of her cracker and then shoved the rest in her mouth and chewed. "I'm so glad you didn't feed me oatmeal."

"I should've taken you out for a better meal. But why would I bring oatmeal on a date?"

"No reason." She laughed softly. "Never mind. And this is a perfectly fine meal. Not too heavy, not too light. Also, this isn't technically a date."

"You kissed me," I said. "So I think it does make this a date."

Twisting her lips to one side, she narrowed her eyes again. "Have you always been so... persistent? I don't remember that about you."

"You never really got to know me."

She nodded. "You're right. I was young, and I was in my own little world. But now I'm thinkin', if I'd peeked out of it once in a while, my life may have been very different."

"Maybe," I said. "But I think we get to where we need to be *when* we need to be there. So maybe you had to go through some shit to get you here, but you made it through, and don't that feel good?"

CHAPTER NINE

AUBREY

"THE SKY'S BEAUTIFUL TONIGHT," I said, scooting back to sit against the bulkhead.

Tipping my chin up, I tried only to see the stars above us and not Rye's blue eyes, which was difficult because he sat facing me, his elbow resting comfortably on his raised knee, still watching me.

The night was silent. A warm breeze barely rustled the trees through Stillwater Pass behind us, and it felt magical. In early May high up in the mountains, we should've still been clutching jackets around us with hats and gloves this late at night. And I was surprised it wasn't raining, but the sky was clear, and the silver stars sparkled like they'd been set to music.

Rye agreed with a quiet hum as I leaned back further and relaxed into the pillows he'd stacked behind us. I felt his heavy gaze on the side of my face as he took the plate from my hands and set it on top of his picnic basket.

Oh, who was I kidding? I felt his stare in every cell inside my body, down to my pink toenails, which I'd hurried to paint and dry after I closed up the shop today. For what earthly reason, I had no idea. Why would he see my toes?

I couldn't remember the last time I'd felt so at ease though. Being with him was easy and comforting somehow. Maybe because he hadn't exactly been shy about how he felt about me. I knew he'd protect me to within an inch of his life if necessary.

He'd always been kind of a quiet kid. Observant like he was now, but there was no kid here. Rye Graves was *all* man. Masculinity radiated out from the middle of his chest. He was alluring, and I felt safe and warm.

Thoughts of taxes, my shop, and the twins flitted from my mind, like dust in the wind.

"What ideas do you have for the ranch?" I asked, sliding flat down on my back so the stars and Rye's voice were the only two things I could sense.

He lay next to me, not touching me, but I felt him all the same. Like the left side of his body had been set on fire, he warmed me so much I was glad I'd worn short sleeves. He smelled good, too, like some kind of sexy, mossy scent mixed with the leather of his truck's seats and the stiff felt of his hat.

"You ever heard of regenerative or restorative agriculture?" he asked.

Still looking up at the stars, I said, "No."

"Well, now I don't wanna put you to sleep, but basically, it's a more responsible way to raise cows. You let the land and the animals work together naturally, how it was done years ago. There are ways to make it all work in my favor, so that the land can actually sustain the cows, and they can enrich it instead of destroy it and our environment.

"It would also bring in more money eventually. I've trolled the internet till my fingers were sore, and I've called so many ranch managers. At this point, they might shoot me on sight 'cause I've annoyed 'em all with my questions."

"How did you become interested in this? I guess I've never really thought about how meat production affects the rest of the world."

"Flippin' channels. I saw a documentary one night after a big argument with my dad. No matter the subject, he and I don't see eye to eye on much. I couldn't sleep that night, and I turned on the TV, and it was like a sign or somethin'."

"You didn't go to school for agriculture?"

"No. Didn't go to college at all. It wasn't for me. The land teaches me all I need to know. Although, dirt don't know much about business, so that's one area I could stand to learn more about."

"I'm not a business genius," I said, "obviously, but I might be able to help you with some of that."

"My dad deals with that side of things now, and he has people on the payroll to help him, but someday, the business will be my responsibility, so I might just take you up on that. In the meantime, there's some farms up in Oregon I can learn a lot from, but my old man won't ever allow me to leave the ranch long enough to get it done."

"What's he gonna do? Fire you?" I giggled but caught myself and slapped a hand over my mouth. I didn't giggle. I hadn't giggled in twenty years.

Gently, Rye tugged on my arm and pulled my hand away. When he slipped his fingers between mine and squeezed, they were as warm and strong as the rest of him. Held within his, my hand looked like a little girl's.

"This okay?" he asked quietly.

Gathering what little courage I could, even though I was certain I'd lost my mind, I whispered, "It's okay. For now."

It felt okay. More than okay. Some kind of buzz seemed

to be building between us, and it almost startled me when I realized how much I liked the feeling.

He squeezed again and tucked our hands between our bodies, and then we just lay there, both of us thinking a million things and saying nothing.

Finally, because it was burning a hole in my mind and because I kind of liked it, I asked, "Why do you call me Spitfire?"

He chuckled, and I felt the rumble shake the bed of the truck.

"Well, the fire part 'cause you're bossy and stubborn. But the spit part… You remember the watermelon-seed contest we had at the ranch? You were probably twenty-two. Twenty-three maybe, but I remember you spittin' those damn seeds so far, and you got 'em in the bucket too."

I laughed and nodded. I did remember that. I beat all the cowboys and won a gift card for thirty bucks to a rib joint in Jackson.

"I dunno why, but that day has always stuck with me. I laughed so hard. And the smile on your face when you won? You glowed with pride."

"Rye, you were just a kid then."

"Yep."

"Don't you think it's weird that you remember that stuff, but my husband never did? It doesn't feel weird to you that I'm so much older than you?"

He got serious and became still. "It ain't like I was pinin' for you when I was ten. Back then, I just thought you were my brother's friend's pretty girlfriend and that you were nice to me. It wasn't till probably high school that I thought of you differently. But by then, you were livin' your life."

Turning on his side, he swiped my hair behind my shoulder with one finger.

"I love your hair," he said. "The color and the texture. It's soft but strong, and that's how I've always seen you. But I'm not a kid anymore, Aubrey. There's a few years between us, sure, but I'm a man now, and you're one hell of a woman. There ain't a damn thing wrong with me wantin' you. And it wouldn't be wrong if you wanted me too."

Want? No.

The word didn't do justice to the feeling taking over every inch of my body. His nearness made me stupid with desire, something I hadn't felt this strongly in a very long time. Maybe ever. I wasn't only attracted to him because he was an insanely good-looking man and had the correct body parts to do to me all the things I'd been starved of, and it didn't hurt that when he looked at me, his eyes quite literally sparkled like the bright night sky.

But it was his goodness, his eagerness, and his hopefulness luring me in deeper than I'd let myself be lured in over twenty years.

Suddenly, I *needed* him like the blood in my veins needed to flow. Sexy me time could be right now if I let it.

A parade of people and neighbors flashed in my head: the perfect moms from the PTA when the boys were in school, whose husbands actually participated in their kids' lives and who looked down on me because mine hadn't, my parents, fellow business owners in town. And every single one of those people, in my head at least, disagreed with the indecent things I wanted Rye to do to me. And the surprise and betrayal I knew I'd see on Benji's and Micah's faces if I slept with a man who wasn't their father? All of it had me feeling like I might pass out. My heart had become a jackhammer in my chest.

But just one more kiss. What could that hurt? If there was another reason to explain why I'd found myself in the bed of a ridiculously handsome cowboy's truck, I'd completely forgotten what it was.

"Can I tell you somethin'?" I whispered because what I wanted to say was entirely too scary to admit, and if I spoke too loudly, I might ruin the magic.

I couldn't bear that. It had been so long since I'd experienced anything remotely this magical, with Rye's eyes on me and the twinkle lights he'd taken the time to set up for me illuminating the dark forest.

Was the magic coming from Rye? Or was it because someone finally wanted me physically? I had to be honest with myself; it felt amazing, and it was trying to make me brave.

"You can tell me anything," he said softly.

"I… I don't understand what I'm feelin' right now."

He whispered back, his mouth hovering beside my cheek. "What're you feelin'?"

Still staring up at the stars, I didn't dare move my head or even my eyes. If he looked in them, I'd lose my nerve.

"I feel…" Clearing my throat, I licked my lips. "I want…"

His breath rushed out in a warm puff that caressed my neck, and he lifted our hands onto my stomach, low, over the waistband of my jeans.

Pressing down lightly, his fingers flexed around mine, but he let go and slid his hand to my hip, his elbow expertly placed to elicit more of the want he kept talking about. "What do you want, Aubrey?"

"Oh God."

What the fuck was I doing? *You're a mother! You're old. You cannot be serious right now.*

But my heart was *pounding*. Lungs pumping. Aw shit.

Heart attacks happened younger in women than in men. Maybe I was having—

"Before you freak out about it, this ain't part of our deal, but it's just you and me here, Aubrey. We can be together right now, live forever in this moment, if you just say the words."

Oh Jesus, when he said my name like that, over and over, tingles spread from the base of my throat to all kinds of inconvenient places.

But what would people think?

"Say it, Aubrey," he rasped in my ear, the scruff below his mouth tickling my jaw.

I dared to peek at his face, and I wasn't sorry I did. His eyes, so blue, seemed darker somehow, and his eyelashes hid them from me slightly when he blinked slowly, like he wasn't freaking out like I was. The sharp cut of his jaw flexing with tension was the only thing giving him away.

I imagined his mouth on mine again. From our kiss earlier, I knew his lips were soft. He parted them as I stared at them, and I moaned softly. He could destroy me between my legs with that mouth.

"Say the words," he begged, nuzzling his nose beneath my ear.

Shivering at his touch, I whispered, "I don't think I can. It's been so long." And now drivel came out of my mouth. "I can't orgasm. I haven't had a good orgasm in, God, over ten years. Not one that makes me lose my mind. Every time I get the opportunity, I get so stressed out, and I hate my body. I'm in menopause, Rye. Like, this is real old-lady shit, and it's all I can think about, and I can't come! What's the point of sex if you can't come?"

I gasped when I realized what I'd just said, and I wanted to crawl underneath his truck and then beg him to run me over. Covering my face with my hands, I contemplated crying or screaming. Either would've been appropriate.

But I didn't get the chance, because when I peeked out around my fingers, he was above me, his legs straddling mine, and the look in his eyes was feral.

"The point of sex, with or *without* an orgasm, is to feel good. To make the person you're with feel good. Stress release. Cure for anxiety. It's a way to tell someone you love them. Take your pick, but if you say what I've waited my whole adult life to hear, I will make you come so fuckin' hard the stars in the sky will disappear."

"Y-you don't understand."

Pulling my hands away from my face gently, he locked his eyes on mine. He clasped both my wrists in one hand, and in the slowest, sexiest gliding movement, slid his other hand into my jeans, beneath my underwear. "Don't I?"

"I don't even know if I…" I groaned miserably. "This is so embarrassin', but I don't even know if I can get wet enough for you. I've heard that, you know, that older women have trouble—"

The little breath I'd been able to drag into my lungs rushed out of me as he cupped his hand over my pussy possessively.

"You ain't that old." The quiet growl rising from deep within his chest made my barren insides clench with anticipation. "And you're *plenty* wet for me."

All the fear and anxiety I'd held in for ten years, the disgust I had for my mom body, my menopausal and cancer-surviving body, it all swirled so quickly inside my head that I felt dizzy again.

"Oh God. Oh jeez. But I didn't even say it yet."

"Mm," he rumbled, "I'm still waitin' for you to say the words, but I figure I can give you a little taste of what you'll be missin' if you don't tell me what I wanna hear." He extended one long finger between my pussy lips and breathed deeply as he slipped it inside me.

I wondered if he could sense my desperation, the desperation currently sucking his finger in deeper. Could he sense the wildness trying to talk me into letting this continue? Did he know the agony he'd cause if he pulled his finger away and stopped touching me?

Was I really that beautiful to him, with a five-inch scar down my belly, cellulite everywhere, and—

He withdrew his finger slowly and smeared the wetness over my clit, and then he began to rub. His eyes never left mine, and even though I wanted to hide and cover my face or close my eyes, I couldn't.

He had me trapped in his cobalt gaze, but when he replaced his finger with two more, they didn't *feel* like fingers. They felt like—

"Oh my God." I gasped. "Oh. My. God. How… how are you… doin' that? *More*," I demanded. "It feels so good. More fingers. More everything. *Please*."

Leaning over me, he pressed his lips against mine and whispered, "Not till you tell me."

His mustache tickled my upper lip and his beard scratched against my chin when I almost sobbed, "What? What do you want me to say?"

"Tell me you want what I can give you."

"What, your cock?"

"No, although that's one option, but tell me what it is you want *right now*."

"I want to *fucking come*! I want you to fuck me with your tongue and make me feel so goddamn good that I have no choice but to come. I want it hard and fast. I wanna explode in your mouth."

"As you wish," he breathed and tilted his head, his tongue sliding into my open mouth easily.

I closed my lips over his and sucked on them, nibbled them, and opened wider for him while I worried the heat he'd caused inside my body would melt his truck bed and I'd burn with it and cease to exist.

The rhythmic thrusts of his tongue and the way it dueled with mine made the whole bottom half of my body tingle and had me imagining other kinds of thrusting, but the kiss ended way too soon as he slipped his hand out of my underwear and moved quickly down my body.

Pulling the shoes off my feet and then the jeans from my legs, he caught my high-waisted tummy-control briefs with them, and suddenly, I was bare beneath him.

I didn't have time to feel self-conscious because he descended, fixed himself firmly between my legs, then hooked them over his impossibly wide shoulders. I felt the soft, well-worn cotton of his T-shirt under my calves as he pumped two fingers inside me again and lapped and sucked at my body like a man dying of thirst.

"Ohmygod. Ohyeah. Ohno. I can't... I don't know how to..."

"Let go," he ordered between licks. "You are so fuckin' beautiful right now that I can barely breathe. Your body is so sexy. Your voice is gonna make me come in my jeans, and the look in your eyes has me questionin' the existence of the devil."

I moaned and whimpered and called out his name as he fucked me with his fingers and mouth. How was it even possible that I felt an orgasm building already? My thighs shook around his head, and I clutched his hair in my hands, rolling my hips again and again.

Anybody could have driven by. Those bitchy, judgy PTA

moms. A hiker could have emerged from the forest. Maybe someone had. I wouldn't have noticed because my entire body felt like it was being lit from within.

I couldn't think. I couldn't worry. I could only feel.

For so long, I'd felt like I had disappeared. I was a mom, a daughter, a friend, and a widow, but I hadn't been beautiful or desirable to anyone. Sometimes, I felt invisible.

Tonight, in Rye's arms and in his eyes, I had reappeared.

I was unhidden.

"Come for me, Aubrey. Better yet, come for you—"

The first orgasm had me convinced I'd been right about that heart-attack thing. Was it normal to come *that* fast? It made me realize just how deprived I'd been of anything that felt good.

The second made me laugh uncontrollably for five minutes while he kissed every inch of my body, until slowly, he began his delicious ministrations again with those naughty hands between my thighs.

I'd never been so aroused. Cum flowed between my ass cheeks as he fucked me again with his tongue and fingers slowly, swallowing everything I gave him down his throat, moaning wildly and urging me on.

The wet noises my body made while he rained heavenly orgasms down on me were so far from my comfort zone, I couldn't even remember where my comfort zone was, but I couldn't be bothered to care because his truck rocked in the dirt while I begged him to set me free, straining higher and harder to reach another release than I ever had in my life.

And the third orgasm he gave me when he slid his free hand beneath my shirt and splayed it wide over my chest between my breasts, pressing me to the truck bed and holding me still as he sucked my clit between his lips, adding a third and then a fourth finger to the violent implosion building inside me, made me clench around those thick fingers so hard that I'd surely cut off circulation.

I came again, tears leaking down the sides of my face and screaming his name so loudly, I'd probably scared all the cows at his ranch fifty miles away.

Not once did he ask me to return the favor, but little did he know, there was nothing in the world I wanted more. What exactly did he think I'd been reading every week at my romance book club?

If there was one thing I'd learned to do well from all those books, it was how to give amazing head.

CHAPTER TEN

RYE

AUBREY TREMBLED BENEATH ME, riding out what I hoped was the best orgasm she'd ever had, and I licked the last of her cum from my lips as I rose up on my knees.

I wouldn't get a chance to taste her again. Not for a while anyway because she was about to freak out about what I'd just done to her.

Trying not to imagine rubbing one out above her with her cum coating my fingers—and trying *really* hard not to focus on the fact that my dick felt like it was ready to burst—I closed my eyes and savored her on my tongue, counting down in my head for the anxiety attack I figured was coming.

Three, two, one…

But nothing happened.

I looked at her then because I needed to see the flush on her cheeks and the satisfaction on her face, the satisfaction *I'd* given her.

Three times. Me, the younger man she saw as a "kid."

She'd never look at me that way again, but when I opened my eyes, I found her sitting up, too, tracking me like she wanted to eat me, like she was a cougar and I was a big ol' buck she wanted to take down.

As she drew her legs out from underneath mine, she pushed at my chest, and I fell back on my ass. That wasn't good enough for her though. She advanced on me, shoving me with her small hands and delicate fingers, and she rose up on her knees as I fell flat on my back and whacked the back of my head on my tailgate.

"What're you doin'?"

"Givin' you the best blow job of your life," she said, pushing my T-shirt halfway up my stomach, then she yanked down my zipper and slid her hand inside my jeans.

"Whoa, whoa, whoa." I gripped both of her wrists to stop her. "You don't have to do that."

"Please. Don't give me that 'little lady' crap. I know what I want."

Well then.

Licking her lips as her eyes devoured the skin above my fly like she was ready to take a bite, she pulled her hands out of my grasp and scraped her shiny, white teeth over her bottom lip, biting down until I thought she might hurt herself, and she moaned loudly.

Her amber eyes flashed gold as she breathed, "I want you."

When she reached beneath my boxers and wrapped a hand around the hardest erection in the history of the world, my whole body shuddered. I'd fucked my own fist with this exact scenario in my mind so many times, it had become ingrained in my brain tissue like some porno dream I couldn't shake.

I groaned and lifted my ass to give her better access. She pulled my jeans down my thighs and my cock out between us, scooting closer as she lowered her chest over my legs.

But then she stopped, holding my hard-on straight up in the air. It swelled and jerked in her hand 'cause I'd never been so turned on.

"Jesus Christ, Rye. You've been packin' *this* the whole time?"

"Oh yeah," I teased, "have a look at what you been missin'."

She rolled her eyes, shaking her head. "I bet you're really proud."

Smirking, I flexed my pecs, and I twitched in her hand. "Oh, I am."

"But do you know how to *use* it, or is all this bait and tackle just decoration?"

Promising utter devastation with just a look, I said, "Fuck around and find out, Spitfire."

I thought she'd hit me or roll her eyes again, but with my hard, fat cock in her hand, her mouth fell open with want. Sinful pride rushed through my body as the sexiest groan slipped free from inside her.

She released me and planted her hands on either side of my hips, and the loss of their warmth touching me almost made me whimper like a puppy.

I tried to watch her, to prepare for something I'd never imagined would happen in real life, but she leaned down lower, and when I felt her breasts rubbing against my thighs and the warm suction of her beautiful mouth around my dick, I began to succumb to her pleasure. Imagining ripping off the pink bra beneath her shirt and fucking between her tits, I groaned, but when she gripped the base of my cock tight with one hand and swirled her tongue around the tip, my eyes rolled back in my head.

And then she went to *work*.

Her mouth was a dirty, messy, wet dream, and she sucked

so fucking hard that my balls went numb, but then she cupped them in her warm hand, rolling and pulling, and I was pretty sure I died.

I couldn't feel anything other than insane pleasure.

I tried to speak, to tell her to slow down 'cause I wanted the most sensual thing I'd ever experienced to last forever, but the words came out of my mouth as gasps and moans and rumbled nonsense. At one point, I begged her never to stop sucking me.

Cum leaked from the tip of my cock, and that shit just made her wild. She lapped it up and swallowed it down enthusiastically, and then it became her mission to elicit more cum out of me.

"Slow… slower… Oh fuck, Aubrey. How do you know how… to do…"

"Mmm," she moaned, her soft hand pumping harder and faster.

"It's not s'posed… to… this fast. Shit."

I had to hold on to something. If I didn't, I'd hurt her. I'd never had head so good, and there was a savage need growing inside my body to bust into that pretty mouth so goddamn hard.

The sides of my dually's bed liner had been made out of some kind of industrial plastic. There wasn't anything for me to grip, and I couldn't reach any clips or holds, so I found my hands in Aubrey's hair, pulling her up and down my cock, but not to my rhythm.

She was in control.

So I let go, just like I'd asked her to, and rode out what was fixing to be the best and fastest orgasm of my life.

Her wavy, strawberry hair kinked around my fingers, and she sucked so hard, her cheeks hollowed obscenely. *Fuck*. I'd never seen anything hotter than her head bobbing up and down above me, again and again, working me *hard*.

But it wasn't until she placed her hand over mine that the throbbing between my legs really threatened to blow. She wanted me to push her down further, to hold her there and make her take me.

When I did, she released her grip, and I watched her slide her hand between her legs.

"Fuck yeah. Make yourself come with your mouth around my cock. That's so fuckin' sexy, I can't even—"

I almost swallowed my tongue when my dick hit the back of her throat and she gagged and choked. But she wouldn't stop.

She moaned and shuddered, fingering herself faster and faster, and then her whole body froze, and she came again and sucked harder than ever before as pleasure like I'd never imagined erupted from inside me and ribbons of my hot cum shot down her throat.

"MAYBE I BETTER TAKE YOU HOME," I said, watching confusion and embarrassment flash through Aubrey's eyes and rush over her skin in the prettiest rose blush after what we'd just done in the back of my truck on the side of Highway 10.

Way to keep it in your pants, asshole.

"What?" she asked distractedly as she climbed back into her seat and clipped her seatbelt into place.

"I'm takin' you home. We can finish this… *conversation* another time."

Her hand shot out and she placed it gently over my forearm before I could switch the ignition into gear. "No."

"I can see it on your face. You think this was a mistake. I didn't mean for it to go so far, I swear, it's just that when it comes to you, I'm…"

"What? You're what?"

Dragging my hand through my hair and down my face, I sighed. "Hopeless."

She unbuckled her belt and scooted closer to me. "Don't say that, Rye. It was your optimism and your hope*ful*ness that made me do what I did tonight."

I turned my head, and we sat like that, side by side with her hand on my arm over my center console, staring at each other for what felt like forever.

Finally, her gaze dipped, and she said, "I'd like us to finish what we started."

Huh? Was she saying what I thought she—

"I want you to take me back to my house, and I want to have you in my bed. You wanna know the best part about gettin' older? I can't get pregnant. So if you can promise me that insanely big dick hasn't been inside some Coachella-bound twenty-five-year-old in the last year, then I want you to come inside me." Her cheeks pinked to an impossible shade of sexy. "Fuck me, Rye. Finish what we started."

In my state of dumbfoundedness, I put the truck into Neutral instead of Reverse. I'd already released my parking brake, and we began sliding slowly down the embankment toward the forest.

Aubrey shrieked. Her hands shot out toward the dashboard, and I fumbled to start the truck and put us in Reverse. My tires spit dirt as I punched the gas and we backed up, and she gasped and snapped her seatbelt back in place while I whipped my truck around so fast, smoke probably came off the engine.

THE DRIVE back to her place was quiet.

And kind of awkward, for me anyway. I wasn't sure why since I'd wanted her for as long as I could remember, but she stared at the side of my face the whole way, and I couldn't figure out what she was looking for.

Did she see what everyone else always had? Grady Graves's youngest son, his baby boy who wasn't to be trusted or relied on, who couldn't do anything without his daddy's say so?

Or was she looking at me like that because I'd proved myself tonight as a means to her end—the end of her dry spell?

Good job building the tension, idiot.

She'd get what she wanted from the "kid" inside her house, and then what?

I parked behind her little white SUV in her driveway, turned off my truck, and let my hands fall down to my thighs.

"What's wrong?" she asked.

"Nothin'."

"Rye—"

"You know what? I think I should just head back to my uncle's. I've gotta head home early tomorrow mornin', so it's probably best if I… y'know. Go."

She flopped back against her seat. "You're leavin' tomorrow?"

Was I hallucinating, or was that disappointment in her voice?

I nodded. "Yeah, I've been here too long. The next few weeks, there's a lot to do before the drive."

"I don't know what changed for you in the last twenty

minutes. Things feel different now between us, but if you're headed out tomorrow, then spend the night with me. Please?"

I turned to face her. "Look, tonight was a dream, Spitfire. Really. But I want you too much for a one-night stand. If I stay with you tonight, it'll kill me to leave in the mornin' knowin' we can't ever go back. Once you get what you need from me, I'll never see you again. Not like this, not how you are tonight."

She huffed an angry breath at me. "Ryder Graves, get your ass in my house now."

CHAPTER ELEVEN

AUBREY

RYE THOUGHT I wanted to use him? Now that I knew he had the skills to light my body on fire, I what? Just wanted to get my rocks off and then send him on his way?

"Come in," I said when I unlocked my front door and pushed it open, and Rye followed silently.

"I haven't, you know."

"Hm?" I'd left the hall light on, but as I led him to my kitchen, I flipped on more. After setting my purse on the table, I turned back to him. "You haven't what?"

"I haven't fucked any twenty-five-year-olds lately, at Coachella or anywhere else."

I laughed, feeling relieved that he was being playful again.

His hands stayed in his front pockets as he looked around my kitchen and then wandered out to the living room.

I knew what he was seeing: proof that I was a mom. An old mom who'd raised two rambunctious boys in this house. Boys who'd left marks on the walls from their shoes I hadn't yet painted over, and the missing brick from the fireplace they'd removed when they learned how to use an electric chisel. Big mistake having my cousin Maxie teach them anything about tools that had more power if you plugged them in.

Rye looked at photos of my little family on the mantel above the fireplace, back when we were still a *whole* family, with a mom and dad and two boys who hadn't yet lost everything. Their toothless smiles could be so misleading. Our lives now were nothing like they'd been back then.

But then again, neither was I.

Rye moved through the room silently until he stood in front of one of my bookcases by the window. His hand whispered over a wooden shelf and he touched a few books' spines.

"You read all these?"

"Yeah. There's another bookcase on the wall behind you."

He turned and walked toward it without looking at me.

"There's one in my bedroom, too, and another in the office. I don't really use it as an office though."

"Why not?" he asked as he looked at more pictures on the walls.

"Dunno. Guess I'm just more comfortable with my laptop on the couch."

I'd long ago taken down the photos of Tommy and me. Our wedding photos didn't bring me pain anymore, but me not wanting to see them had more to do with knowing who I used to be before we were married, and how much of myself I'd given up for a relationship based more on ownership than love.

Not that I'd be any good at it, but throughout the thirteen years of my marriage, one thought had run through my mind more times than I could count:

I could've been a dancer.

Or a pilot. A senator or the owner of a huge chain of

wildly successful bookstores. The profession didn't matter. It was the years I'd spent with a man who didn't care what I did, so long as I never looked at another man, didn't make him look bad in front of his buddies or his parents, and it didn't interfere with Monday night football. As long as the food was cooked, the house was clean, and the boys were attended to.

But maybe Rye was right that we got to where we needed to be in life when we needed to be there.

In which case, Rye needed to be with me tonight.

The pictures still displayed in my living room were of me and the boys, my parents, customers at special events I'd hosted at the bookshop, and some were completely impersonal. Mostly florals. I had a weird thing for vintage drawings of flowers. Roxi said my house was "a whole girly mood," but I really liked what I'd created since I'd been on my own.

There wasn't a man to disapprove and tell me he didn't like the things that made me happy, and there were no boys to break them or leave sticky fingerprints on them. I missed having Benji and Micah home most of the time, missed cooking for them and laughing at their antics, but sometimes, I reveled in being by myself.

Rye smiled at my favorite drawing made with India ink. "I like this one," he said, reaching out to touch the frame's glass. "It reminds me of you."

He was uncharacteristically quiet, and he seemed so big in my little one-story house. His six-two or -three frame, his wide shoulders, and the confident cowboy air he always exuded were almost another personality in the room with us. When we'd sat in his truck talking, he'd felt so human to me. Normal.

Now, as I watched him move, he seemed extraordinary. Bigger. More powerful.

Maybe it was because now I knew what he was capable of.

Tonight had been a revelation to me. My body *wasn't* out of commission, like I'd been convinced it was. It wasn't withered and unsatisfactory like I'd thought. Rye had made me feel more alive at forty-seven than I'd felt when *I* was the twenty-five-year-old Coachella girl, if I'd even known what Coachella was back then.

I watched him still moving through my house slowly, touching memories and knick-knacks carefully. He'd left his hat in his truck, and his curls lay wild and disheveled from running his fingers through.

It surprised me that I was the one being so calm. I knew he had been expecting me to flip a lid earlier, after he ravaged me in the bed of his truck and I'd done things to him you'd probably only see on Skinemax. *Wait. Is Skinemax still a thing?*

Maybe it was the multiple orgasms he'd given me, probably was, but I felt cool as a cucumber. I felt lighter too. Less stressed. Less burdened.

But Rye looked stiff, like he'd taken all that stress into himself when he'd cured me of it.

"Ryder?"

"Hm?" he hummed as he turned to face me, and again, we just stared at each other. What was he seeing when he looked at me?

Normally, I'd worry he was seeing the gray roots growing out of the highlights Ronnie Evans at Cut It Up had given me, or the bags under my eyes or the way my skin was beginning to loosen and change. Or maybe being in my home, now he saw what he'd never wanted to before: that we really were two very different people from two different generations, and that we didn't belong together.

We could help each other, sure. There wasn't anything wrong with having a little fun in the sack, cracking some jokes, and providing each other something we really needed. Those were the only things I should've been looking to get from this man, but there was a little tug inside my chest telling me I knew better.

Rye Graves was more than just a good lay or a bank account.

He'd been trying to tell me all along. But now he wanted to leave. He'd go back to his ranch tomorrow, and I'd never get to feel his hands and his mouth on me again or hear the hum of his voice when he said such profound things to me like they were nothing at all, when in reality, they were everything I didn't know I'd needed to hear.

"Please don't go."

"Gotta, Spitfire. It's gettin' late." He walked toward me, dragging a hand through his hair again, and one curl stood straight up from his forehead. Stopping in front of me, he reached out and pulled me into his arms.

"But we didn't finish hashin' out our plan."

"That's what phones are for, yeah?"

"Rye, please talk to me. Why are you really leavin'? I thought this was what you wanted. That *I* was."

"Oh," he breathed, caging me between his strong arms, hugging me tighter. He pulled his fingers through my hair softly. "You *are* what I want. More than you know. But I have to go because I feel this… I dunno. I feel this weight now inside my chest, and I know if I stay, things between you and me will go somewhere neither of us needs. I don't wanna just be sex to you."

"That's not why I want you to stay."

"Still, it's better if I don't. Trust me. I go from zero to sixty in a heartbeat, and then when work gets busy, I disappear. Broken a few hearts that way. I don't wanna break yours." He squeezed me against his chest, but then stepped back. "I'm gonna call you tomorrow when I get a break, okay? Answer your phone."

Clicking his tongue, he nodded once, leaned down to kiss me quickly on the lips, and then he left me breathless.

The good kind.

MY PHONE PINGED with a text from Rye at midnight:

> Night, Spitfire. Dream about me tonight like I dream of you every night.

I had no clue how to respond, and to be honest, I was a little afraid late-night texting might turn into sexting, and what if I loaned my phone to Benji the next time he came home or to Roxi and they saw it? The mortification I would feel if that minuscule possibility happened stopped me from texting Rye back, so I hugged my phone to my chest like a teenager and dreamed of things I had no business dreaming about.

"WHERE WERE YOU LAST NIGHT?" Roxi demanded when she rushed into Your Local Bookie right after I flipped the "We're open if you dare to dream" sign the next morning, clutching her phone in one hand. "And why didn't you answer my texts this mornin'? I thought you'd been abducted by aliens!"

I had a whole collection of unconventional open and

closed signs. I'd thought they'd give the shop an edge over some of the other stores in town.

Yeah, they didn't. Lately, unless you sold food, guns, or cowboy hats, you had to sit back and watch all the customers go into other people's businesses.

But maybe that wasn't the whole truth.

Maybe, just like with Rye, my eyes had been closed. I'd let my business fall to the wayside, let the status quo become acceptable.

Maybe it wasn't anymore. Maybe my eyes had been opened, and maybe it was time to *do* something about it.

"Breathe. Jeez. You look like you're about to bust that vein in the middle of your forehead."

"Ugh." Roxi pushed past me at the cash register so she could check her face in my mirror in the back room. "What vein? I put on foundation this mornin'. Although, I was so worried about you, I rushed it and now I probably look like horse shit." When she was convinced the veins in her face weren't purple and pulsating wildly, she stood across the counter from me again and stared me down. "So? Where were you?"

"Did I forget we had plans?"

"No, we didn't have plans, but remember I told you I might stop by if my date with that llama farmer was a bust? Spoiler alert: it was. Guy was a total weirdo. He told me he wanted to cut a lock of my hair so he could weave it into a blanket with his llamas' fleece to keep him warm at night. Ew."

Barking laughter erupted from my mouth. I couldn't help it. "Oh my God."

"Yeah. So I stopped by your house after I told him I'd haul his ass to jail if he did it, once I figured out what I could arrest him for, but you weren't there so I had no one to commiserate with."

"Sorry."

Her head cocked to the side. "You still haven't said where you were."

"Out."

She scoffed. "Right. Without me? You don't go 'out.'"

"Well, I did last night. Had a great time."

Her eyes narrowed in suspicion. She was either mad that I hadn't dished the dirt yet, or she was miffed I'd spent time with another friend. Or both. "With who?"

I bit the inside of my cheek so I wouldn't be tempted to tattle on myself.

"Aubrey?"

"Um…"

She gasped, and her eyes grew to the size of golf balls. "Rye? You went out with Rye, didn't you? I flippin' knew it! Tell me *everything*."

Peeking out the front window, I made sure there were no customers coming in, and then I pulled Roxi by her hand to the safety of the back room and spilled all the tea on planet Earth.

"You won't believe it, Roxi. Juneau was right! He showed up here yesterday after book club. I was on the phone with my mom. That's not important, although, did I tell you my parents are goin' on a cruise? Lucky bastards. Anyway, there he was right in front of me, and he told me he could help me with my little problem. You know how I was stressin' big time about my taxes?"

She nodded silently, but there was a little sparkle in her eye.

"Oh wait. Of course you do. You're the unloyal friend who told him!"

She winced.

"I should probably be thankin' you, but I still wanna clobber you."

She batted her coated eyelashes at me, smirking and shrugging. Her face was so expressive, there really was no need for her to speak.

"Anyway, so he says, 'I got money. I can help you and you can help me. I'll take you to Paris,' like it's nothin' to him, and then he pulled up his bank account on his phone.

"The man is rich. Like, not, 'hey, I just got paid, let's go tuck back a couple ribeyes' kind of rich, but, like, loaded rich. And then he paid my back taxes. All he says he wants in return is me to fake date him so his parents will get off his back about his love life. So I said yes.

"And then he— Oh, Roxi. The things he did to me. We didn't even have sex, and I orgasmed four times!"

Trying to recover from my nearly hysterical monologue, Roxi shook her head quickly and pieces of her hair fell loose from the bun she'd put it into this morning. "I'm sorry. I think I hallucinated the last part. Please repeat."

"Yeah. In the bed of his truck on the side of Highway 10, up past Cade Ranch at the Stillwater Pass lookout, you know the little spot in the parkin' area that's kinda hidden at the edge?"

She nodded. "Holy. Shit. But I mean, what did you do if you didn't have sex? I had no clue my intervention would lead to *that*!"

My cheeks must've lit up like glowing brake lights because Roxi's eyes got even bigger.

"Tell me right now."

"He— I— We… did things." I bit my lip. "Really dirty, naughty things."

She squealed so loud, I thought my eardrums might pop.

"And which of that delicious man's body parts did he do things to you with?"

I whispered because I was so embarrassed, I couldn't say any of it out loud. "His fingers. And his mouth. Specifically, his tongue. *God*, that man's tongue."

My eyes fluttered closed as I remembered him rubbing it over my clit while endlessly pumping his fingers inside me, and the sucking noises his mouth had made while I writhed on my back like a flipped cockroach.

"*Oh my*." Roxi's hand covered her mouth, her fingers pulling at her bottom lip a little. "You're gettin' turned on just rememberin', aren't you? I'm so jealous! Maybe it's not so weird if the llama guy wants my hair. If I can have orgasms brought on by somethin' other than my little rose vibrator, I might be able to look past it."

I laughed but dropped my face into my hands, trying to rub the embarrassment away until I realized I'd probably smudged my mascara.

"I'm too old for this. People my age don't have four orgasms in the span of an hour."

"Oh man," she said. "I think I might need to sit down. This is too good. Wait. Halt. Rewind. Did he stay the night?"

"No. But that's not what I'm worried about. What are people gonna think? I mean, he paid my damn taxes. Five thousand dollars, Roxi. That's... I don't even know. But is it wrong? I mean, is it wrong that I accepted the money, and now he's givin' me orgasms? I feel like—"

She shook her head. "Unless you demand money before the orgasms, it's not wrong. He offered the money freely, right? You didn't ask for it?"

"I didn't. He offered because *you* told him I was up shit creek."

"So then it's not wrong. And I know you'll pay him back."

"Yeah, I will. I've already started a spreadsheet to see where I can whittle down my expenses—"

My phone rang, and Roxi jumped in place while I pulled it from my pocket. All her keys and her handcuffs and mini flashlight attached to her uniform vest tinkled and thunked. "Ooo! Is it him?"

I'd labeled his contact in my phone as only R. I didn't have a picture of him to assign to his profile, but the R told me enough when I saw it on my screen.

I nodded vigorously.

Roxi groaned, clenching her fists in the air, and she shook them. "Goddammit, I have to go to work! Okay, answer it and then call me after. And don't think you're gonna get away with skimpy details."

"Yes, Officer Fitts."

"Good. See ya. Oh, and by the way, you're welcome!"

CHAPTER TWELVE

RYE

AUBREY ANSWERED MY CALL. She didn't say anything, but just knowing she was on the line made me smile.

"Hey, Spitfire."

I was pretty sure I'd rocked her world last night. At least, I hoped I had, but now that I was back at the ranch, staring at the same four log walls I always did, she felt so far away. Already, I missed the lightness of her house and all the pretty things she'd decorated it with. The only thing decorating my wall was an old, metal PBR sign, and I'd nailed a couple hooks next to my front door that I hung horse tack on.

Actually, what I missed was Aubrey and the lightness of her laugh.

I left my uncle's place before dawn this morning, and I cussed myself out the entire drive home for leaving after she'd asked me to stay. Hadn't slept all night thinking about it.

"Hi."

"You get my text last night?"

"Yes."

What was with the one-word answers? Had I blown out

the language center of her brain when I made her come on my tongue? Three times in a row and then watched a fourth time while she masturbated with my cock in her mouth.

"Did I wake you?"

"No."

"I'm not gettin' a real proof-of-life feelin' right now with these one-word answers. Are you okay? Have you been kidnapped by pirates and they're standin' over you, not lettin' you talk to me?"

Finally, she laughed.

"There she is. Mornin'."

"Good mornin'. I'm sorry I didn't text back. I'll be honest with you. I had no idea how to respond, and I don't really know what to say to you now either. I-I think I'm… embarrassed."

I hummed my pleasure into my phone, and instantly, I was hard. This woman! What was she doing to me?

"Can't stop thinkin' about last night either?"

"No," she responded breathlessly. "I don't… I just— I don't know how to talk to you now that we, you know, did… that."

"Mm. Shook ya real good, didn't I?"

"Rye, quit with the playboy crap, okay? Just talk to me like a normal person."

"Okay, then you do the same."

"Fine," she said.

"Good. What time am I pickin' you up Saturday?"

"Huh?"

"Our date," I said. Had she already forgotten? Maybe I hadn't rocked her world as hard as I thought I had.

"What date?"

"I told you we need to go out and get to know each other before the cattle drive in a few weeks. You think you're gonna fool my mama if you don't know the first thing about me?"

"Oh, I know plenty about you."

"The size of my dick, sure, but don't you think you should know somethin' about my personality before we put this whole thing to the test?"

I could almost hear her rolling her eyes, but I was right.

"Fine," she said. "Seven. Wait. What are we doin' on this date?"

"There's a new Thor movie out, or maybe it's not Thor, but it's one of those guys."

"Oh," she said, probably surprised we had that in common, but the last time I was in town, I'd heard her talking to one of her book-club friends about the previous movie when they walked past Red's store. "I actually love superhero movies."

"Yeah?"

"Show me a woman who says she doesn't wanna watch that hunk of a man on the big screen, and I'll show you a liar."

I chuckled. "Should I be jealous?"

"Very."

"WHERE ARE YOU HEADED OFF TO?" my mama asked as I put a foot in my truck Saturday afternoon.

I'd showered and trimmed my beard, and my hair was as combed as it was going to get.

"Town."

"You better be back early," my dad added. "We've got a lot to do tomorrow."

"Yeah. I know we do. I'll be here."

"You finish the chores I gave you? You better not be thinkin' about leavin' if your responsibilities haven't been tended to yet."

I resisted the urge to roll my eyes and thought about the heifer I'd just had to wrangle. She'd twisted her ankle earlier in the day, so I soaked it in a salt bath and ran the cold hose over it for a spell. She was still limping though. If she wasn't better by morning, I'd have to call the vet. My dad had never had the patience for the animal-care part of the job. He was better with numbers and the overall running of the ranch.

"Everything you asked me to do is done, on top of all the stuff I always do. That heifer's still limpin'. If she ain't walkin' straight in the mornin', I'll call the doc. Until then, I'm off the clock, and I got a date so I'll see ya."

Mama gasped and touched her hand to her chest. "A date? Who with?"

Here we go. Time to plant the seed.

"Y'all remember Aubrey George from Wisper, used to go by Aubrey Abbott?"

"Ryder, she's a married woman." Mama huffed a breath, exasperated with me for something that wasn't even true.

"No, Mama. She's not anymore. Tommy died over ten years ago. You know this. You went to his funeral with Junior."

Her shrewd eyes narrowed. "Well, isn't she a little old for you?"

Jesus. Couldn't I do anything right? She wanted me to find a woman. Now I had and the woman I chose wasn't good enough, even though both my parents had adored Aubrey back in the day?

Damn. If I couldn't get them on board now, my whole plan would be shot to shit, and Aubrey would have no reason to spend time with me anymore.

That would be a letdown of epic proportions. I just needed to try harder because I wasn't sure how much kowtowing I had left in me. If things with my parents didn't change soon, one of these days, I'd walk away and never look back.

"She's in her forties. I'm in my thirties. What's the problem? I thought you liked Aubrey. You just asked me about her not two months ago."

"We did like her. But Rye, she's a mother. She has two children. Are you sure you're... capable of bein' with someone who—"

Wow. Really?

"Her boys are grown, Mama. They're up at college in Bozeman." At least half that statement was true. "And yeah, I think I'm well suited for Aubrey. We have a lot in common, actually." And I could handle a couple college kids, right? We had their dad in common, and we all loved Aubrey.

Uhhh. Wait. I meant we were all *fond* of Aubrey.

Shit.

I couldn't be in love with her. I barely knew her.

Technically, I'd known her most of my life, but I didn't really *know her* know her. Not yet. But I'd daydreamed enough about her to convince myself what I felt was love.

Fuck. Everything was all messed up and chaotic in my head. I really did want to go forward with my plan, but wasn't it just a means to my own end? All I'd ever wanted was Aubrey's attention, but now that I had it, it didn't feel like enough.

"I gotta go."

"Don't forget dinner tomorrow night," Mama said. "It's your birthday." *Oh, so they did know I wasn't just their employee, and they hadn't forgotten they had a third son.*

That got my dad's attention for a second. He had forgotten, and a little tic of his cheek was the only outward appearance of recognition.

I nodded. "I'll be back late tonight, and I'll be ready to work in the mornin'."

Like I always am, with my mouth shut, my intelligence insulted, and my hope for the future of the ranch in the toilet.

"HEY, MAN," my oldest friend, Bax, said when I called him on my way to pick up Aubrey. "Happy birthday tomorrow."

"Thanks."

"How you been? I called you last week, but I never heard back. Thought you mighta dropped off the face of the planet."

"Naw, I've been around." Man, I missed the days when Bax, his brother, Brand, and their little sister, Abey, and I would ride out on our ATVs and get lost in mud and hills. They and their youngest brother Dixon had provided some of the best memories of my life growing up. "Just been busy and kinda stuck in my head. How are you and Athena? What's she, like, eighteen already?"

"Don't joke. She's thirteen, and she's already a handful. I can't even imagine eighteen." But he'd been doing a great job with his only kid since his wife, Candy, passed. "Anyway, what's up?"

"Nothin'. Just wanted to call you back. I'm on my way to town, actually. Got me a date."

"A date for your birthday? You sure you wanna risk tyin' the memory of the day you were born to a disaster? Who you goin' out with? Please tell me it's not the woman who disabled your engine when you told her you wouldn't impregnate her after three weeks of ridin' the Rye train?"

"Ugh, don't remind me. That was Tiffany, the barrel racer.

Nope. Not her. And what's with this Rye train? You're the second person to use that stupid phrase in a week."

He laughed. "Who is it then? If you're comin' to Wisper, do I know her?"

As much as I'd dreamed about her, I'd never told anyone how badly I wanted Aubrey. Devo had guessed because I usually spent time with her when I came to town since her job was across the street from Red's store, and apparently my face gave a lot away.

"You might. It's Aubrey George."

Bax was quiet for a minute, and I pictured the confusion and then the dawning on his face while he put two and two together. "Wait a minute. The bookstore chick? Isn't she, like… older?"

I laughed. "Yeah, Bax, she's a few years older than I am. But you and me? We ain't so young anymore. You yourself, sir, are pushin' forty."

"Yeah, don't remind me. Some days it feels like sixty. But we used to go in her store all the time," he said. "Remember she used to sell us comics?"

Oh, I remembered. To this day, I'd never even opened a comic, let alone read one, but I'd bought one from the lovely bookseller every other week so I didn't miss out on Aubrey's warm smile. She must've thought I was the biggest nerd, coming to town to buy comics at twenty years old when she worked part-time at the bookstore while her boys were in school. She bought it from the previous owner six months after Tommy died and revamped the whole thing.

I also remembered the argument I'd overheard between her and Tommy at José's Diner a couple years before that when Presley and I had gone for lunch one Saturday. We sat at the booth behind Aubrey's, and when she told her husband she'd gotten a job at the bookstore, he was pissed. She'd tried to tell him how much she loved being around books and that she really needed time for herself, but all Tommy had focused on was that his friends might think he couldn't provide for his family if his wife had to work. I still remembered the look of disappointment and sadness that flashed across her face that day.

And I'd never forget Presley's reaction to overhearing an argument between two people he didn't know from Adam. He wanted to drag that fucker, Tommy, to the alley behind the restaurant and teach him a lesson for talking to his own wife like she was a disobedient child.

Good ol' Presley. He didn't talk a whole hell of a lot, but when he did open his mouth, I'd learned to listen because he was wise.

I wasn't sure what had changed Tommy's mind, but Aubrey did take the job. Whatever the reason, I was still grateful because it had allowed me to see her, and that I'd gotten glimpses of her in her happy place, around books, was probably the reason the fake-dating idea had come to me. She'd do anything for her store.

"Listen," I told Bax, "we're doin' the spring drive in a few weeks at the ranch. You wanna bring the family, eat some barbecue, and listen to Presley fuck up a fiddle?"

"Yeah. That sounds good. I'll ask Mama. Brand might like to tag along too. He's been stayin' here with Athena and me while he's workin' on the new cabin rentals and Abey's and Mama's houses. He could use the opportunity to get out and see someone other than his problematic brother. I think I've stressed him out enough lately. Maybe we can get him to drink a little and cut loose."

"What'd you do to your brother?"

"Nothin', it's just that we lost some of our funding for the new business. Brand's already put a good chunk of his own money into the project, not to mention his time and skills. The dude put up the bare bones of a cabin by himself in a day. It's insane."

"What happened? How'd you lose the funds?"

"Oh, some big shot investor from South Dakota skipped town. Nobody seems to know how to get in touch with him. But I've got it figured out. I'm gonna sell off a piece of the farm. We're not using all this land anyway, and the family agreed. It'll be on the market by the end of next week."

Hm. Suddenly, my brain got stuck on the spin cycle. So many ideas popped into my head.

Good farmland for sale right outside Wisper?

CHAPTER THIRTEEN

RYE

"WHATCHA WANT?" The teenager at the concession stand inside the Jackson movie theatre looked dead bored while I tried to figure out what to buy.

I held out my credit card. "Just give us one of everything."

"Are you out of your mind?" Aubrey had been perusing the "Coming Soon" movie posters lining the theatre's walls, but she jerked her head in my direction. "I'm not eatin' all that!"

"Okay, young lady, then what would you like?" Like a gameshow host, I waved my arm out toward the menu board and the lit-up case full of boxes and packages of candy.

"Popcorn, Rye. Just popcorn with butter and a Coke, please."

The teenager shrugged and turned to round up the stuff.

"A big popcorn! Extra-large, and make that two Cokes," I called after him, then I second guessed myself. Turning back to Aubrey, I said, "Unless you want your own?"

"Rye," she whispered, peeking around the lobby discreetly to make sure no one could hear her, "your hands have been inside my body. I think we can share a bucket of popcorn."

That put a smile on my face a mile wide. "Good."

Yes, my hands had been inside her, and yes, I still remembered every second of our red-hot encounter in the back of my truck on a dark night at the edge of wild Wyoming, and how soft she was and how responsive to my touch.

Hadn't had a "good" orgasm in ten years? Woman, you just didn't have the right motivation.

We watched as the kid pumped a river of butter onto our popcorn. Aubrey didn't seem concerned about the cholesterol. Myself, I wasn't usually one to eat junk. The physical work I did every day demanded protein and complex carbs, not sugar and butter. But for her, I'd make every exception in the book.

"Ooo," she said, pointing to a white box in the candy display. She smiled up at me, a girlish grin lifting her lips. "And maybe some Junior Mints?"

I leaned down to kiss those lips, like I did it every day, and she blushed crimson.

The kid tossed her box of minty chocolates on the counter and swiped the card from my hand. He tapped it on his card reader, handed it back, and rolled his eyes, which was our signal to move on with our goodies.

"I haven't been to a movie in so long," Aubrey said.

Juggling the bucket of butter in the crook of one arm with the Cokes tucked precariously next to it, I handed our tickets to the attendant, while Aubrey held onto her box of Junior Mints with two hands, like it was her only present on Christmas, and her face was as bright and excited as lights on a tree.

"Me either," I said, opening and holding the theatre door for her. "I always tell myself I need to take more time to relax, but then a cow gets pneumonia, or the barn door gets busted by a bull, and then I forget all about the fun things in life."

"Self-care is important," she said as she pointed to the dimly lit top row. The very empty top row, I'd noticed, which suited me just fine 'cause I planned to steal a few more kisses. "At least, that's what my friends tell me."

"Yeah, but they aren't business owners, are they?"

"No. Well, Juneau is a writer, so I suppose she does own her own business, but it's a very different kind than mine. Billie probably does, too, but I'm not sure exactly what kind of business hackers run. Anyway, it doesn't really matter. Everybody's jobs keep them busy, but no, I guess you're right. Running a store is definitely a full-time job, especially doin' it all on my own. The sign might say 9–5, but they aren't the only hours I work."

"What's your favorite part?" I asked, and we sat right in the middle of the row, below the patched-up hole in the wall from where the movies used to be projected.

"The books. It's always been about the books. I went to school for business because I knew someday I wanted to have my own shop. But the downside is, by the time I actually opened my store, all the business 101 I learned back then had changed several times through the years. I feel like I'm constantly startin' over."

"Yeah, Spitfire," I said, handing her our gargantuan bucket of popcorn, "but you're smart. You can do it."

"Thanks," she said, taking the popcorn and digging her hand in. When she had a handful, she passed the bucket back to me and ate one piece at a time.

"Was there one book?"

"Huh?"

"What was the book you read when you were a kid that got you hooked?"

She smiled. "*The Secret Garden*. Have you read it?" The love in her eyes for that book lit up her whole face, and she looked as happy as only a little girl could.

"No."

"Oh, when I was a girl, I thought it was about adventure and I used to imagine I was the main character, Mary Lennox, and I'd go outside and climb trees and crawl under bushes, looking for my own secrets. But as I got older, it became more than that. It's really about lettin' yourself heal from heartache and loss and growin' from that."

The story seemed to fit her perfectly, and I wondered if I could find a first edition copy of the book for her.

"What about you?" she asked. "You said you have all these ideas about how to run your family's ranch, but have you ever thought about startin' your own? I have a feelin' you'd be good at it."

Grabbing a couple kernels, I popped them in and chewed. "It's funny you say that. Just today I had the same thought."

"Really?"

The lights dimmed in the theatre and the previews started up on the screen.

"Yeah," I whispered, leaning back in my chair and closer to her so she could hear me. "You know Bax Lee?"

"Abey's brother?"

I nodded. "He's a friend, and when I called him on my way to pick you up, he mentioned puttin' up a big parcel of his land for sale. It's good farmland. Until last year, they raised sheep on it. It'd be a hell of a lot smaller than my dad's outfit, but I think that might be ideal for a start-up while I work out the kinks. I've got the money for the land, with enough left over for labor and stock."

"So," she whispered back, inching closer to me too, "what's stoppin' you?"

Good question.

The previews seemed to last forever, but I didn't mind 'cause I spent most of them leaned back, watching Aubrey experience them. Her eyes would get big during action scenes, her mouth forming a delicate 'o,' and she'd flash a little secret smile at the romantic scenes. When the "shut the hell up and turn off your damn phones" announcement came on, she turned to look at me.

"What?" she whispered.

Shaking my head slowly, I tried not to let it show on my face just how much her smile made me feel full inside and how much I adored her. I set the popcorn on the seat next to me and reached for her hand. When she placed it in mine without argument, I held on tight, and we settled back and waited for Thor and his friends to entertain us.

And I did, in fact, steal a kiss, but I waited till her favorite superhero was up on the big screen flexing his biceps, driving home the fact that whoever that movie star was, he could be her dream, but in real life, I was the guy who could make her blush and swoon and come alive.

***

"THAT WAS SO GOOD!" Aubrey practically skipped to my truck after the movie.

It wasn't Thor's movie, technically, but his friend's, another dude in too-tight pants and ridiculously unmanageable hair, but she didn't care. Thor made a couple cameos and that was enough for Aubrey. She liked to laugh, and those superheroes with their raunchy back-and-forth and their constant pop culture references had her snickering the whole two hours.

"Glad you liked it," I said.

"Thank you for takin' me."

I still held her hand, and in my other I carried the half-empty popcorn bucket 'cause it was a metal superhero edition, and she thought her boys might like to have it. Thinking back to when I was twenty-three, I couldn't seem to remember wanting shit like that, but she knew her boys. And if they didn't use it for popcorn, they could always use it to hold cold beers or Doritos or something.

"You wanna drive over to Town Square and walk around a bit?"

She bit her bottom lip. "Would you mind walkin' around downtown Wisper instead?"

"Sure, Spitfire. Whatever you want."

I was right. She hated crowds, and it was late enough in the season that the tourists would've already started pouring into Jackson Hole. I didn't blame her one bit for wanting to avoid the throngs of people you had to actively work to dodge on the sidewalks around Town Square or all the people out in front of their stores trying to convince you to come in and buy shit.

If you wanted peace, Wisper was the place to go.

In my opinion, the laid-back easiness of Wisper was its number one selling point. Sure, they got their share of tourists, too, but way less. If you didn't run into at least one person you knew on the street every day in Wisper, you'd think you were in a twilight zone. Even me, and I'd never even lived in town.

She smiled up at me. "Thanks."

The drive back was relaxed. She held my hand for most of it, humming along to popular country songs on the radio, while I stroked her wrist with the pad of my thumb.

"So what are your boys up to lately?" I asked, releasing her hand and turning the song down a notch.

"Um. They…" Suddenly, she groaned, and her head fell back against her headrest. "I have no idea. They deliver pizzas up in Bozeman. Benji failed most of his classes. You know, that's what happens when you don't actually *go* to class. God, it took so much energy to get them to agree to go in the first place. And then instead of tryin' again, Benji dropped out. Then Micah followed. His grades weren't nearly as bad, but he has to do everything Benji does. They have that weird twin mind-meld thing."

I laughed.

"Yeah, well, their school was paid for by their dad's military benefits, so they're really lucky they didn't have to take out loans. Anyway, I don't know what they wanna do now. They're still livin' right off campus in an apartment, partyin' it up and actin' like they don't have a care in the world."

Sounded to me like they both needed a kick in the ass, and maybe a summer out at the ranch with my old man as their boss. He'd cure them of their carefree twenties real fast.

"What were they studyin' before they dropped out?"

"Actually, agriculture."

"Really?"

"Yeah. Benji's always been enamored with the cowboy life. Micah, not so much, but like I said, he does everything Benji does. Actually, I think Micah would excel in business."

"I can't speak to the business stuff, but Benji might benefit from a summer on a ranch. He'd learn more than he ever dreamed about agriculture and the life. It might give him an idea about where to go next."

"Can we talk about somethin' else?" Aubrey asked. "This subject makes me feel like a complete failure."

"What? Why?"

"Oh, that's right. You don't have kids yet." She rolled her

eyes and huffed out a breath. "When you do, you'll understand. Everything your kids do is a reflection on you."

She paused, maybe realizing there was an opportunity for a divide between us around the subject of me wanting kids. Fortunately, I didn't, and I already had my argument lined up to battle hers, just in case.

"If they punch a kid on the playground in third grade," she said, "everyone thinks there must be problems at home, even though that kid had bullied them since kindergarten. If they fail Mrs. Simmons's biology class in high school, then you must be workin' too much and can't help guide them through their studies. People gossip and talk no matter what I do. I tried to ignore it, but then after their dad died, it just got worse."

"I'm sorry. That had to be hard on you, all that talk."

"The worst part was how everyone suddenly worshipped Tommy. Please don't misunderstand me. I respected him for serving his country. A lot. I still do and for his sacrifice. I know that sounds cliché. But back here at home, Tommy wasn't a hero at all. Sometimes, he wasn't even kind. He wasn't abusive. Not physically. I don't mean to imply that he was.

"But he was dissatisfied with our life in a lot of ways. He never wanted me to work, but all he did was complain about not havin' the finances to do the things his friends were always doin', like expensive vacations or huntin' trips. Things like that.

"And he was a good dad to the boys," she went on, really saying what she was feeling now, "but he wasn't a *great* dad, you know? It was always me who took them to the movies. I helped with their homework and cooked and cleaned and basically catered to Tommy, while he played around with his truck or—

"Sorry," she said. "I didn't mean to get carried away."

"Spitfire, you can talk all night if you want to. I love listenin' to you no matter what you wanna talk about. Besides, I like knowin' how things were for you. I've imagined your life, but it was just a daydream in my mind. Although, I'll admit, I don't like knowin' you spent all that time feelin' alone. You don't have to censor yourself, though. Ain't nobody here judgin' you."

Cautiously, she placed her hand back in mine. "Thanks. It's nice to be listened to. But I'm changin' the subject. It's been such a nice night. I don't wanna ruin the mood."

"Impossible," I said, squeezing her hand. "My mood could never be ruined with you sittin' next to me."

HOW WEIRD WAS it that I'd gone forty-seven years without Rye holding my hand, but now that he had, I never wanted him to let go?

We parked in front of Your Local Bookie and then continued our conversation while we walked slowly through town. It was a peaceful, starry spring night, but the slight chill in the air disappeared around Rye.

"So what about you?" I asked. "You want kids someday?"

"Nope."

"What? Why not?"

Most guys I knew wanted four or five kids, boys to carry on their name and girls to dote on and protect.

"Dunno. Just never have. I guess my focus has always been on the ranch, and now, it's shifted a bit, but it's still ranchin'. I want marriage, or even if it's not marriage, I want a partner. I want someone to love, to walk through this life with me. But kids, naw. I'm almost thirty-five. That window's closin' quickly anyway."

"You know men can have children pretty much up until

they die, right? You could be eighty and still father a whole brood of kids."

He laughed. "Not if my woman can't."

Did he mean me because I was... *well, we'll call it mature*.

"Your woman? You want a little lady waitin' at home for you when you come back from a cattle drive?"

"Not at all. I want a woman to go *with* me on that drive. Or if she doesn't want that, I want her to do things that make her happy while I'm away, and when I get back, I'll make love to her and listen to her when she tells me about all her adventures. I'll cook her breakfast and rub her feet and make her come so many times, she won't be able to walk straight for a week."

The smug smile on his face as he looked down at me had me blushing and digging through my mind for any subject I could change the conversation to. If he kept turning me on with his tongue and his words, I'd never learn enough about him to be able to pull the wool over his parents' eyes.

But I didn't have to search too hard because we ran into Daisy and her husband José in front of a closed Coffee Shot. Like, nearly ran right *into* them because I was too busy blushing and trying to hide it from Rye, and I almost bowled Daisy over.

She gripped my shoulders so I wouldn't fall on my ass, and José said, "Hey, Rye. Aubrey. How are y'all tonight?"

Daisy didn't say a word, she just smiled up at Rye with a look full of gossipy satisfaction, giving me quick sideways glances every few seconds.

Rye reached out to shake José's hand. "We're alright. Thanks. Oh and thanks for that meat-and-cheese-board thing the other night." Rye winked at me. "It was a hit."

"Glad to hear you enjoyed it, Aubrey."

I could already hear the book-club talk. The impending squeals and demands for information made it difficult to concentrate on what José had said. "Thanks."

Daisy's smile grew while she looked back and forth between Rye and me, not even trying to hide her curiosity anymore. And when she noticed him holding my hand, her eyes flared.

"Rye, this is my wife, Daisy. I don't think you two have met yet, have you?"

"No," Daisy said. "We haven't, but I've seen you at the diner and around town, *young* man. It's a pleasure."

She held out her hand to Rye and he shook it, but he seemed to be catching on to the undercurrent of her teasing smile as he looked back and forth between Daisy and me. José seemed oblivious. He'd probably heard the gossip from his wife, but he wasn't really one to get involved.

"Alright, well, nice to see you," I rushed to say. "We've gotta get goin'."

"So soon?" Daisy asked innocently.

"Yes, Daisy. See you at book club," I nearly growled, and I squeezed Rye's hand and yanked him down the sidewalk.

Dammit. As soon as she could, she'd be calling everyone we knew to report who she'd run into and how cozy Rye and I had looked together.

"C'mon," I said, pulling Rye as hard as I could, which barely budged him at all.

"Nice to see y'all," he called behind us with his usual cocky grin. To me, he asked innocuously, "Where we goin'?"

"My shop," I whispered. "Hurry up."

"Why you in such a rush, Spitfire?" he asked, and I could actually hear him smiling. Great, now he was teasing me too.

"Just come *on*."

I pulled my keys from my purse as I speed-walked back

to my shop, pulling poor Rye like a puppy, but he just laughed under his breath, like he was enjoying my embarrassment. I almost fell through the front door after I unlocked it, and his sexy chuckle sent a chill down my spine.

He followed me to the storeroom, and when I found the light switch, I flipped it on and rounded on him. At least no one could see us through the big front windows back here.

"Daisy's lightin' up the gossip tree as we speak. I just know it."

"So?"

"You don't get it."

"Enlighten me," he said with a grin. "We're supposed to be datin', right? So if someone sees us or talks about us, how's that a problem?"

"I don't care if people see us. I agreed to your dumb plan, and I'm stickin' to it, but now they're all gonna be talkin' about what they think we're doin'."

"Such as?"

"Rye!"

"I don't think I know what you mean, Spitfire. I'm gonna need it explained." The side of his mouth lifted in the cockiest smirk I'd seen yet. "In great detail. Now, please."

"Dammit, Rye. You know what I mean."

Turning away from him, I tried to calm down. He was right. What did it really matter? The whole point of fake dating was to convince everyone we were together. The gossip could probably help us.

But there was something intimate growing between Rye and me and knowing that everyone would be talking about it made me feel protective of him.

Just as I was about to turn back to him, his big hand warmed my hip. He held me in place, sliding the length of my hair over my shoulder and trailing a finger lazily between my shoulder blades. The warmth moved slowly up to my neck where he gripped and squeezed softly.

"So," he whispered, "if I do this"—leaning down, he pressed his lips to my neck and placed a soft kiss there— "someone will talk about it?"

The instant his mouth touched me, tingling pressure began to build between my thighs.

I didn't answer him. I couldn't speak. The panic I'd been feeling about my body, about sex, and about being the focus of gossip dissipated. I wanted all my concentration on how Rye's touch made me feel.

What the Pavlovian crap was that?

But whether he'd trained me to want him, to *need* him, or not, I did, and the wanting was making me shake, making breath come out of my mouth in shudders.

"Or this?" His other hand snaked under my arm, around my ribcage, and he cupped my breast in his hand, thumbing my nipple through my shirt.

"Or this?" Dropping that hand, he fit it over the warmth now quickly forming between my legs, rubbing with his thumb exactly where he knew I couldn't ignore it.

Heat rushed around the inside of my body like an out-of-control wildfire. It didn't know where to go, so it went every-where. "Oh God."

"Not God, Spitfire. I think what you meant to say was 'Oh, Rye.'"

I was practically hyperventilating now as I remembered the last time he'd whispered in my ear and touched me there.

"Does the invitation to spend the night with you still stand?"

"Yes."

"May I see you home then?"

"Yes."

"Was there anything else you wanted to talk about before we go?" He paused for dramatic and annoying effect. "We still haven't discussed our plan."

"I don't care," I said, moaning and pushing back to better feel the rigid length of his cock grinding against my ass.

His hand still on the back of my neck applied strict pressure, and he guided me to look at him. When I did, his mouth came down over mine so fast, he gave me vertigo. But that didn't matter, because he released his hand and turned me into his body, kissing me harder and holding me tightly.

My heart took flight inside my chest, and I opened for him, delving my tongue into his hot mouth.

Strong hands gripped my hips, and he lifted me. I wrapped my legs around his waist, locked my ankles together behind him, and ground myself against his erection through our clothes in an embarrassing display of need versus proper old-lady behavior. An orgasm had already begun to build deep inside.

It had been so long since I'd had a man's body inside mine, and I was having a hard time imagining the sensation.

"*Rye.*"

"We ain't makin' it back to your place, are we?"

I shook my head wildly. "Here. Now."

Into my mouth, he breathed, "You're so needy, baby. I fuckin' love it," and he reached beneath me to pop his fly and unzip his jeans. "I want you up against that wall." He nodded behind us. "And I'm gonna take you a second time from behind while you're spread open for me over that desk."

He looked to the right, to where my mom's old writing desk had been sitting for years, piled with papers, receipts, and schedules I never bothered to look at. I pictured him sliding his arm across the mess, knocking it all to the floor so he could take me just like he said he would.

Somehow, seeing my storeroom in this new, erotic light felt like a dangerous adventure. It was so exciting to be wrapped up in this man, to be enticed and seduced by him in this plain, everyday place.

I groaned. "Yes, *please*."

Moaning in my ear, he unhooked my legs and set me on my feet. I swayed and reached out for him again to steady myself as he took my hands and placed them gently on his shoulders.

And then for the second time in less than two weeks, he got down on his knees for me and began to undress me.

"Ever been naked in here before?"

I shook my head, unable to speak while I watched his eyes eat up every inch of my body when it was revealed to him.

"Mm. I like that. It'll be our first time together in more than one way." He tossed my shoe behind me, and then tugged the other one off my foot and tossed it too. "If you'd fucked anybody else in here, I'd have to rut you like a stud bull to stake my claim. I'm gettin' harder just thinkin' about it."

He unzipped my mom jeans, leaning forward to kiss my stomach. I tried to hide it, to move my hands in front of the loose skin below my navel and the disgusting fat pocket I hadn't been able to get rid of, no matter how many diets and exercise routines I tried, but he pushed my hands away.

"Don't you dare. I have dreamed of this body for far too long for you to hide it from me now. I understand your tummy ain't your favorite feature, but you need to understand that I think it's sexy as hell. We're just gonna have to agree to disagree."

The serious-as-a-heart-attack look in his eyes had me

nodding my consent, and he went back to kissing and dragging his lips and scratchy beard across my skin.

Slowly, he pulled my jeans down, catching my underwear with two fingers and pulling them down, too, until he removed them completely, tossed them away, and nuzzled his beard between my legs, looking up at me like I was a goddess and he was on his knees at my altar, ready to worship.

Rye gave me courage, so I lifted my shirt over my head and tossed it, unsnapped my bra and tossed that too.

He studied my breasts like he'd never seen a pair before, his mouth working to hold his tongue inside. They were okay. I'd never thought much of my breasts. A little saggy from pregnancy forever ago, but not too big, not too small. There were visible stretch marks, but Rye seemed to think they were the best things since sliced bread if the clenching of his jaw while he looked at them meant what I hoped it did.

"Arms up," I told him, and when he complied, I bent to lift his shirt, too, and he latched onto my hip with his mouth, sucking and licking and working his way north.

Lord above, the chest on this man!

His muscled pecs and shoulders, and, truly, I'd had no idea trapezius muscles could be that hard and strong.

He was the most beautiful human being I'd ever seen. And the tattoo covering his whole upper right arm and pectoral muscle was so sexy, I had a hard time looking at anything besides the life-like black and gray rendering of the Tetons, with tiny cows grazing in the valley below, and a banner with the phrase "where the heart is" below it.

Lust slipped between my lips in a moan, and Rye tilted his head. He looked up at me, and I pushed my fingers into his hair and fisted it in my palms.

"Like what you see, Spitfire?"

"Mm."

"It's all for you. It's always been you," he whispered, and he slid his hand between my legs, growling when he felt how wet I already was for him.

I pulled him closer, he nuzzled his mouth between my breasts, and I widened my legs as he slipped a finger inside me.

"Yeah," he breathed, his lips whispering against my skin. "That's what I've been dreamin' about."

"B-but your jeans."

"What about 'em?"

"They're still on."

"They'll come off soon enough, but first, I want you ready before I fuck you, so you can take me easier."

"O-oh okay."

He chuckled and got to work with his mouth on my clit. He held me up, stopping me from falling over because it didn't take long before waves of euphoria began to pulse through my bloodstream.

His tongue should've come with a warning: ⚠ *Slippery when wet. Do not use unless you're prepared for utter satisfaction, and please beware that just when you think you can't take another second, this tongue will double down. * ⚠

Sure enough, he did. He thrust another finger inside me, and his tongue fluttered against the most sensitive part of my body as quickly as a hummingbird's wings. His saliva coated my pussy and dripped from his mouth, and he rubbed me with his chin, his bristled beard doing things to me I'd never even imagined.

"Ride the mustache, baby. That's what it's there for."

"*Oh.*"

"Use your words," he demanded.

"Th-that's sinful, Rye. So good." My hands gripped his

hair harder, and before long, I was guiding his head to the most delicious rhythm.

He hummed his satisfaction, the vibration made me gasp as he added a third finger, and then I was riding his hand, my hips rolling to the tempo of his tongue, while his beard and mustache rubbed me in *all* the right ways.

How had I not noticed that before? But I'd been so utterly shocked at what he'd done to me in the bed of his truck that I didn't blame myself for missing such a wonderful part of his sexual tool set.

I couldn't miss it now, and I wanted *more*.

"Harder," I begged, practically riding his face now.

Fast flicks and licks of his tongue drove me higher, and I pulled his hair so hard that if I hadn't been in the throes of orgasm already, I would've worried I'd made him bleed when I yanked it all out.

"You're so fuckin' beautiful when you come," he breathed when I called out my release and my head fell back, my hair swaying behind me, tickling his hand still bracing me from behind.

His knees had to be killing him on the hard tile floor, but he never complained.

When he stood, those knees popped audibly while I tried to get my sea legs back. He shed his jeans and a pair of navy blue boxers, then towered over me silently and still, like a mountain.

I couldn't not reach for his cock. It was nearly purple, he was so hard and ready, the thick veins running up his length raised and ribbed for my pleasure.

He stopped me with his heavy hand on my wrist as I grasped for him. "Oh no you don't."

I gasped, and he ran his tongue over his bottom lip, leaving a trail of wet shine to draw my eyes there.

"This time, I want your pretty pussy 'round my cock when I come."

He released my wrist and arched an eyebrow, daring me, and I climbed him like a fucking tree.

His hands found my ass, and he squeezed while I wrapped my legs around him again, securing my body around his. He walked us to the wall between two old, yellowing "buy local" posters and pressed me against it, watching my face and listening to the moans falling out of my open mouth as he pressed his bare chest to my breasts.

Just to feel the warmth of his body, skin to skin against mine— I couldn't describe how amazing he felt.

Leaning down, he took my nipple into his mouth, and his hard cock slid between my legs as it twitched and pulsed.

He drew his hips back, released my breast, and straightened.

And when I felt the smooth, full pressure of his thick length gliding into the core of me, my eyes rolled closed.

"Yes!" The voice that came out of my mouth was guttural, like I'd been possessed by the devil. "Oh dear God, *yes*!"

CHAPTER FIFTEEN

FUCK THAT TAKING-IT-SLOW, "I don't wanna just be sex to you" shit.

I wanted to be sex and release and laughter to her. I wanted us to breathe together and come together, and I wanted her to fall asleep in my arms after.

And I wanted it all right now.

Aubrey's overuse of the Holy Spirit's name would've made me laugh, but the urge to fuck hard and loosen her up tried to derail my concentration. Her body tightened around mine instantly. She felt so goddamn good, I could barely breathe.

But I needed to remember it had been a long time for her.

She was wet enough. Her creamy silk coated my cock, letting me glide in and out even though her pussy was tighter than a bench vice. I could only imagine what my body felt like inside hers, but she took me like a fucking dream.

I forced my eyes open so I could watch her, to make sure pleasure showed on her face, and when it did, I wanted to drown in her. I'd stay down on my knees for her forever if she asked it of me.

"Aubrey, oh God."

"Use your words," she bit back, running her hands through my hair, clutching it between her fingers, pulling me ever closer.

"You want words, Spitfire?"

Eagerly, she nodded. She wanted me to tell her how she made me feel.

"I fit inside you like I was made for you. I wanna fuck you forever."

Her eyes fell shut, and she sighed a moan.

"Your pussy suckin' me in and your ass fillin' my hands is goddamn perfection. I love how you gasped when you felt how good I fit inside you, like it shocked you. I wanna give you more. Can you take more of me, woman?"

"Yes," she breathed. "*More*."

"Hold on tight."

I didn't think I could get any harder, but when she obeyed and dug her fingernails into my shoulders, a thrill rushed through me. The need to fuck wild traveled through my body like a stampede, and I punched my cock inside her, but her head hit the wall, and her eyes popped open.

"Shit! Did I hurt you?"

"Do it again," she whispered, and after the second it took to recover from the shock her answer caused, I *pounded* into her, over and over, and she rode my dick like I was a prized rodeo bull.

I'd never been so turned on in my life.

"Gimme your mouth," I said, and she complied, latching onto my lips and taking over the kiss.

Her tongue tasted like mint and honey, like the pleasure I gave her made her sweeter somehow.

She took everything I had to give, which was no small feat. It had been a while for me, too, and all my anger at my family, the frustration, and the aimless hope I'd been feeling seemed to load up inside me, ready to break free when the right catalyst presented itself.

She was my catalyst, and she couldn't know, but she was the one I'd been waiting for. She and I were meant to be. Maybe she didn't believe it yet, but if it was the last thing I did on this earth, I'd convince her.

Tearing my lips away from hers, I was gasping now, too, as I tried to see between us. I pressed her hard against the wall so I could look down and watch my cock make a mess of her, but she hooked two fingers inside my mouth and pulled my eyes back up to hers.

Jesus Christ. I couldn't take much more. Already, my balls had pulled up tight, and that tingling buzz had started at the bottom of my spine.

But I was doing my damnedest to hold out for her. I sucked her fingers and let them fall from my mouth, then breathed, "Slide those wet fingers between us. Rub yourself and come."

"No," she said. "*You* make me come. Just you. You're all I need."

"Fuck." If she said things like that, I wouldn't last another five seconds. "You're destroyin' me with that mouth."

Smiling a devil's smile, she liked the power she had over me. Damn if I didn't love it too.

She angled her hips, tipped them forward a little so the hair above the base of my cock rubbed her clit with every push inside her, and I watched how her eyelids dipped the tiniest bit and her mouth went slack.

"That's it. That what you need? A little dirty friction?"

She moaned loudly. Her body relaxed more every passing second, and she nodded as her head fell back against the wall, banging like a knock on a door with my every move.

I gave her what she wanted. Hard and fast. Her tits were warm pressed against my chest, and they bounced between us again and again as cum loaded up inside me, getting ready to blow.

She fell out of our rhythm, and her body squeezed mine more tightly than anything I'd ever felt.

It seemed I'd lost the ability to form coherent thoughts. *"Fuck."*

"Rye!" She screamed my name and dug her fingernails harder into my shoulders, just like I'd dreamed about, and I trapped the inside of my cheek between my teeth and bit down. The metallic tang of blood filled my mouth, but that was okay by me if it stopped me from coming so I could take her over the desk next.

I carried her there as she fell limp against my chest, but I felt her mouth on my skin, kissing and licking. She scraped her teeth over my tattoo, and it made goosebumps rise at the back of my neck.

She was warm. She smelled so fucking good with the scent of our sex clouding around her like perfume, and her hair tickled my chest as she rode out the last vestiges of her orgasm on my still-hard cock. It was almost painful, but I knew as soon as I had her face down, I could fuck her proper, and that would feel better than amazing.

A cell phone rang on the floor behind us.

"Shit." *Not now.*

She whispered, "Don't answer it."

"Ain't my phone, darlin'."

"Oh. Well, just ignore it. It'll stop."

She didn't have to tell me twice. The phone stopped its chiming as I lowered her ass to the desktop and leaned over her to swipe the papers on top to the floor with my arm.

She laughed and moaned and swayed with my movement,

like her body was a magnet attracted to mine, and when the mess was cleared, I lifted her again and set her on her feet. Reaching up for me, she gripped my biceps hard as I kissed her, my tongue snaking in to steal more of her sweetness, but then the damn phone rang again.

We both groaned, but I released her, grabbed her purse from the floor, and handed it to her.

As she pulled her phone from the inside pocket and dropped the bag back to the floor, I turned her and guided her chest down onto the desk with my hand hard and splayed wide between her shoulder blades. She bent over for me with no hesitation, her lush, round ass ripe for my taking.

I molded my hands over it, rubbing and loving how her cheeks bounced when she moved. I used my thumbs to spread her open, but when her phone rang again, she said, "Rye, wait."

"Ain't gonna happen, Spitfire. Gimme that phone."

She surprised me when she handed it back to me, but I took it from her slender fingers and saw Abey's name on the screen.

Clicking to accept the call, I greeted my old friend pleasantly. "Hey, Abey. What's up? Aubrey's busy right now. Can she call you back?"

Using my other hand, I fisted my cock and slipped it between Aubrey's wet thighs. Good God, from this angle she was a vision, her ass raised for me, her pussy coated in her own slick. The sheen on that soft, pink skin almost made me drop the phone.

I needed inside her heat again.

"Um, Rye? I'm gonna need to *actually* speak to Aubrey," my friend, the deputy sheriff, said. "Someone reported screamin'."

That stopped me. "No shit? That's kinda epic," I said, and I pushed the tip of my cock inside Aubrey. "Hold on."

Aubrey moaned loudly at my invasion and pushed her ass back for more of me, but when I held her phone over her shoulder she snapped, "What?" and ripped it out of my hand.

I couldn't hear what Abey was saying anymore, but with Aubrey's hair pulled over one shoulder, the darker the deep blush on her neck and the side of her face became, the more I could guess.

"I'm fine, Abey," she said, and I guided her down lower on the desk.

When a quick punch of my hips pushed me inside her again, Aubrey gasped and moaned into the phone.

Abey said something, and it threw my Spitfire right over the top.

"Don't you dare come here, Abey. You *know* what we're doin', and it's none of anybody's goddamn business." I pumped again and again, gripping her naked hips hard, hopefully leaving fingerprints on them, 'cause after tonight, she needed to know I was hers and she was *mine*.

She groaned loudly and her forehead hit the desk. "Rye, yes!" she called out, but then she whimpered into her phone. "Abey, *please* hang up now."

Abey tried one more time to say whatever the fuck she'd called for.

"I said I'm fine! My physical and emotional safety are intact," Aubrey yelled into her phone, and when I rammed inside her again as hard and as fast as I could, she moaned so loudly, the sound vibrated around my cock from inside her body.

"Jesus, Abey! If you need me to say it, I'm gettin' railed by your brother's best friend. Rye's fuckin' me within an inch of my life right now, and if you ruin it, I will never speak to you again. Go ahead and tattle to the gossip girls. I don't even care anymore. Goodbye, Sheriff."

I pistoned my hips, punching inside her again, the knowledge that everyone knew what we were doing urging me on. Aubrey groaned and threw the phone across the room. It hit the back door, then thunked onto the floor.

She muttered, "Shit," but then she gripped the edges of the desk and pressed her ass up higher for me, which just made me fuck her harder.

Her backtalking scary Sheriff Abey turned me on even more than I had been before the phone call. My vision went in and out the louder she moaned when I slid out and back home again, rocking into her pussy like the answer to world peace was tucked high and tight inside her and I was about to hit it, break it free, and cure everything.

Her moans got lower and breathier the harder I pressed her chest to the desk, which worked in my favor 'cause I could see hints of her breasts spreading out beneath her and holding her still was making me insane with lust.

"Goddamn, Spitfire. You're makin' every dream I've ever had about you come true right now."

"Rye! I can't stop it. How are you doin' this to me?" Her fingers were white now from blood loss as she clung to the desk for dear life. "Watch me take you. I want you to watch your cock break me open, and I want you to come inside me. *Now*." She moaned and begged again, "*Please*!"

Fuck my life. Was this woman even real?

I did what she begged, bent my knees a little so I could hit the spot deep inside her I knew would make her lose her mind, and I watched how I glided so smoothly in and out of her pink, swollen pussy and how her cum dripped down her thighs, coating my cock and pubic hair, making everything slick and shine.

Her back muscles flexed hard when she gripped the edges of the desk even tighter, enough to make the old wood creak, and her body spasmed around mine and sucked my dick in, over and over and—

I'd never been one to make a lot of noise when I came, but the sheriff was sure to come breaking down our door tonight 'cause the roar that let loose from the deepest hollow inside me when I shot my load inside the sexiest woman I'd ever known was bound to knock down walls and mountains alike.

CHAPTER SIXTEEN

AUBREY

WITHOUT A WINK of sleep and possibly too many orgasms between us, Ryder left my house at three on Sunday morning, loaded with a Thermos full of coffee and half a box of strawberry breakfast bars, so he could get home in time to start work. I worried he'd fall asleep at the wheel, so I stayed on the phone with him the whole hour.

"Are you sure you should be drivin' right now?" I asked for the fifth time.

"I'm fine, Mom. Quit bitchin'."

I rolled my eyes and scoffed loudly into my phone. "Do you speak to your *actual* mother with that mouth."

He laughed. "I *fuck* somebody's mother with this mouth."

"Ugh, Rye, don't even say that."

"You started it." He chuckled and yawned. "Seriously though, I'm okay. I get up this early most days. Maybe a little bit later, but I'm usually up and movin' by four. What about you? Tell me about your workday."

"Mm, I usually wake up around six. Take a shower while the coffee's brewin'. Oh. And I have to feed the birds. I get a lot of Stellar's jays in my backyard, you know the blue jays that look like opposites of themselves? The blue and black ones."

"Yeah, the little nuisances."

"They are not." I sipped coffee from my favorite "Book Bitch" mug. "They're beautiful, and they're really smart. They come back year after year, and if you sit quietly and watch, you can see their different personalities. I like to feed them whole peanuts. I've even had one take a peanut from my hand."

"Wow. I made love to Snow White last night. My fair maiden."

I snorted. *Yeah right.*

"You don't see yourself very clearly, fair maiden."

"What's that supposed to mean?" I asked, kind of offended.

I'd always thought I had a good grasp on who I was. I was honest with myself. I knew when to pat myself on the back and when not to. I knew if I'd made a mistake, and I knew how to not end up in the same situation again.

"What do you see when you look in a mirror? Tell me true. Don't lie."

"I'm not a liar."

"That's not what I meant. I meant tell me what you think about yourself. Who you *really* are."

Tapping speaker, I set my coffee on my bedside table then tossed my phone on my comforter. I lay back, resting my head on my favorite feather pillow that still smelled like Rye and breathing the scent of his shampoo deep into my lungs. I smiled when it relaxed me.

After the sex we'd had in my store and again in my kitchen before we hit my bed, I was more relaxed than I'd ever been in my life, but feeling his presence in my home, smelling him and imagining him coming back to me put me over the relaxation edge.

I yawned. "I don't know. I guess I see a mom. A friend. A business owner and member of the community."

Rye gagged, like he'd stuck his finger down his throat. "I didn't ask for the bio you submitted to the Chamber of Commerce. Who are you, Aubrey? What do you love? What do you hate?"

"What's with the third degree so early this mornin'?"

"I've wanted to know the answer to these questions for a very long time. The least you can do after the way you came for me last night—*several* times—is tell me who I'm fallin' for."

Falling for? Heat flooded my cheeks. It rushed around my chest and made my heart race. Love wasn't part of our deal. Sex, yes, he'd mentioned something that day at my store about things getting "heated."

But wasn't this the part of the story where one of us was supposed to pull away, create some kind of self-imposed obstacle we had to overcome? Nothing came to mind though. I just wanted to lay there listening to Rye's voice. I wanted to remember how amazing he'd made me feel—like the main character of an epic, wildly sexy romance novel. At my age? I wasn't about to waste it.

But had he put me on a pedestal I'd never be able to climb down from? The thought kept popping into my head.

Besides, if Rye's and my story was a romance, then there had to be a happily ever after at the end. I wasn't so sure I was ready for that. I had a pretty good guess my boys weren't ready for it either. Micah still brought up his dad at every opportunity, still romanticized the life he'd thought we'd had back in the "good ol' days."

Maybe our genre wasn't romance. Maybe Rye and I were

in the middle of a grisly crime novel, but the bloody parts hadn't happened yet. Or maybe it was self-help. *How to Navigate Menopause and Your Later Years, Erotic Edition*, with a note to the reader: Dear Reader, please hide this book under your bed or in your sock drawer. Better yet, hide it with your cleaning supplies. Kids never look there…

Yes, my boys were grown, but they'd always be my "kids." Some things never changed.

"I thought we were *fake* datin'."

Rye didn't seem to like the word "fake." He rumbled when I said it and almost growled his next sentence. "Just answer the question."

"Okay, okay. Jeez. Um, well first, I'm a mom. That's true. I'm a good mom. I'm not Martha Stewart, but I washed my kids' sheets every week, and I make a mean apple pie—"

"Ohh," Rye groaned, his grumble quickly acquiescing to his insatiable libido. "I'm gonna need you to make that for me and feed it to me, naked in your bed."

I tried not to imagine the mess that would make, but then I smiled like a fool when I actually pictured the act and how hot it could be if I covered my body with strategically placed dollops of apple-pie filling and demanded he lick it off.

Like he knew exactly where my randy mind had gone, Rye chuckled deviously.

"*Anyway*, I was always good at helpin' my boys with school projects. They probably got their best grades on the dioramas and posters I helped them make. But then after Tommy passed and I bought the shop, I didn't have a lot of time for that kind of stuff.

"That made me feel like a shitty mom, but I guess it also taught them that they couldn't wait around for me to do everything for them. They had to figure stuff out for themselves." I rolled my eyes. "They're still workin' on that."

He laughed, and I let the sound wash through me, from my ears all the way down to my toes and back up again. It made me feel warm and cozy, and I snuggled into my soft mattress and pulled my covers up to my chin.

"What else?" he asked.

"I dunno. I guess… I'm a great friend. I didn't really have girlfriends until I became a widow. Tommy didn't like me spendin' time with other people. God, sometimes I forget just how isolated I was back then."

"I remember that," Rye said. "But I also remember your wild smile, the way you were so free before you got married."

"You do?"

"Oh yeah. Like it was yesterday."

"I don't understand," I said. "How are you this person? How have you been here the whole time and I never knew?"

"Well, technically, I wasn't 'here.' I was an hour away, and also technically, you weren't ready to know, but I'm glad you do now. It's a great birthday present."

"Birthday? When?"

"Today. May twenty-third."

"What! Why didn't you tell me?"

"Age is just a number, baby. Haven't we already decided that?"

"Yeah, but your birthday is special, no matter how old you are, or how young. It's supposed to be a celebration of you, of the person you are now and of the day you debuted in the world. It means somethin'."

He hummed. "I like that."

"I'm glad you were born, Ryder Graves. Happy birthday."

"Thank you. I'm glad you were born too, in October, ain't that right?"

"Yes, how…? Never mind." I smiled again, thinking of the book I carried at the store that talked about compatibility between zodiac signs; Libras and Geminis were said to be extremely compatible. Not that I believed in all that crap…

"I also like that I got to ring in my thirty-fifth year inside you."

He couldn't see it, but I blushed so hard. "So what would you like for your birthday?" I asked to distract him. His filthy mouth was going to change my skin to a ruddy red color permanently.

I had already started making a list in my Notes app: books about regenerative farming, the cowboy coffee he'd told me he loved. And maybe I'd be brave and order some kind of sex toy or, like, edible panties.

"You," he said. "I want you on a big, round cake plate. Gargantuan sized. And I wanna eat you and give *you* apple-pie orgasms till you're nothin' but a moanin', pantin' mess with a warm, gooey center."

It seemed my birthday gift list was spot on.

"Be serious," I scolded.

"Fine. For my birthday, I'd like you to come out to the house tonight for dinner. My mama makes a big spread and a tres leches cake that'll make your head spin. It's delish."

"Tonight? Won't you be passed out by then?"

"No time for sleepin', lil' lady. There's work to be done." He yawned again. "Please? I miss you already, and we can flaunt our date in my parents' faces. It'll be the first real test."

"If it's fake, just an arrangement, why'd you stay the night? Not that I'm complainin'."

"Mm, 'cause I like to keep a good eye on my investments," he said. "Besides, we barely slept, and I know when I've struck gold. And when a man strikes gold, he don't love it and leave it. He keeps it close."

SILENCE GREETED me when I walked into book club after my first ever railing—during which, and with Rye's giant-sized dick inside me, I'd spoken to my friend, the fucking sheriff! Who was also a lesbian. She was probably still icked out. I'd already texted her to apologize for my rude behavior on the phone last night, and for the moaning she'd no doubt heard.

Abey at least had decorum, and she took her job seriously, and since she'd called while on duty, I felt pretty sure she wouldn't rat me out, but everybody knew already anyway. Of course they did, just like I knew every other piece of gossip that happened in this town, if not when it was happening, five minutes after.

Someone cleared their throat.

Standing behind my usual chair, I rolled my eyes and braced myself. "Just get it over with."

Chaos ensued, wherein people jumped out of their chairs. Some giggled. Some squealed. One of them slapped my ass. I had a feeling it was Billie, but I was too busy being hugged by at least six women to know for sure, and after they'd taken their seats again, all ten of them grinned up at me, buzzing in their chairs, waiting for more information. I heard a few, "Mm-hm, girl"s, and Phil said she was "pleased" I'd had "a nice time."

"Jeez. Y'all act like I was a virgin before the weekend and Rye came down from on high to bless me with his golden dick. This isn't the 'magical-cock trope' in real life. You do know I'm a mother to two children, right?"

Billie snorted, and Cal tsked her disapproval.

"Alright, here's the deal. Yes, I had sex. No, I'm not gonna regale you with the tale. It's private and you should know better."

"You're absolutely right," Sam said. "Shame on us. Now,

let's get to our new book." She held up a paperback copy of a pale blue book, and on the cover next to an illustrated couple standing on a train track and wearing cowboy hats, the hot-pink title read, *Railed by the Cowboy*.

"Abey!" I accused and glared at her.

She held up her hands. "I swear it wasn't me. I didn't say a word."

"It was me!" Roxi said, bouncing in her armchair with her hand in the air as I sat next to her. "I'm sorry. I just couldn't hold it in. I'm so proud of you."

"Jesus." I breathed slowly, trying to quell my embarrassment.

"Well," she tried to explain, "sorry, but I just happened to be standin' next to Abey when you talked to her durin' your... the *railing* in question, and you were really loud. And then you didn't call to tell me about it this mornin'. I had to talk to somebody!"

I scoffed. "The whole town qualifies as 'somebody'?"

She winced. "Not the whole town. Just book club."

"She spilled the beans," Billie drawled. "Get over it and get to the good stuff. How *exactly* did he rail you?"

"What is railing?" Cal asked.

Phil leaned closer to her and whispered, "I'll explain it at home later."

"It basically means Aubrey got good and... fucked, for lack of a better word," Juneau said. "Please," she whined, "tell us *something*. How do you feel? Was it a positive experience?"

Billie snorted again, and I shot daggers at her eyeballs.

"Yeah. It was... great."

The word didn't begin to describe the whirlwind marathon sex fest I'd had with Rye, but I wasn't ready to share him. The girls now knew he and I were "dating" but that's all they needed to know.

And I was so not going into how sore my entire body was. I had to be careful not to groan when I sat. I hadn't checked in my mirror, but I was pretty sure I had bruises in the shape of Rye's fingerprints all over my hips and ass. The pain was my constant reminder of the railing I had indeed received, and I never wanted it to go away.

"I'm not goin' into details, so don't even ask."

"He's so young," Daisy said. "I can only imagine his stamina! But you girls should've seen the way Rye looked at Aubrey. He's smitten."

I shook my head. "He is not."

"He is too," she argued. "Even José said so."

Rye had said as much, hadn't he? That he was falling for me. But when someone on the outside of the situation said it, it felt silly, like some teenage Romeo-and-Juliet farce we were playing in.

I wasn't someone people adored. Not since the early days with Tommy, and even then, it hadn't really been me he adored, but the idea of me. The idea of the life and family he'd said he wanted, but then failed to live up to even his own expectations.

As usual, Carly had hearts in her eyes. "Do you like him?" she asked.

"She does," Roxi practically shouted, but then she turned toward me. "You do like him, right?"

Looking around the room, I knew I couldn't lie. My friends would see right through me.

"Yes," I said. "I like him. He's funny and kind, and he treats me well."

Abey smiled at me. She knew Rye better than I did, had for years. She'd corroborate his goodness.

"But," I added, "he's way too young for me. He lives an hour away, and I have my boys to consider. My business."

Roxi glared at me and her mouth popped open, probably so she could point out that there wouldn't be any business had it not been for Rye. She'd promised not to mention to anyone the deal Rye and I had struck, but Roxi was nothing if not passionate about her friends. Especially me, but before she could blurt it to the entire town, I shut her down with a glare of my own.

"Look, guys, he hasn't even had kids yet, and you know I can't be the woman to give those to him."

He said he didn't want kids, but that would change. He'd meet some young thing soon, with tight thighs and really perky boobs, and she'd want kids, and Rye would want to give her whatever she wanted. He was that kind of guy.

But why did that image in my head make me sad? He wasn't mine. He couldn't be, and I wanted him to be happy, didn't I?

"Did he say he wants kids?" Aislinn asked. "Maybe he doesn't. And aren't *your* boys in their twenties? Why do you care what they think? And don't you think they'd want you to find happiness?"

Yeah, sure, if Rye had gray hair, the boys might find it partially acceptable, but since his hair is golden brown and beautiful, he still has a full head of it, and there's literally one decade between the boys and Rye, and Rye and me, yeah, I don't think they're gonna be on board.

Not a lot of people understood the closeness the boys and I had between us since their dad died. It was them and me against the world. It was the way things had to be for us to get through the loss we'd been dealt.

"It's complicated," I said. "Look, I won't lie and say I'm not havin' fun. I am, but I'm not sure it's meant to last."

It was the closest I could get to telling my friends about my fake relationship, which had to stay fake in my mind, but seemed to be anything but fake in Rye's.

Everyone else, including Cal, sighed in disappointment. Except for Billie. She grumbled that she'd only come to book club to get the hot gossip, and I'd let her down, but I hoped my revenue-generating idea would distract her.

"Listen," I said. "Since we're on the subject, I have this idea for my shop. I wonder if y'all could help me refine it. It involves custom tote bags and cowboys."

I told them my Bag a Cowboy idea, and everyone loved it. Carly and Juneau even said they'd talk to Buckey and my cousin Max to see if they knew any available cowboys in the area. Billie loved the idea, and she promised she'd get her husband, Jay, to rat on some of the guys and the one cowgirl working out at Cade Ranch. She was sure she could strong-arm a few of them.

Eventually, we got back to our new book, which was not *Railed by the Cowboy*, but a billionaire romance between a British real estate tycoon and a nerdy American who went to the UK to nanny for her sister's college room-mate's boss.

WHEN I GOT BACK to the shop, my phone pinged with a text.

I pulled it from my purse and saw that Micah had sent a message. I decided just to call him back. I was too tired to type and try to be funny with slang I didn't understand and silly emoji.

But first, I called Billie and left a message when she didn't answer her phone. "Hey, it's Aubrey. I've been thinkin'. You were right about the online store idea. How do I go about settin' that up?"

Now that Rye had single-handedly saved Your Local Bookie, I figured I'd better figure out some ways to keep it in the black. Besides e-commerce, I'd had an idea a while ago about outfitting a trailer or an old food truck to be a mobile bookstore. There were a lot of farmers markets in the area and festivals throughout the year I could sell at, maybe make the book genre match the event. It would take more thought, and I wasn't sure where to get a free trailer, but I knew one cowboy in particular who'd probably be willing to help me look.

"Anyway, call me when you get a chance. Thanks, Billie." I figured if I didn't hear back, she'd be barging into the store soon to commandeer my laptop. When she had a mission, she was pushy and unstoppable, and it was my favorite thing about her.

Micah answered when I called him next. "Hey, Ma. Get my text?"

"Yeah, but I didn't read it. It's easier to call, plus I get to hear your voice. What's up?"

"Oh, nothin'. Just wanted to check in. See how you are."

Why he bothered texting in the first place was a mystery to me because I could hear in his voice that he wanted to talk, which meant he'd hoped I would call instead of text anyway.

"I'm okay, sweetie. How are you and Benji doin'?"

"Benji's Benji. And I'm okay, I guess. Um, I met a girl."

"You did? That's great, Micah," I said. "What's her name?"

"Izzy. Isabel, but Izzy."

"That's a pretty name. How'd you meet?"

"She's goin' to school at MSU. She grew up not too far from Bozeman. Her family runs a cattle ranch."

"Well, she sounds great. I hope I can meet her when you're ready."

He hesitated. "Yeah."

He'd always been the more emotional and quieter of my twins, but not this quiet.

"Micah, what's wrong? You don't sound like yourself."

"I dunno, Ma. I mean, I guess I've just been thinkin' a lot lately."

"About what?"

"Do you think it's wrong if I don't do what Benji does? I mean, like, if we went in different directions in our lives?"

"Of course not. Just 'cause you're twins, it doesn't mean you have to be glued at the hip your entire lives. And I think Benji wants you to be happy, whatever you decide to do."

"Yeah. I know. I think."

"Is this about Izzy?"

"No. Well, kinda, but not really. But, I guess, yeah."

That was painfully vague, but it didn't take much momaging to know he wasn't ready to go into details. "I won't push, Micah, but when you're ready to talk, I'm here. Okay?"

"Okay. But you're doin' good? How's the shop?"

What a question, and my answer was loaded with all kinds of land mines. "The store's fine." No need to worry him. "Same as usual. Oh, I saw the new Thor movie."

"There's no new Thor movie."

"Right. It was the other guy. You know, his best friend? The space guy. But Thor was in it."

Micah snorted in my ear. "Which is the only reason you went, right?"

"Guilty."

"You're so predictable, Ma."

And wasn't that the sad truth?

CHAPTER SEVENTEEN

RYE

AUBREY HAD INSPIRED ME.

The way she let me take her last night, and how she'd taken me too. Like sagebrush, once her protecting walls had begun to tumble away, I didn't think anything could hold the woman back.

She'd pushed me down on her couch and sucked my cock so thoroughly, I'd practically passed out. Her living room curtains stayed open. She said she didn't care if anyone saw us, that it would help our dating ruse if anyone got nosy, but I thought maybe it had more to do with her wanting to live free. To see and finally be seen.

I saw her. She was on full display for me, and I couldn't tear my eyes away.

And it wasn't a goddamn ruse. I hadn't been secretive with my feelings for her, but maybe in further attempts to protect her heart, calling it fake was what she needed, even between the two of us.

Or maybe I was completely delusional, and this thing between us would fizzle out and fade away once we both got what we wanted from the deal.

The problem was, I wanted a fuck of a lot more than what she'd agreed to.

I wanted forever.

I'd left her house, after one last go with my mouth between her legs and her fingernails digging into my scalp, and we talked as I drove home. I made it almost all the way back to the ranch, but then turned around and drove back to Bax's place after Aubrey started falling asleep on me.

It was my birthday and a Sunday. My parents would head to church, but I never went. There was too much to do usually, and it hadn't ever been something I made time for.

For me, religion was in the mountains and the trees, the dirt beneath my feet and the air above me. I communed with my higher power all the time. Sitting in some too-hot, dusty church in a shirt and tie that made me feel like I was suffocating didn't make God love me any more or any less than anybody else.

And as always, Presley was at the ranch. Since he stayed in our bunkhouse and managed the seasonal cowboys, he started work early every day to beat the heat of the sun, sometimes before I'd even climbed out of bed, so that meant I could be late to work today, but I shot him a text to let him know.

I knew Bax would be up early, too, so when I knocked on his front door and asked him to show me the land he wanted to sell, he stepped into his boots, grabbed his coffee, and I followed him out there in my truck.

Maybe he could tell I had some contemplating to do, and *his* mama wasn't so forgiving if he missed church, so he left me there alone, sitting on my open tailgate, watching the sunrise and dreaming of something I'd been too chicken shit to even think about before.

Going it on my own.

That was the real inspiration Aubrey had filled me with. She'd been at one of the hardest points in her life when she opened her bookshop, but it had been her dream for forever.

She took the leap and did it, even though she had no way to know if her business would soar or fail. And when times were hard, she doubled down. She immersed herself in furthering her education so her store would have its best shot. She told me she'd taken free online classes and had attended lectures given by business gurus when they were close and she could afford the travel. Maybe things hadn't been so easy for her lately, but I knew she'd make her comeback.

I was impressed by her. And in awe of her.

Daybreak came as I sat on Bax's land with my boots dangling above rich farm soil, thinking about Aubrey and what an apt nickname Spitfire was for her.

Western Wyoming slipped off her starlit nightdress, letting me see her sweet underbelly. New morning light washed itself over her mountain peaks in oranges, pinks, and purples while I *really* thought about what it would be like to have my own ranch. My own cattle. My own business.

I knew it would be hard. I'd excel at some things and struggle with others, but I was willing to go through it because I wanted it *bad*.

And it wasn't because I needed to one-up my dad, or 'cause I was sore at him for not wanting to hand over the thing he'd spent his whole life building.

Yeah, sure, that hurt a little, mainly because I'd spent most of my life expecting him to pass down the reins of G&S. But now I thought I could understand it, because if somebody had asked me to give up the land I was currently deciding to buy, I'd put up a fight too. Especially if I'd spent forty years cultivating it, farming it, and making it mine.

I looked back over my shoulder, toward the only home I'd

ever known, fifty miles in the distance. I'd build my house there, in the southeast corner of my property, with the back porch facing my past, and I'd put big, sweeping windows in the front room so we could look toward the future and see the Tetons when we sat in there, drinking our morning coffee, or when we sat on the front p—

I laughed out loud, probably scaring the crows, when I realized I'd been picturing Aubrey living in my nonexistent house with me, relaxing after a long day with our feet up, rocking on a porch swing together, holding each other and watching the sun set.

FUCK, I was tired.

I couldn't remember dragging ass this bad in a long time, but spending the night fucking my Spitfire six ways from Sunday was worth the fatigue.

When I finally got back to the ranch, I scrambled up six eggs and armed myself with about a gallon more coffee.

I sucked it down as I made my rounds, sent the cowboys out on twenty different tasks, and then I went in the barn to check on my injured heifer. Her ankle looked like it had a cow-colored pool floatie around it, so I called the vet and then finished up some chores while I waited for him to make the drive. His office was in Wisper, so travel time took him the same hour it took me.

Soon, when I bought Bax's land and started my own ranch, I'd be much closer. That was a bonus I hadn't thought of. When you lived out in the middle of nowhere, vets charged extra to cover their fuel, time, and the wear and tear on their vehicles. At least, our vets did. I understood, but man, it'd be nice to pay normal prices. Not that I was the one forking out the cash yet, but still.

When he finally showed up, Dr. van der Wouden X-rayed Miss Thang's ankle and declared it a sprain. I'd figured that but wanted to be sure. And then in his weird accent while he lasered the swollen joint, he tried talking me into buying my own. It'd save him trips like this, when he couldn't really do much for the animal. He wasn't wrong. I doubted my dad would buy one though.

It occurred to me then that *I* would. When I was the guy calling the shots, I'd buy my own damn laser and plant whatever crops I wanted to. I could raise cattle the way I saw fit.

But what would that mean for my parents?

I needed to think on it a bit more before I made my announcement, but Bax and his family were ready to sell to me, and now, my own ranch had replaced the vision I'd had in my head for thirty years. My own business I could run however I wanted to.

Regenerative agriculture.

That's where it's at, and you know it. Do it.

Do it.

Just fuckin' do it!

"What's goin' on with you?" Presley asked as we watched the doc's tires kick up dust down my dad's long drive on his way back to town.

He clapped me on the shoulder and handed me a grape-flavored soda pop. Presley brought one for me every year on my birthday because, twenty years ago, the day we'd met, he'd had one in his cooler in the bed of his busted-up old Ford on his first day at G&S. He was ten years older than me, and since neither of my brothers had ever had interest in cattle, I'd looked up to him.

Back then, I was a scrawny fifteen-year-old, lamenting the lack of celebration for my birthday because there were no less than twenty cows in different stages of labor that day, and every available pair of hands had been tending to them instead of carving up a cake for me. It seemed every birthday went that way since it came at the tail end of birthing season every year. Presley felt bad for me, so he gave me his grape soda and a tradition was born.

Luckily, this year all the calves and their mamas had decided to give me a break, and we had enough ranch hands now that, if one did decide to share my birthday, I'd still get to eat my cake.

"Thanks," I said, popping the top with my thumb and taking a drink, but it burned my throat on its way down. "This shit gets sweeter every year."

"Naw, man, you're just gettin' older, and you can't handle the sugar you used to."

Smirking, I wiggled my eyebrows. "I ate sugar all night long last night."

"Oh really?" His eyebrows pitched up in surprise. "Who's the unlucky woman?"

"You don't know her. She lives in Wisper."

"I go to town just like everybody else up in this place."

"I don't kiss and tell. Or *eat* and tell." I smirked at him, and he shook his head, but then I realized I could come clean with Presley. He was one of my best friends. "Her name's Aubrey."

"So, she's what's up?" he asked again.

"Yeah, she's part of it. Listen, I wanna talk to you about somethin'."

"Shoot."

"What would you say if I told you I'd like to buy my own

ranch and start up the alternative agriculture program I keep dronin' on about?"

"I'd say you'd lost your mind."

"Call me crazy then. I'm doin' it."

"YOU INVITED A GUEST?' Mama asked when I told her Aubrey would be arriving soon. "Ryder, that's rude. You should've asked me first."

"I invited Aubrey, my *girlfriend*. I thought that's what you wanted. Besides, it's my birthday, but I apologize for the late notice."

"Don't backtalk your mama," my dad said, like I was nine years old, as he snagged a beer from the cooler he kept set atop the kitchen counter.

No matter how many wine and beer fridges he could afford, that beat-up plastic beer trap drove my mama nuts every day of her life. The bags of ice he bought every week and kept in the deep freezer in the garage to fill the cooler didn't make her much happier, but Dad said the beer tasted better from a cooler.

"Well," she said, sliding the roast back into the oven after she tested the temp with a meat thermometer. "That's fine, I s'pose, but Marta's already gone home, and I'm not prepared for guests. I didn't set the table or even sweep the floors. What will she think?"

"She'll think you've been busy, just like she has, and she'll be gracious and thankful that you made dinner, just like I am."

Mama grumbled something, but then we heard a knock on my parents' front door, and now I *felt* like a nine-year-old on

Christmas, my pretty present waiting for me to grab her and hug her so hard she'd break, but then I'd just fix her right back up and do it all over again.

I had plans to break her and build her back up *all* night long.

CHAPTER EIGHTEEN

AUBREY

RYE ANSWERED HIS PARENTS' door when I knocked, but his mama pushed past him to grip my hands and pull me inside.

The bag over my shoulder containing the bottle of red wine I'd picked up at the Liquor Depot in Wisper slipped down my arm, and for a second, I panicked, imagining walking into Calla Graves's home and then dropping the bottle and spilling middle-of-the-aisle Merlot all over her expensive Brazilian walnut floors.

Grady Graves Sr. stood several paces behind his wife, looking irritable and put out. Rye's parents reminded me of the well-known painting, *American Gothic*, the one with the strict farmer holding a pitchfork, standing next to his daughter, who I'd always thought was his wife, like a scene from *The Grapes of Wrath*.

But the Graveses' home was nothing at all like one the Joads would've lived in. It was grand and featured shiny, impossibly tall, waxed-log walls.

Taking up most of a focus wall in the great room, the decadent fireplace had been made with large, polished stones, and the enormous, long-horn skull above it felt excessive, like some kind of display to speak to the Graveses' wealth and standing within the Wyoming cattle community, but did I really need a desiccated cow head to tell me that?

Suddenly, the old cowboy boots I'd dug through my closet to find because I thought they'd be appropriate on a cattle ranch didn't seem to fit this gilded wooden castle that looked like it came straight out of *Mountain Living* magazine.

Whiskey colored couches and pale-gold fabric armchairs surrounded a classic and ornate Persian rug. Hand-carved wooden end tables bookended the long couch, and there were enough trinkets and expensive knick-knacks expertly placed around the room that Rye's mama could've started her own gift shop if she wanted to.

Simple art hung on the walls, from a beautiful Native American blanket hand-woven in oranges, white, and reds, to large monotone photographs of what I assumed was Graves land, framed in a similar wood to the end tables. And in the middle of it all sat a knotted-wood-style coffee table that looked big enough for me to sleep on. How the hell had they gotten that thing into their living room? It had to weigh a ton and looked to have been cut from the base of a five-hundred-year-old redwood tree.

I saw excess everywhere I looked, though Rye's mama had made an effort to keep her home's decoration understated and not too flashy, but still, it was clear the Graves family had money. I'd known that. Rye had said it, but I'd had no clue just how affluent his family was now. The house hadn't been this big or fabulous when I was here in my teens and early twenties. They'd added onto it and shined it up nice and pretty.

"Come in, come in," Calla said, pulling harder. "Welcome. Forgive the mess. I was only informed five minutes ago that we'd be entertainin' tonight."

"Oh, please don't mind me," I said, flashing a smile that somehow reminded me of picture day in elementary school. And there wasn't a "mess" for ten miles in any direction. I couldn't find one single thing out of place. "Your home is beautiful. Thank you for havin' me. It's nice to see you again."

When Calla finally let go of my hands, I adjusted the tote bag's strap over my shoulder and then remembered why it was there in the first place and pulled out the bottle of wine. I handed it to her, and she took it, but her face did a thing; her nostrils flared the smallest bit and her forehead scrunched up. Maybe white wine would've been a better choice? *Dang it.* But I thought red paired better with beef, and I was standing smack in the middle of the place beef came from!

"Yes," she said, "it's been too long. How are you, honey? We haven't seen you since Thomas's funeral."

Yeah, great. Thanks for the reminder. In Calla Graves's eyes, I was still Tommy's widow. How could I betray him by dating her son?

We were off to a great start.

She handed the wine to Rye, who shook his head almost imperceptibly, his eyes full of apology for his mama's rude-ness, but then she grabbed my hand again and tugged me further inside, past the dining room to the kitchen.

Rye followed silently with his dad on his heels, like any good husband who knew if he abandoned his wife now, there'd be hell to pay.

Calla guided me down onto a chair at her kitchen table, then opened her fridge and began to empty it of all its contents. "What can I get you to drink, Aubrey? Coffee? Or I made a fresh batch of sweet tea yesterday."

The kitchen was just as fancy as the rest of the house, but more lived in. Photographs of cute kids covered the fridge along with stick-figure drawings of a large family surrounded by cows.

I saw a few dishes in the deep basin sink, and the small kitchen table looked similar to the one in my kitchen, but the appliances were all state of the art. The only thing that looked out of place was a red cooler resting on the granite countertop.

"Thank you. Water's fine, if you don't mind. The caffeine would just keep me up tonight."

"Oh, well I know that's true," she said. "The older we women get, the less we can tolerate such things. It's important to drink enough water. Keeps the skin elastic." Under her breath, she mumbled something that sounded eerily like, "Too bad it can't unshrivel your eggs."

Oh, so not only was I Tommy's widow, which in Calla Graves's view meant basically still married to him, even though he'd been dead ten years, but I was also too old for Rye. I couldn't give her grandchildren, so what good was I to her? She didn't have to come right out and say it. I spoke "judgy mom" just as fluently as the next girl.

"Mama," Rye warned, and he handed me a glass of water he'd filled from a filtered jug in the fridge.

She didn't respond to him, so I said, "Thanks, babe," laying the fake-girlfriend schtick on thick. I smiled at him, and he leaned down to kiss my cheek.

Rye's mama watched us out of the corner of her eye. "So how did you two…"

"Hook up?" Rye asked, knowing it would push her buttons. The little wink he threw me gave him away.

Again, her face pinched into definite disapproval, but she

caught herself and forcibly morphed her expression back to bland indifference.

Rye was having the hardest time not laughing, which made it hard for me too.

"We ran into each other in town," he said. "I've always had a thing for her, so I asked her out, and she said yes."

He beamed. It was all true. Kind of. But his mama scoffed and that pinched-up look was back.

"Ryder, you did not have a thing for her. She was Junior's friend and way too old for you."

"Yeah, well, that's what happens when you go through puberty with a goddess like Aubrey hangin' around all the time."

I felt my cheeks heat and probably blush the color of a red chokeberry. It sounded like Rye's mama actually choked, and his dad mumbled something that sounded a lot like "Can't blame him for that."

"Grady Graves!" Calla scolded, and now I had to bite down on my lip to hold back my laugh. So, it wasn't Rye's dad who needed to be won over after all.

It felt like it took forever to get to the actual eating part of the evening, but Rye and I made good use of our time, flirting and touching every chance we got. Given the amount of time I'd spent worrying what Rye's parents might think of me dating their much younger son, I was pleasantly surprised to find myself having fun.

While Calla beat her mashed potatoes into submission with a hand-held mixer, Rye leaned against the counter, holding me in place in front of him, his chin on the top of my head, his legs touching the outsides of mine, and his arms wrapped around my stomach, while his mama droned on loudly about her auxiliary club and how they'd just made her president for the seventh year in a row. She checked every few minutes to see if her son was still touching me.

Another of Rye's delicious appendages was perceptible behind me, and visions of another marathon session filled my head, but then my manners got the best of me, and I offered and tried to help Calla set the dining table and get everything ready to serve.

She said, "No, thank you. You're our guest. Don't worry your pretty little head," and pushed my hands away.

The phrase "cold shoulder" kept coming to mind. Surprisingly, though, Rye's dad seemed to warm up as the night wore on.

"Tell us about your boys," he said after Calla had served the main course of beef roast, potatoes, and baby carrots she'd sautéed and drenched in local Wyoming honey. "They're in college now?"

Now that we'd moved into the formal dining room, it was hard to notice anything but the impressive drapes hung almost as high as the ceiling, highlighting a massive window that faced northeast and offered a stunning view of what I thought might be Pass or Tosi Peak. Whichever mountain it was, I knew it was part of the Wind River Range, and it was gorgeous.

"Well, yes, the boys were enrolled at Montana State, but they've… decided to pursue other avenues."

Rye tossed a kind smile at me across the table, because of course Calla wouldn't let me sit next to him. "Men and women should face each other durin' a meal," she'd said.

"What does '*other avenues*' mean?" she pressed, and she speared a carrot with her fork so forcefully that it scraped and screeched across her plate.

I didn't remember her to be so disapproving, but then, twenty-something years ago, she'd been a young wife and mom with three sons, a husband, and a huge ranch to tend do. She probably hadn't had a lot of time to judge people.

Okay, well, let's just go ahead and let Mrs. Judgy McJudgerson have her fun.

"They dropped out," I said, and suddenly, it felt like I'd crawled out from under the guilt and nonsensical shame I'd been carrying about that particular subject. I felt like I could breathe again.

Helping Rye stand up to his parents was helping me stand up for myself too.

What did it matter if other people thought my or my boys' decisions were wrong? They didn't have to live our lives or pay my bills. The twins and I had gone through hell and back. All three of us were stronger for it, and we deserved to live our lives without worrying about what other people might say.

Fuck the haters. I'd played the part of the good wife for a long time. Far too long.

I wasn't playing anymore.

If I wanted to screw Rye in plain view of everyone on Main Street, I could. Our "arrangement" had made me feel like a new woman. I felt alive again. Beautiful inside and out. There wasn't a goddamn thing wrong with us being together, fake dating or not. What good would it do me to be awoken from a long, lifeless dream just to spend my time trying to appease other people?

Reaching over the table to serve myself an extra helping of mashed potatoes because, when you were gearing up to throw caution to the wind, potatoes were always necessary, I said, "The boys will do what they're gonna do. I'm their mom, not their warden. I don't always agree with their choices, but I love them. Rye didn't go to college, and he's smart and strong. He's exactly the kind of man I want my boys to grow up to be. They've been through hell, so I'm gonna support them in whatever they do. Besides, it's the mistakes we make in life that teach us the most, like my marriage."

Calla gasped, Rye's dad chuckled under his breath, and Rye grinned from ear to ear. He seemed to like this new, bolder, guilt-free Spitfire.

He had a hard time chewing with that smile plastered across his face the rest of dinner, but he managed. Calla served us her tres leches cake, which was maybe the most delicious thing I'd ever eaten, but before she could take her first bite, I stood from my chair and demanded we sing Happy Birthday to Rye. He deserved to be celebrated, and by God, Crab and Crabbier could show their son they loved him. It was awkward as hell, but we toasted the day this glorious cowboy was born with glasses of my sub-par wine, and then they joined me while I sang to Rye, like I was Marilyn Monroe singing to JFK, minus the overtly sexualized voice and charming vibrato.

As soon as Rye stuffed the last bite of milky cake into his mouth, along with the last stray slice of strawberry that had adorned the cake when Calla served it, he tossed his napkin onto his empty plate and stood. "C'mon, Spitfire. You haven't been here in a stone's age. Lemme show you around."

"But we haven't finished our conversation," Calla protested.

Grady spoke up finally. "Darlin', let the kids go have some fun. I'll help with the dishes."

Me, a kid? I laughed out loud. I sure felt like one tonight.

It felt like a weight had been lifted from my shoulders, like I was that wild, young girl Rye kept remembering.

"Thank you for dinner, Calla. It was lovely," I said as Rye walked around the table. He came at me like a bull in a China shop and lifted me into his arms. My legs dangled over his forearm, and I wrapped my arms around his neck and held on for the ride. "You have to send me the recipe for that cake. It was the best thing I've ever tasted."

Rye raised an eyebrow, clearly questioning my last statement. Oh yeah, I bet he could think of *one* thing I'd liked tasting better.

"Thank you, Mama. Love you both, but I want some time alone with my *girlfriend*."

He stared deep into my eyes when he said it, and nothing in the world could've stopped my smile.

As he dashed us out of the dining room toward the front door, I heard Calla mumble, "You're welcome, I guess. Happy b—"

CHAPTER NINETEEN

RYE

HOT DAMN! *There's the Spitfire I remember.*

When we got outside, I stood in front of my childhood home, looking out at the dusty, barren landscape and the mountains in the distance, both lit up and shadowed by the moon.

And I knew for sure it had come time for me to leave it.

I had no clue what I'd say to my dad, how to explain the need I felt to go out on my own, but whether he understood or not, I was doing it.

And when I looked down at Aubrey in my arms and her brilliant smile, I knew the name of my new endeavor:

Spitfire Ranch.

Wyoming SusBeef didn't have much of a ring to it. Any name that spoke more to the type of sustainable farming I planned on doing would probably have been more conducive to the whole business-model thing I'd heard people talking about. I had to admit, that shit had never come easy to me, but the woman currently in my arms knew a thing or two about business, and I planned to utilize her beautiful brain if she'd let me. And I'd pay her for it too. In fact, if I could convince her to love me, she could have it all.

And if she'd inspired it, why not name it after her?

"You got me in some kinda mood, Spitfire."

Reaching up, she scratched her fingers through my beard softly and trailed one finger over my lips. "Show me."

"Feel like a roll in the hay?"

She smirked. "Do I ever."

I looked down at her legs hanging over my arm, her skirt inching up her thighs and the cowgirl boots I still remembered her wearing with that pink dress decades ago dangling in the night air.

"Okay, but you're leavin' those boots on."

Her head tipped back and she laughed, and I could've died of satisfaction. This was it.

She was it for me.

Did she have any clue how much I'd been yearning for her? If she didn't, I was about to show her.

AFTER I CALLED Bax and made him an official offer for his land, I asked him to meet me for a drink in town.

My sister-in-law out in the Midwest worked in real estate, and I'd asked her to do some research for me so that the number I gave Bax was competitive. My mama wasn't Sorelle's biggest fan even though she'd given my parents three really cute grandkids (it seemed Calla Graves wasn't a fan of *any* woman who tried to claim one of her sons), so bonus, I knew Sorelle would keep quiet until I was ready.

I wasn't quite there yet. I needed to have all my shit situated before I went to my dad.

Bax and Brand met me at Manny's Bar in town the next weekend, and we had a rowdy good time, remembering our teens and early twenties and all the trouble we'd gotten into. Brand had always been the quietest of the three Lee brothers or their younger sister, Abey, but when you got a couple beers in him, his personality leaked out.

"Oh, no, don't you dare blame that tractor explosion on me," he said, laughing after finishing his third beer. "That honor goes to Abey. Our baby sister was the real trouble-maker in our household. But I've got a good one. You remember the time we let all the chickens out of the coops at Lee Farms after we got into our mama's wine coolers?"

"Oh man," I remembered, "your dad called my dad, and he drove up to whip my ass. I was thirteen! It was embarrassin'."

Bax laughed. "You think our dad was any more pleased than yours? The sheep were terrified of those chickens, and they chased all the ewes out of the pen that Dixon forgot to latch. Some of those fuckers were loose for a day before we finally caught 'em all. One of 'em ended up over on old man Marley's property. If we hadn't figured it out, he would've eaten that animal."

Bax and Brand shot their arms up in the air, shouting, "My land. My rules!"

"Shit," Brand said, "I lost baseballs, frisbees, and hard-earned money to that man's land."

Bax took a swig of his beer and nodded. "Me too. What a grump-ass. You know, even after Dad died and I took over the farm, that man was still a damn pain. He had to get around with a walker in his later years, and he couldn't see for shit, but he never missed the opportunity to screech and holler at us. He got up in Candy's face one time when she got a flat tire and had to pull over at the end of his drive until I could get there. She had Athena with her, a truckload of groceries, and she was six months pregnant with—"

Bax's long pause said everything I needed to know about how my friend had been dealing with the loss of his wife and unborn son. I couldn't remember ever hearing him mention the baby, but it seemed to be getting a little easier for him to talk about Candy.

"What a dick," I said, watching Bax carefully as he saw the memory in his head.

It had been three years. Raising a spunky thirteen-year-old on his own couldn't be easy, but Bax had pulled himself up by his bootstraps with the help of his family.

"Anyway," Bax said, trying to shrug off the painful subject, "that brings us to the land part of this conversation, and Brand and I have an addendum to add to your proposal."

"Oh yeah?" I asked. "What's that?"

"A joint venture."

Wait. What? "A joint... Seriously? You wanna go in on this with me?"

"Yeah, man," Brand said. "Bax mentioned that whole eco-farming thing you wanna do, and I did some research. It looks profitable, and it looks like a *good* thing to be involved in. I've got my construction company up in Sheridan, but it's big enough now that I don't need to be there every day to nitpick."

Bax rolled his eyes. "Mr. High and Mighty over here's got people for that. And his people got people."

Brand agreed with a shrug.

"Yeah," Bax said, "and I've got the new rental-cabin business goin' up on the other side of our property, but I thought we might tie the two together. It's somethin' we wanna talk to you about, maybe turnin' the farm side of things into a teachable moment, and we could use it to lure people to the cabin side and vice versa. Like a dude ranch but for sustainable cows."

Bells were ringing inside my head. What a great fucking idea! If I *didn't* have to go this thing alone, I could make Spitfire Ranch profitable a lot faster than I'd been thinking. And knowing I'd have support and camaraderie didn't suck either.

"Y'all are geniuses, and you honor me," I said, holding up my beer for a cheers. The guys joined me and we tapped bottlenecks, but there was one stipulation I needed to make before I decided to start a business with my friends. "I'm all for your joint venture, lads. Fair warnin', though. It might mean you gotta deal with sheep again. It's important to raise more than one type of animal because—well, it's all about the soil…"

Bax nodded.

"Alright, I hope you know the amount of homework and heavy labor you're agreein' to, but if you're up for it, I'd be proud to call you partners. There's just one term you're gonna have to shake on first."

"What's that?" Bax asked.

"The name. The ranch part of this deal will be called Spitfire. Ain't nothin' gonna change my mind."

Looking across the table at each other, they both shrugged and at the same time turned their heads back in my direction and said, "Deal."

SUNDAY EVENING BROUGHT with it late-May gloom and chill.

I'd busted my ass all week, getting everything ready before the drive, and I'd spent some time with the Lee brothers at their farm earlier in the day, talking dreams and ideas, but I needed to head back home early the next morning and planned on having "the talk" with my parents later at dinner, but before I went and did the biggest thing I'd probably ever do, I had to see my Spitfire.

When I knocked on her door, her porch light was off again. I tried to fluff the bunch of bright pink peonies in my hand, like the flowers in the drawing hanging in her living room she loved so much, but all I accomplished in the darkness was knocking off petals, so I left them be and waited for her to open the door for me so I could see her face and breathe again.

The bouquet of flowers I'd spent two-hundred bucks on became a distant memory when the door swung open and she appeared in a deep-green silk robe, fresh from a shower, her cheeks blushing and her hair messy and falling out of the clip she'd put it up in.

Aubrey was all I knew.

"Damn, I missed you." I stepped over the threshold, dropped the flowers onto a chair in her living room as I kicked the door shut with my boot, and picked her up.

I carried her to the hallway leading to her bedroom without her saying a word, but she pulled the clip out of her hair 'cause she knew what my intentions were. She gazed up into my eyes while I walked, and in that moment, I knew that she knew how I felt about her.

I hoped she was right there with me. The coy smile on her lips, the need coming off her body in waves of heat, and the sultry look in her eyes made me think she was.

"I want in you," I said roughly.

She breathed, "Yes."

When I had her sprawled across her bed, knees bent and open for me, I leaned over her and untied the robe. It slid over her luscious curves as her body was bared completely to me, lit up softly by a flickering candle on her bedside table, and I felt overwhelmed.

How was I the guy lucky enough to have this woman?

I had no clue, but I wasn't about to waste time digging around my brain trying to come up with the answer.

"Strip," she said.

Towering over her at the end of her bed, I obeyed, but I worried for a second that I might hurt her; she looked small and precious, but the want inside me felt so big.

I undressed as slowly as I could manage, teasing her a little. I pulled my shirt over my head and loved how her hips flexed in response and her legs spread wider for me. I was never disappointed with the way her slow gaze ate me up, and when she saw my chest and arms, those amber eyes always ended up on my tattoo.

I sat and slowly pulled off my boots, and she crawled up behind me silently, wrapped her arms around my waist, and unbuttoned my jeans.

In a soft voice, she demanded, "Off."

I shucked the jeans and my boxers and socks, and then I twisted and caged her between my arms. She backed up the bed until her soft, strawberry waves cascaded over her pillow, and I moved the robe free of her skin with one slow glide of my hand, then splayed it wide over her belly.

She tried again to move my hand and cover her stomach.

"Baby, what is it you're tryin' so hard to hide from me?"

"My…" She sighed. "My scar."

I found the faded, raised line below her navel. "This?"

"Yes," she said, and she closed her eyes.

The skin around it was soft and a little loose, but I liked it 'cause it moved to the rhythm of my fingers and mouth when I went down on her. "Is that from havin' your boys?"

"No."

"Does it hurt?" I asked, trailing my finger softly down the scar. I kissed it, and she shivered.

"No."

"Tell me."

"I had… cancer. Three years ago. They took my uterus out."

Fuck. She'd gone through cancer all alone? The boys had been away at school. I hadn't noticed she'd closed her shop for any length of time, although, back then I didn't get to town as much as I did now.

"Aubrey, if I'd known— I'm so sorry you had to go through that. Are you okay? Are you sick?"

Everything would stop if she was. I'd give her anything she needed, take her anywhere her doctors told her to go.

"I'm not sick anymore," she said, and her eyes opened cautiously. "I survived. I'm a survivor. But does that— Do you see me differently? God, Rye. You're so young, and I'm… not. And my body's changin'. How can I be beautiful to you? I don't get it."

That was what she'd been worried about?

"I know you said you don't want kids, but I definitely can't give them to you if you change your mind. Not that I could at my age, even if I still had all the necessary parts." Blushing, she shook her head against the pillow. "Not that we… I mean, we're not—this isn't a *real* relationship."

"How else can I say it to make you understand? You are, hands down, the most beautiful woman I've ever known. Now. Not just when you were twenty or twenty-five." Pushing up on my hands, I hovered above her. "Hear me when I tell you, Aubrey, you're forty-seven, yes, *and* you are drop-dead gorgeous. When I look at you, I can hardly breathe.

"And this has been real for me since that day in your store when you said yes. Maybe you can't see it yet, but everything I want is in my arms at this very moment. I don't want kids. I don't need kids.

"I just need you."

CHAPTER TWENTY

RYE

"YOU DON'T CARE that I'm a barren woman?" she asked quietly.

"Spitfire," I said, shaking my head and rubbing my lips back and forth over her scar, "you may not have a uterus, but you're anything but barren. You're lush and full and perfect. Everywhere I look when I'm with you grows greener. You *are* a survivor. Now, open those lovely legs for me, and lemme show you just how much I don't care."

She smiled a smile so bright, I thought the sun had come out at midnight, and she caught her bottom lip between her teeth. She loved my mouth and beard on her pussy, and I was fixing to give her what she wanted, but she slapped her hands on my shoulders before I could descend.

"Wait. Don't do that. If you do that, I'll come too fast."

"And the problem with that is…?"

"I want you slow, and I want you inside me right now."

Well now.

She was a fucking warrior goddess. Who was I to deny her anything?

I climbed over her, loving how her legs wrapped around

my hips and gearing up to drive home, but she held my face between her hands and kissed me, and I got lost in her for a few moments, almost forgetting that my cock was hard and primed and waiting impatiently.

Almost.

But I was in awe of this woman, utterly and completely. And silently, I vowed that she'd never have to face anything alone again. Not a bad day, a shitty quarter at the bookstore, a fender bender, or even fucking cancer, God forbid it came back.

Not ever.

"Before you," she said softly, "sex was… not much fun. It's never felt this good. Now that I have my body back and know what it's capable of, I wanna savor it."

"Spitfire," I whispered. "If that's what you want, you got it."

I entered her slowly, my eyes fixed on hers and her hands still holding me.

"I love how you make me feel, Rye. It's not wrong."

Shaking my head, I said, "Nothin' wrong with you and me."

We made love then, like you see in the movies, all slow moves and lovers becoming one. Our phones rang more than once. The world outside tried to interrupt us, but we ignored it.

Sweat slicked us together while she controlled my pace with her hands clutching my ass, and she came with my body buried so far inside hers that I felt her orgasm in every one of my own nerve endings.

"How do you do that?" she asked as I pumped into her slowly, guiding her down from her high and getting ready to take her right back up.

"What?" I asked, swiping a sweaty lock of hair from her cheek.

"How do you know how to make me come like that? I'm embarrassed to say it, but with… Tommy, it took quite a bit more effort, but most times I faked it or he finished and didn't bother to finish *me*."

Man, I hated hearing that guy's name while I was loving her, but I knew I needed to get over myself. He had been her husband. Her first love. He was the father of her children. He'd always be a part of her life, a good and a bad part.

When I arched an eyebrow in confusion, she explained. "He rarely got it right. If he happened to find the right 'spot' and I responded, he'd stay there for a few seconds, but then he'd move on, and I'd be left thinkin', 'Are you kiddin' me right now? Go back! My clit's between my legs, not on my stomach or my boobs.'"

I held back a laugh. The way she'd described the subpar sex she'd had was funny, but the subject wasn't. I was still hard as stone inside her, but this was a touchy subject for her, I knew.

"But I could never say it to him. I could never say what I needed. Not like with you."

"Did you love him?" I asked. I had to know.

"Of course I did. He was my husband."

"I know. I'm sorry, but I meant, were you *in* love with him? Truly in love? Was he in love with you?"

"I-I, I mean, we… A long time ago, I thought I loved him."

"It's not wrong to say you weren't in love with him, Aubrey. And there's the difference. I *am* in love with you."

Her eyes widened. She didn't say anything, but her hands never stopped caressing my back.

"I know how to make you feel good because I love you. I

think maybe I always have. I'm in awe of you, of how strong you are and how beautiful. I'm not thinkin' about my own pleasure when my hands are all over you and I'm inside you, when my lips touch your skin. The whole point of all of it is to make *you* feel good, inside and out.

"Bein' with you makes me feel happier than I've ever been, so you see, my Spitfire, it's a win-win for me." She smiled, but something made me remember her dark porch. "Can I ask you somethin' else?"

She trailed her fingers over my collarbone, then slipped them between us, and they slowly traveled lower. "Hm?"

"Why do you leave your porch light off?"

My question stopped the warm caress of her hand over my stomach, and my cock jerked inside her.

She moaned and hummed, "Huh?"

"Every time I come over, it's off."

"What does that have to do with—"

"Why?" I asked again. "Don't you need it to see who's at your door?"

She laughed. "I mean, no one really comes to my door. My boys don't come home as often as they used to. It's just me here. Roxi comes over, but she's never seemed to mind. If I need it, I turn it on, but when I don't, what's the point of wastin' the energy?"

"I don't like thinkin' about you here alone with no light. If you let me, I'll be with you. You'll never have to be alone again, and you can leave your light on for me."

Her eyes fell shut, and she rolled her hips, begging me silently to move inside her again, and when I did, she whispered, "You're the most romantic person I think I've ever met."

I planted my knees on the bed and flipped us. I wanted her above me, riding me to ecstasy and back when I came.

"Don't you tell nobody."

She teased, "Your secret is safe with me, cowboy."

She groaned when I flexed my hips and pushed inside her sweet heat again, and I watched her whole body relax when I filled her up. She became liquid in my arms.

Sure as fuck, *I* knew where her clit was. Hell, that first night she'd screamed my name, I'd dropped a pin so I'd never forget its location. And now, I moved my hand between us and massaged it in slow, wet circles while she ground down on me, rolling her hips and taking me deeper inside, and her head fell back, her chin tipped toward the ceiling.

What a fucking vision. How she could think she'd become unwanted with age or sickness was beyond me. I'd never seen such full, soft, utterly feminine beauty.

She grasped at my thighs behind her, arching her back and dragging my cock in and out with every glide, and I rubbed round and round, whispering how beautiful she was while she rode me.

"Goddamn, look how good you take me, baby. So fuckin' sexy."

The urge to come became difficult to ignore as I watched her. My eyes zeroed in on the hardness of my cock stretching her again and again, her pussy accepting me with every roll of her hips, and the sound of her moans made me wild.

I couldn't take my eyes from the sight, but then her breasts bounced and swayed to our movements. I reached up to pinch one taut, peaked nipple, and she began to pant and fuck me harder.

"Take what you need from me, Aubrey," I said, my voice a reverent whisper.

Something was happening between us tonight. Our connection had changed. Nothing about the way she let me love her was fake.

She was riding me now, getting off on me, thrashing and leaning further back while the orgasm grew deep inside her. I felt her body clutch and grasp at my dick while I licked my thumb and rubbed harder over her clit.

She dug her nails into my thighs. "Come with me. *Please.*"

"As you wish."

She gasped and froze above me, and then she called her release into the quiet night, and I let myself go inside her.

It sounded like we'd brought the house down around us. I nearly bucked her off the bed, I came so fucking hard. I swore I heard the roof shaking and doors slamming shut, and I was still coming.

But then I heard a weird voice outside the bedroom door.

Had I hallucinated it? Was the most intense sexual experience I'd ever had messing with my ears? Aubrey twisted her head in the same direction just as the door was thrown open, and two guys barreled into the room and headed straight for me.

Aubrey shrieked and rolled off my dick, which was still hard as slicked steel and standing up straight. Cum shot up in the air, but I managed to pull the covers over me quickly.

"What the fuck!" one of the guys shouted.

Aubrey yanked her robe from the end of the bed, covering herself as quickly as she could, and I was fixing to bust in some heads. I threw the covers off again.

Both guys stopped in their tracks, and their hands flew up to cover their eyes. In unison, they yelped, "No, no, no! Don't do that!"

"It's okay," Aubrey whispered to me, and I covered my manly parts with the blanket again, but I was dead ready to wrassle both their twiggy asses to the ground. Was this a home invasion? I figured the shotgun rack in the back window of my truck would deter that kind of thing. It was parked right in front of Aubrey's house.

One guy reached and fumbled around with one hand until he found the other's head, and then he whacked his friend on the back of his noggin. "I told you we shoulda called her before we left, idiot!"

"I did call!" the second guy said in a pissed-off voice, swinging his arm aimlessly toward Aubrey. "Apparently, *she* was too busy to answer."

The first guy whimpered and said, "I'm scarred for life, Ma," still with his hand over his eyes, like if he removed it, he'd be shocked to death.

In the most mortified voice I'd ever heard, Aubrey said, "Boys, what're you doin' here?"

<hr>

"STAY HERE. PLEASE?" Aubrey pleaded as she hit the switch on her bedroom wall, and a too-bright light flooded the room. "I'm so sorry. Just give me a few minutes?"

"Yeah, Spitfire. Whatever you need," I said, and I watched as she tore through her closet for fresh clothes. When she was fully covered in jeans and a sweatshirt with a picture of a stack of books that said, "I have no shelf control," she tossed me a sorry smile and dashed from the room.

Figuring I'd better get dressed, too, I found my clothes on the floor and pulled them on, but I heard the twins going at Aubrey in her kitchen.

"What the hell, Ma?" one demanded.

The second backed him up. "Yeah. Who the fuck is that guy?"

"Boys, I'm only gonna say this once, so listen up. Don't

you speak to me like that. If you want answers to your questions, ask them respectfully."

"Okay," the first twin said. "Who the fuck is that guy,
please."

I snorted. It was funny, but I really didn't like his tone.

I had no clue which twin was which 'cause they were
nearly identical, and when they'd barged in on us, it was
dark. I hadn't seen them in several years, and we'd never
been properly introduced.

"Benji, that does *not* count as respectful. Try again."

Ah, so the softer voice came from Micah, and Benji was
the balls-to-the-wall twin.

"Mama," Micah said, "was he hurtin' you?"

Aubrey's soft, awkward laugh floated down the hall. "No,
Micah. That's Rye, and I'm pretty sure you already know
what we were doin'. We were havin'… sex."

All kinds of groaning reached my ears.

"Dammit, Ma," Benji whined. "You're not supposed to do
that. You're our ma!"

"Yeah," Micah added. "And he ain't our dad."

I scoffed out loud. "Oh, come on."

I'd heard enough. Aubrey didn't deserve ridicule from the
two people in this world who were supposed to love her the
most.

After stomping my feet into my boots, I adjusted my still
half-hard dick under my jeans and walked out into World
War III.

CHAPTER TWENTY-ONE

AUBREY

I HEARD Rye's boots behind me in the hallway, and I braced for impact.

"That's enough now," Rye rumbled in his deep voice.

Micah puffed up his chest and stepped up to Rye, who was a good five inches taller and twice as wide and muscled. "Who do you think you are?"

"I'm the guy who wants you to treat your mama with a little more respect."

Oh man.

"This joker has some nerve, Ma," Benji said with his hands on his hips. He glared at Rye, but Benji knew he was outmanned. It seemed Micah hadn't figured it out yet.

"Boys, sit down," I said, tugging gently on Micah's arm, but neither of them obeyed, so I yanked harder. "*Now.*"

Benji took the chair behind him. He almost fell into it, and Micah backed up with narrowed eyes, like he needed to keep his eye on Rye in case Rye decided to pick me up and make a run for it. If I hadn't been so embarrassed that my kids had walked in on me riding a cowboy, I would've laughed.

Leaning down to kiss my hair, Rye said softly, "I'll head out, Spitfire," and he turned to leave.

"I'll walk you out."

One at a time, I looked at each of my boys, communicating through the motherly rage on my face that if they moved, hell would rain down on them both. Apparently, they still had good survival instincts because neither of them so much as twitched or said a word.

Rye led us to my front porch. The light was on now, and when the door had been securely shut behind us, he turned to face me.

He touched his fingers to my cheek and smiled. "Sorry 'bout that."

"It's not your fault. I'm sorry they were so rude to you."

"Naw, baby, I get it. They're young men, and you're their mama. Protectin' and defendin' is kinda in their job description, but I wish they'd been kinder to you. Ain't a thing wrong with you livin' your life however you see fit. You deserve to be happy."

"They know that." *I think.*

"Alright, well, you sit 'em down and let 'em know what's up. I'll call you tomorrow."

I blushed. I felt heat rising from my core all the way to the top of my head. "I'm sorry we didn't get to finish our…" God, even just talking about sex with the boys around felt weird.

Rye chuckled. "We did finish. We just didn't get to bask in the afterglow."

"It's not funny!"

"It's fuckin' hilarious." He kissed me, but all I could think about was that the boys were probably watching, peeking through the curtains in the front window. "Spitfire, that was the best sex of my life, until the last thirty seconds anyway. We made love tonight. I'll never forget it."

He lifted my hand and placed a sweet kiss across my knuckles, and then I watched as he climbed into his truck and drove away.

Goddammit!

BACK IN THE HOUSE, in a voice Benji thought was a whisper but was definitely not, he said, "That guy's a douche."

"Shut up, dumbass. She'll hear you," Micah whispered loudly too. "She's happy to see me. You, not so much."

An audible scuffle broke out between them. I heard grunting and what I imagined was the two of them trying to kick each other's shins under the table. If I hadn't given birth to them, I wouldn't have believed anyone who told me the twins were adults.

As soon as my foot hit the kitchen floor, I crossed my arms and cocked a hip, and Micah tattled like a six-year-old. "We got kicked out of our apartment. Moronic Monty over here forgot to pay the rent. Three months in a row." He rolled his eyes and kicked his brother again.

"Ow! Whatever," Benji said. "The place was a shithole anyway." He smiled his infamous grin, the one meant to manipulate me. "Besides, Mom misses us, don't you, Mama? And I bet you wanna cook us dinner too. I've been drivin' all night. I'm starvin'."

"I told you I'd drive," Micah said. "You act like it's some great service to mankind to drive four hours."

"It *would've* been four hours if you'd remembered to put gas in the truck." Benji flashed me the most pathetic puppy dog eyes. "Mama, we had to walk two miles to fill up the gas can and back. I'm so tired," and he leaned closer and hugged me, throwing his arms around my waist and dropping all his weight there, like a baby orangutan. "I love you, Mama." He batted his eyelashes. "Wanna make me some pancakes?" But then he stiffened and released me, probably remembering whose hands had been all over me a few minutes before his.

"What did you do with the money I sent?" I asked in a tight voice. "If you didn't use it to pay your rent, where did it go?"

"Benji likes bettin' on games," Micah said, "but he's not so great at pickin' the teams."

For fuck's sake! That's what I've been spending my money on? That's why all the goddamn oatmeal?

"You're payin' that back, Benji," I seethed, almost ready to cry as I realized just how much money I'd wasted. "And boys, next time call ahead. Also no, I'm not makin' pancakes. It's almost one a.m."

"I'm sorry. Please, Mommy," Benji whined.

Micah seemed to be feeling bolder than usual. "We did call, several times, but you didn't answer. Besides, this is our house too. We shouldn't *have* to call."

"It is and it will always be, unless I sell it. But we're all adults, so maybe we could act like it and respect each other's boundaries?"

"Sell our home?" Benji said incredulously. "I don't think so. And moms don't have boundaries."

Well, that's the end of your newfound sex life, Aubrey. You shoulda waved goodbye when it drove off in a shiny RAM dually with a HEMI V-8.

"OH MY GOD!" Roxi screeched into her phone the next morning when I told her what happened.

The cool front that had moved into Wisper the night before was perfect because no one would think anything of me hiding in an oversized hoodie and beanie. Maybe if I pulled it down over my face, I could avoid looking my kids in the eye.

"Did they see—?"

"I have no idea! I'm too embarrassed to ask."

"What'd Rye do?"

"Pulled the covers over his straining erection, I *hope*."

The bell jangled on the front door.

"Gotta go. Customer," I told Roxi. "I'll call you later."

Whoever had stepped into Your Local Bookie was hidden behind a tall spinning rack of Harlequins and used cowboy romances. You'd think they'd sell more given our location, but maybe Wisper's female population got enough cowboy in their real lives. Maybe my Bag a Cowboy idea was a non-starter. I'd have to get some outside input. But if the genre was wrong, maybe I could tweak it to something else.

"Welcome to Your Local Bookie. What kinda fictional trouble can I help—"

"Hello, Aubrey," Calla Graves said when she stepped around the rack, holding a used western stepback romance in her hand.

"Mrs. Graves. Hi." *Uh oh*. Her being in my store first thing Monday morning did not bode well for me, especially not after my performance at Rye's birthday dinner. "How are you?"

"Oh, I'm fine, dear, but please call me Calla. How are you?"

"I-I'm… okay. It's nice to see you again so soon. Are you lookin' for somethin' specific?"

"I am, in fact." She looked me up and down, focusing on my Montana State sweatshirt that was three sizes too big and my disheveled hair beneath my hat. "I'm lookin' for you."

"Oh?" I asked, slipping the beanie off and tossing it behind me.

I combed my fingers through my hair but gave up trying to tame the frizz when I realized my appearance wouldn't change the direction of wherever this conversation would go.

Glancing around the shop, she took a few graceful steps toward the contemporary fiction shelves. Even the way she moved seemed rich. Her cream-colored slacks and matching blouse with its wide, sweeping sleeves felt out of place in my dusty store. She looked more like the head of a publishing house than she did a customer.

She touched the cover of a popular women's fiction title written by a fabulous Crow author from Montana. "I'll take this," she said, and she held up the cowboy romance still in her hand. "This as well. Do you have anything that's maybe... a little risqué? Somethin' different than what you might imagine I'd read?"

"Um. Yes, of course."

Without Rye here to make me brave, I felt like a teenager again in her presence. *Man, you really picked the wrong day to show up to work lookin' like a ragamuffin.*

When I walked around the counter, straightening my sweatshirt, though nothing I did would make me look like her, she smiled demurely. "Are you not feelin' well, dear?"

"No, ma'am. I feel fine. Why do you ask?"

"Oh, no reason." Except there was a reason. She clearly didn't approve of my work attire.

"Here," I said, hoping to take her attention away from anything she thought distasteful. I reached for a wildly popular book called *Truth*, about a woman who moves into a wealthy family's home in the Pacific Northwest to home-school their children, but she falls for the husband, and a whole bunch of hot—but disturbing—stuff happens. "This one had me up at night for two weeks. It's very good."

She took it from my hand and studied the hazy pine forest on the cover and the title's blood-red font. "Thank you." And then she continued her assessment of my store. "It's very quaint in here, isn't it?"

"That was my goal, to make it feel like you'd stepped into your auntie's or your sister's house to borrow a book."

"Well, thank you for the recommendation. I think I'm ready to check out."

"Sure."

She followed me back to the register and handed me a very black and very stiff credit card. "Just ring it up."

"Thank you." I finished the transaction and pushed the receipt in front of her to sign. She penned her name with a flourish and pushed it back to me. "Was there anything else you needed?"

"Now that you mention it, there is. Rye returned home quite late last night. I assume that's because he was here in town with you?"

"Yes, he was."

"He hasn't mentioned anything to his daddy yet, but I know my son's thinkin' about movin' on. He's been obsessed about a new farmin' idea for a while now."

Rye had told me all about his plans with Bax and Brand Lee. I'd been excited to know he'd be closer to Wisper. But he'd also said that he still needed to talk to his parents about his plans and how he worried about what it might do to their relationship. I wasn't about to get in the middle of it.

"Oh, I don't… It's not really my place—"

She waved away my hesitance with a flick of her thin,

elegant wrist, and the gold bangles there jingled against each other. "I wouldn't ask you to tattle on Rye. He'll come to us when he's ready, but I have a feelin' it'll be soon. And I'll be very happy when he does."

Wh-what?

My face must have displayed my surprise because she smiled and grabbed hold of my hand on the counter.

"You mistake me, Aubrey, but I don't blame you. I know what you see when you look at me and our ranch and house. But underneath all of that, I'm still just Calla. A mom first. A rancher's daughter who also married a rancher. And I'm a wife who *loves* her husband, stubborn ol' goat that he may be.

"But I see the way he and Rye butt heads. Grady has no plans to retire anytime soon. He believes strongly in our way of life. He will never give the farm over to our son if Rye insists on changin' the entire structure of the way we do things.

"The only chance Rye has to change his daddy's mind is if he goes out and does it himself. If Rye can show Grady how this plan of his can work, it's the only way his daddy will ever respect the idea.

"It's sad but true. I've known for a long time that this is what it would take. But you see"—releasing my hand, she tapped her temple with one finger—"I know better than to get in their way. If they don't figure these things out for them-selves, well, I'm sure you know men can be a little proud."

"Why are you tellin' me this?" I asked. "I don't have anything to do with Rye's plans."

"Oh, but you do," she said. "He's in love with you. And soon, if he hasn't already, my son will lay his heart on the line for you. He'll want you to be a part of everything he does."

"And you don't approve?"

"Well," she said, shrugging, "that all depends on you, I

suppose. But don't you think there's too much... *distance* between you?"

Distance? She said it like she meant that there were miles of road between Rye and me, but what she refused to come out and say straight to my face was that she thought I was too old for her son. The grandkid thing slammed home again. Why I was letting it bother me when it never had before was beyond me, and it made me so mad, letting her have that power over me.

I'd spent far too long thinking the same things about myself. Finding things to love about myself and the fact that I was getting older was really fucking hard. I didn't need Calla Graves pointing out all the reasons I shouldn't.

"And besides that," she said, "you have your own family to tend to, and if my son really does leave the nest, so to speak—"

I tried hard to hide my scoff, but it caught in the back of my throat anyway. Was she under the impression that her thirty-five-year-old son was a baby bird? Or just a baby?

Calla heard it and she arched an eyebrow. "All I mean to say, Aubrey, is wouldn't you feel awful if Rye went after his dreams, but instead of focusing on them, he focused on you because he's so infatuated with you?"

She straightened and grabbed her bag of books from the counter, then dropped her hands to her sides. She took one slow, last look around my store then fixed her stare on me. "You have boys. You can understand that Rye's a proud young man, and if he had to come home with his tail between his legs, penniless and defeated... Well, you wouldn't want that, now would you?"

CHAPTER TWENTY-TWO

RYE

MONDAY NIGHT, after my parents had finished eating the chicken cacciatore the indomitable Calla Graves had slaved over for hours (we knew because Mama told us), I cleared my throat.

"Mama, Dad, I need to talk to y'all."

When they weren't entertaining company, we ate in the kitchen, at the little table I'd grown up eating on.

Mama had filled the house with fine things she loved, but she'd never gotten rid of this kitchenette. It was the heart of our family, and I could still see the crack in the wood my dad had repaired with putty when I'd gotten pissed at Junior for sitting on my favorite hat and crushing it. I'd pushed him so hard he fell against the table. It slammed against the wall, almost taking out our brother Shelby's arm, and made a hole in the drywall. The table cracked right down the middle and nearly broke in half.

"What would you like to talk about?" Mama asked, straightening her empty plate and silverware in front of her.

I looked my dad in the eye and took a deep breath, all the

happy memories of growing up on this ranch swirling like dust devils in my head.

"I quit."

Those memories had been trying to make me lose my nerve and change my mind, but I knew deep in my bones that the path I'd been laying out for myself was the right one.

"The hell you do!" my dad boomed, and he threw his napkin onto his plate. It soaked up leftover tomato sauce and turned the folded paper towel a dirty red color.

Mama intervened. "What's this all about, Ryder?" When I looked at her, she nodded. "Maybe if you explain, Daddy will understand it better?"

"Yes, ma'am." My eyes found my father's again, and they flashed the same blue as my own when I was mad. "I've made an offer on land I'm plannin' to buy, and I'm gonna start up the regenerative cattle project you want nothin' to do with."

My dad stood, pushing his chair out behind him with his legs. It scraped across the floor. "This ranch is called Graves *and* Sons! What the hell you think I'm gonna do without even my youngest workin' here with me?"

"See, that's part of the problem right there, Dad. I'm just your youngest. To you, that means least. If Junior and Shelby don't want anything to do with the ranch, then you'll take what you can get with me. Ain't that right?"

"Son—"

Dropping my napkin on the table, I stood too. "No, Dad. Let's be honest with each other. It's about time, don't you think? You don't want anything to do with my ideas, but I can't continue in this line of work doin' the same damn things every other cattle rancher has done for ages. There's new ways. *Better* ways. And if I don't go off on my own and show you, you'll never understand.

"But I'm done tryin' to *make* you understand. I need… I need my own goddamn air. My own land. I need to prove to myself that I'm not *just* Grady Graves's son. It's time I planted my own roots."

His enraged stare didn't convince me he understood at all.

Throwing my hands up in the air, the frustration I'd felt all my life while I'd waited for him to notice me began to break loose from my chest. "I don't get it! You're the youngest in your family. The baby just like me. So why all my life have you treated me like I'm nothin'? Like I'm not good enough. Smart enough. Strong enough. All I've ever wanted was to honor your legacy."

"Yeah, I'm younger," he clipped, and he swung his arm out. It knocked over his empty beer can, which almost fell over the edge of the table, but Mama caught it. "And I had to scrape and climb to make this business and the lifestyle you take for granted."

"Take it for granted? How have I ever done that?"

He bristled, shaking his head. "You wouldn't know the first thing about buildin' somethin' from the ground up. You've had it easy."

"Easy?" I laughed. "If you think workin' for you was easy, maybe dementia's settin' in. You're right. This ain't my business. Ain't my ranch. You never let me forget it. I didn't build it. You did. And dammit, I've always been proud of you for that, but you've never been proud of me for anything. Nothin' I do is ever good enough. So I'm done. I love you. God knows why some days, but I'm just done."

I downed the rest of my beer in one long gulp, then crushed the can in my hand. "Oh, and I'm takin' Presley and Blue with me."

My dad said nothing, and Mama reached a hand toward me.

"No, Mama. You can't patch this one up. Thank you both for givin' me a job all these years. I couldn't have done this without your generosity, but I'm out. It's time I go somewhere I'm appreciated."

"Son," my dad said again, and I wanted so badly to hear regret in his voice that I actually imagined I had, but it was only a manipulation he thought might make me change my mind. "I didn't mean to—"

"I know you *think* you didn't mean to run me like every other cowboy who's ever worked this land, but you did. But that's all fine. You taught me everything I know about this business, and I'm grateful. You gave me a foundation to build on, and that's what I plan to do, so with the deepest respect, *boss*, I quit."

Mama's soft voice broke through the rough air between Dad and me. "What are your immediate plans, Ryder?"

"I'm leavin' in a week. I'm gonna drive up to Oregon, to those farms I've been tellin' you about. There's a lot I can learn up there. I'll be back before the drive, and that will be my last contribution to G&S. I've already worked it out with Presley. He'll take over for me until y'all can find a new foreman. He even agreed to move into my cabin temporarily so he can be close when you need him."

My dad turned and yanked his chair back, then sat silently. He scooted his legs under the table, looking defeated, which was something I'd rarely witnessed.

"I'll still be close. Wisper's only an hour's drive away. If you need me, I'll *always* be here for you. I love you both, but I gotta do this."

Finally, Dad's eyes met mine again. "There's nothin' I can say, is there?"

"No, sir. My mind's made up."

He nodded solemnly and stood again slowly. He pushed

in his chair, walked around the table to kiss Mama's cheek, and then he shoved out the kitchen door.

I watched him go, thinking his exit tonight was no different than any other day. As much as it hurt, it was also what made me know he'd be fine without me. Graves & Sons Cattle would continue. It would always be the Wyoming institution my dad had made it into, just without the "sons."

Maybe Junior would make a reappearance. He hadn't been home in a long time. He'd grown up in the business, too, but he'd given up our way of life for a chance to do something different and make his own money. But plans change. I was proof of that, so I'd call my oldest brother and see what he was up to. Maybe if he came home, it'd lessen the blow I'd just dealt my dad.

"Ryder," Mama said softly.

"Look, Mama, I know what you must think but I—"

"You don't know a damn thing, son. Sit down and listen up."

Being treated like a child by my mother made my blood boil, but deeply ingrained manners wouldn't let me react. "Yes, ma'am," I said, and I sat. I relaxed my shoulders and waited for the verbal slap I was about to receive.

"*I'm* proud of you," she said, and I about fell out of my chair.

"What? You're—"

"Proud of you," she said again. This time she smiled. "Daddy will come around. He may never get on board with your ideas, but he'll see the hard work you put in with the Lee brothers."

"How do you know—"

"I know everything, darlin'. You can't hide from your mama. And after some time, your daddy will see the benefit of your choice too."

"Thank you for sayin' so. I don't know if you're right, but I love you."

I listened to the crickets chirping outside while she studied my face, probably trying to determine how serious I was about this new venture.

Finally she said, "I know you love me, son, and I love you. I hope you've thought this plan all the way through. I don't know if Wisper is where you should go, but a man needs to find his own way whether it works out or not."

Way to be supportive, Mom. Hadn't she just said she was proud of me?

"You always were a stubborn thing," she said. "Always had to do things your way. Remind you of anyone you know?"

Yeah, it sure did.

CHAPTER TWENTY-THREE

AUBREY

"MA, YOU GONNA EAT THAT?" Benji asked, reaching slowly for the bacon still on my plate after the boys devoured a week's worth of groceries in one meal. I was still shocked they'd woken up before noon.

"No. Go for it."

Benji snatched up the bacon I hadn't been able to stomach and stuffed both pieces in his mouth.

"Hey!" Micah grumbled. "What if I wanted more? You're so inconsiderate."

Benji shrugged and snickered. With a mouthful, he said, "You snooze, you lose."

The house was a cacophony of laughter and arguments again, and funny TV shows the boys wanted me to watch. In fact, they left the TV on every minute of every day, even when they listened to music or watched videos on their phones.

Gone was my peacefully silent reading time, with nothing but the wind rustling the leaves in the trees outside or the far-off calls of my jays.

And just like it used to be when they were teenagers, my house was a disaster zone. As I set my empty plate in the sink, it balanced dangerously on a stack of coffee-ringed mugs, milk glasses, and more dirty plates. They couldn't use one cup for the day. No, they had to empty the cupboards for every sip they took. All the silverware was dirty. I'd had to wash three forks for the pancakes. It wasn't like either of them would've done it. They would've eaten the damn pancakes with their hands before they washed a dish. I should've let them.

Dirty laundry littered every corner, hung from the couch and chairs, the hall bathroom looked like a grown man had exploded in there, and there was already a stain on my plush Oyster Dove-colored carpet in the living room that I hoped was chocolate and not something else, like dog shit from the neighbor's yard because my boys wouldn't think to take off their shoes when they came in the house, even if I tattooed a reminder on both their foreheads.

A memory came crashing forward from the recesses of my mind, of Tommy and the boys coming home after two days of camping and fishing. The twins couldn't have been more than nine years old. I'd heard them pull into the driveway, so I stopped vacuuming and waited for them by the front door.

When they came in, Tommy dumped his tackle box on the floor. He hadn't even smiled at me or kissed me hello. He stepped out of boots covered in dried mud and kicked them to the wall. Dirt went everywhere. The boys watched him and then did the same. And then all three of them, still dressed in dirty, damp clothes, plopped on the couch and complained about how hungry they were. They sat there, waiting for me to kick it into high gear and cook for them.

The boys had learned to disregard me from their father. He did it, so that made it okay, right?

And now, neither one of them had mentioned anything about what they might be planning to do since they'd lost their jobs and their apartment and had hauled most of their belongings back home, which were still packed under a tarp in the back of their dad's old truck in my driveway. It had only just occurred to me that maybe they'd been waiting on me to unload and unpack their crap.

As soon as they'd stepped foot inside the house again, I'd turned into the same woman I'd been when their father was alive.

While my newfound happiness seemed to be leaking out of my pores, the boys kept eating, blissfully unaware of the heartbreak I felt or the fact that their lives falling apart meant mine would too.

I loved them. Nothing would ever change that, but did that mean I couldn't love anyone else?

Didn't I deserve to be loved? Didn't I deserve the kind of love people had been writing about in books for centuries? Now, here it was, courting me and knocking on my door with flowers, lighting me up in ways I'd never even imagined, but I wasn't allowed to claim it?

But as I wandered around the house, picking up dirty boxer shorts and stray unmatched socks, I couldn't stop thinking about what Calla had said to me before she left my shop.

God! I wanted to slap her for telling me Ryder's future was up to me. It wasn't!

How the hell was being in a relationship with me going to ruin his chances of making his business a success? I hadn't missed the way her eyes had darted around Your Local

Bookie. She thought I was a failure in business, so what? That meant I'd bring Rye down with me?

And although she hadn't said it outright, her meaning had been clear: I was a mother before all else, and if my kids still needed me, then it was my job—no, my *obligation*, even though the boys were old enough to vote and buy beer—to mother them and attend to them until they were ready for me to be something else to someone else.

Which might be never.

Rye had stayed away all week. He was busy at the ranch, and he thought giving me time with the boys would help us all deal. He texted me several times a day and called to say goodnight, but last night I'd missed his call because I'd been refereeing an argument and didn't hear my phone. And I didn't call back because telling him what his mother had said to me felt wrong, like I was some gossiping teenager, but the words stayed on the tip of my tongue all week.

And not saying it created a space between us that hadn't been there before.

Micah called out for me. "Mama? Where you at?"

"What! I'm busy."

"Sorry," he said softly as he came up behind me in the living room. "Am I botherin' you?"

Great. Now my mom guilt had really been activated.

I sighed. "No, Micah. I'm sorry I snapped. What do you need?"

He followed me to the laundry basket I'd left next to the boys' bedroom door that they hadn't yet used. "I just wanted to know if you've seen my tablet. Benji had it and now I can't find it."

Dumping an armful of socks and dirty T-shirts in, I said, "Haven't seen it."

"Shouldn't you be at work?"

Lovely, another person to point out my 5,786[th] failure of the week.

"Oh, what's the point?"

"What's that mean?"

"It means I haven't been sellin' tons of books. Maybe I should start lookin' for a job."

"You love the bookstore."

"I do, but it seems there are a lot of things I love that I can't have." As soon as it came out of my mouth, I wanted to take it back.

Had I fallen for Rye too? Was that why I felt so fucking sad and defeated? It felt like the realization had stopped my heart. I lifted my hand to press against it, trying to hold it together so it didn't break into pieces.

Micah touched my arm as I turned, intending to head back to the kitchen to start the dishes. "What's wrong? Is this about that cowboy?"

"It's about a lot of things." None of which I was willing to go into with my children.

"Ma, don't you get it? This is hard for me. I miss Dad. Benji does too. No one can ever live up to him."

Arghh! I wanted to tear out my hair. Live up to their dad? Please. Rye had already surpassed Tommy in every real way. But the boys would never see that. They'd only see that Rye *wasn't* Tommy.

Looking into my son's eyes, I did see it, the hurt and longing for a man he grieved and would always yearn to be able to look up to. Yet, here I'd been for ten years, busting my ass, trying to build a life they could be proud of me for, but all the twins had done was take me for granted.

It was my fault. I raised them. I shouldn't have let them have ice cream when they hadn't finished their chores.

I snorted at myself. *Yeah, right, like that would've made a difference.*

"Micah, I'm sorry you miss your dad. I know it hurts." I shook my head. I couldn't tell him what I felt in my heart, that there were things he didn't know about his dad that I didn't want him to look up to. I couldn't ruin his dad's memory just so I could have unlimited cowboy booty. "Listen, I need some time. I can't talk about this with you right now, okay?"

He nodded and dropped his arm.

"Besides, you're right. I really should go and open up the shop. I'm gonna grab a quick shower and head over there. I'll see you tonight."

"Okay. Sounds good," he said, happy with the way the conversation was ending—in his favor, just like his dad had always won our arguments, basically dismissing anything I'd said. "Oh hey, would you make chicken pot pie for dinner like you used to, with the green beans, potatoes, and corn inside?"

Oh yeah, 'cause you know, whipping up a homemade crust and basically baking a pie is what I truly look forward to after a busy day of being a failing bookseller.

But old habits really were hard to break. I said, "Sure."

And maybe it wasn't the boys' fault so much as it was my own. I saw the habit that needed to be broken, but here I was adhering to it instead of smashing it. It was the same thing I'd done with my business.

But keeping things status quo certainly hadn't earned me anything besides a sink full of dirty dishes and a ridiculously expensive tax bill I couldn't have paid on my own.

"Awesome!" Micah pumped his fist in the air like a little kid, and then he turned and called out for Benji. "Ma's makin' my favorite for dinner!"

Benji's voice echoed back to us from the kitchen, where he was no doubt licking every last crumb from his breakfast plate. "Ew, it's not that chicken-pie thing I hate, is it? Ma! I want short ribs."

Fuck my life.

WHEN I DROVE past Your Local Bookie to turn into the alley to park because I'd been too depressed to walk the five blocks, I saw Rye sitting in his truck out front, waiting for me, and my heart dropped into my stomach.

My legs felt like they'd been filled with lead as I got out of my car. I unlocked the loading-dock door and realized I'd forgotten to bring my lunch—*shit*—and when I walked through the dark store to unlock the front, I found Rye on the stoop. He'd seen me pull in.

"Hey, Spitfire. Good mornin'."

I didn't feel like a spitfire. Not even close.

Rye was every dream I'd ever had, with his soft brown curls that seemed to do their own thing no matter how many times he tried to tame them. He'd groomed his beard. It was a little shorter than he usually kept it, but still, he was a sexy vision standing before me in his worn-in jeans and his hat in hand.

"Mornin'," I said while doubt clawed at me.

I knew what I needed to do, but actually doing it was a different story.

I couldn't break his heart.

I didn't want to. I wanted to wrap myself around him and forget the rest of the world. I'd become addicted to his kisses and the way he always made me feel like his princess and how everything seemed brighter when he was around.

"How'd you sleep last night?" he asked, dropping his hat upside down on the counter as he followed me to the back room, and he reached out to touch my shoulder.

"Rye," I said, flipping on the overhead lights, "we need to talk."

When I turned to face him, he saw the defeat and sadness on my face, and he took a step back.

"Naw, Spitfire. Don't you do it."

CHAPTER TWENTY-FOUR

RYE

GETTING ready for a cattle drive was always busy, but this year was worse 'cause of my plan to take a step away to drive up to Oregon, and 'cause it was my last drive on my dad's land. Soon, I'd have my own herd to worry about.

I'd come this morning to kiss and hold Aubrey before I left to meet with some of the farmers I'd been calling and emailing for the better part of a year, but a week had gone by since I'd last seen her, and it had been a mistake to stay away. I'd thought giving her time with her boys would help all three of them, but now I saw that all it had done was give Aubrey time to doubt us.

She fought tears, her throat tightening and working to contain the storm trying to spill out. "Rye, I have to. Micah and Benji aren't ready for this."

My hands fisted at my sides. I wanted to roar! Her husband had been gone ten years, but here he was between us, and through her boys, she was still letting Tommy treat her like his property from the grave.

Or was that just her excuse? Had she become another person who thought I couldn't handle what needed to be handled? Did she *still* see me as a kid? Or was she so used to feeling sadness that she couldn't fathom a life without it?

"*Dammit*, woman. You're just gonna walk away? Why? Because I'm not him? I don't bring you heartache, so you don't want me? That's pretty fucked up."

She shook her head, and damp strands of her hair fell out of the loose ponytail she'd pulled them into. They whispered forward over her shoulders, drawing my eyes to her neck, and I watched as she swallowed hard.

"No. That's not what I'm doin', but maybe it's not the right time. Maybe we could just take a step back? You have the new business to focus on, and I need to rebuild mine. I haven't even fulfilled my part of the bargain. I didn't help you at all. Aren't you mad at me?" She was trying hard now to come up with a reason to let me go. "This isn't even real. You're the one who said it. You're the one who said we should '*fake* date.'"

Fake? I rolled my eyes. Still trying to cling to that distinction wouldn't work, and she knew it. I didn't usually go around telling women I loved them if what I felt was fake.

"Let's you and I be clear here, Spitfire. You helped me more than you'll ever know. Your belief in me is worth a fuck of a lot more than five-thousand dollars, but it was never about that for me. Don't act like you didn't know it. I'm beggin' you here. You're lettin' your boys treat you the same way their dad did. You don't deserve that."

"I'm scared, Rye. I don't know who to be. Don't you get that? I'm not ready for this, for you and me."

"You and me?" I said, trying hard to rein in the panic I felt to lose her. She was all I'd ever wanted. "Maybe you didn't ever expect to feel it again, but our love is one for the ages. That's what's been goin' on since the night I picked you up in my truck and turned your light back on, when midnight surrounded us and the spring air kissed us.

"We've been fallin' in love, in case you missed it. It feels scary to you, I know, a little bit out of control, but that's what love is, baby. It's takin' a chance."

"I'm too old for—"

"That's a load of horse shit, and you *know* it. And your boys are grown. They can handle this if you can, and I *know* you can. And don't you even try to bullshit me," I said, swinging my arm behind me. "You're just as big a romantic as I am. It's why you love all these books. *Nobody's* too old for love, and there's no one in this world who deserves it more than you. You deserve a man to worship you, to tell you how much he loves you. You deserve a man to do for you the way you've always done for the men in your life.

"I *am* that man," I promised.

She shook her head again. She was trying to talk herself out of loving me. She was afraid to love me.

"I've been alone a long time. Maybe I'm just not cut out for this—" She waved her hand between us. "For us. You didn't ask me if I was ready for it all to be *real*."

"It's been real since day one and you know it in your bones. And now you're askin' me to let you go, to walk away from the most powerful thing I've ever felt? What, because of a little fear? I can't do that."

There was no way I'd let her do it either.

"But here's what I *am* prepared to do."

The look of trepidation on her face made my lungs seize up. I pressed my hand to my heart, trying to make it work again.

I wanted to give her what she wanted, but what she thought she wanted was ridiculous.

"You're right," I said. "You need to get things straight in

your head and your heart, and I'm drivin' over to Oregon when I leave here, like I told you about, but I'll be back for the drive. It's my last hoorah at G&S. I'll expect you to be there. I *hope* you'll be there. And if you're not, then I guess… I guess I'll need to figure out what love means all over again.

"I *love* you, Spitfire, and that's who you'll always be to me: someone who's bold and brave and wild. Someone who doesn't let life tear her down. No, you take it by the balls and make it yours."

She stared up at me, tears finally filling her wide brown eyes.

Holding both her hands in mine and gripping them tightly, I whispered, "Make it yours, Aubrey. Make *me* yours," and I leaned down and kissed her.

She whimpered into my mouth and slipped her tongue inside, and I tilted my head and let her breath and her taste wash me clean from the inside out. She planted her hands on my shoulders and jumped up, and I held her in my arms.

It was right where she belonged, but the kiss felt like goodbye.

"There's all these grays between us when you let your worries rule you," I said softly, looking in her eyes, trying to find any hope I could, "but I'll be plain. I want you, and when I look at you, all I see is color. I see your rose-gold hair and your amber eyes that smile and light up for me. I see that pink dress, the one that haunted my dreams for half my life. I see green grass out in front of me, and you're runnin' to me on bare feet, with the yellow sun at your back and the blue sky above you. Why can't you see it too?"

"Why do you have to say things like that?" she said, tears finally falling, and she threaded her fingers through my hair. "Make love to me, right here, right now."

Setting her back on her feet, I untangled her hands gently and placed them at her sides. "No."

She pulled back, took a step away from me, and hurt and fear and regret washed over her face, one devastation at a time.

"As much as I wanna take you and claim you right fuckin' now, sex can't fix this." No matter how much I wished it could.

"That's not what I—"

"It is what you meant. You want me to fuck you so you can tell yourself that's all it was between us, just some good, fake sex between the goodbye girl and the young cowboy. But that's *not* all this is, and you damn well know it in your heart."

"Rye—"

"Be at the ranch, ten o'clock Sunday mornin'. That's when the festivities start. Come hungry and ready to dance with me. Come ready to claim *me*."

Her tears fell like rain now, and I kissed her nose and her cheek, her forehead and her hair, trying like hell not to cry too. I wanted to memorize her smell, the feel of her skin on my lips and in my hands. I wanted to convince her all the things running through her mind were fleeting worries and nothing more.

I wanted her to know we belonged together.

But I couldn't make her believe it any more than I could make myself believe that I'd be okay if she wasn't at G&S in less than a week.

"I'm goin'," I said. "I have to 'cause you got some thinkin' to do." Kissing her lips softly, I said, "I won't be here, but I'm *here*." I laid my hand over her heart. "You call me if you need to talk. Text me if you need to laugh, but think about what I said. Okay?"

Finally, she nodded.

"Love you, Spitfire. There ain't nothin' fake about the way I feel, but I need to know you love me too. For real. That I'm important enough to you for you to make room in your life for us, to let all the bullshit go, say 'fuck the fear,' and *love* me. I'm yours forever if you can."

Turning away from her, I grabbed my hat off the counter and fixed it on my head. I pulled the brim down low, and then I made myself walk away.

I just hoped like hell it wasn't the last time.

CHAPTER TWENTY-FIVE

AUBREY

MY BEST FRIEND answered my call, and my voice cracked. "Roxi?"

"Yeah? What's wrong?"

"Everything's all messed up. I dunno what to do!"

"Wait. Slow down. Are you cryin'? I'm comin' over. Are you at home?"

"The shop."

"Be right there."

When she showed up, Roxi didn't say a word. She had a to-go cup from Coffee Shot in one hand and a bottle of Jack Daniels in the other. She held the whiskey out to me, but I shook my head, and she thrust the coffee into my hand.

"Tell me," she said.

I'd hidden behind the checkout counter, butt aching on the cold, hard floor, and Roxi lowered herself beside me. Cradling the coffee in my hands between my legs, I leaned my head on her shoulder, and the waterworks started up again.

She tsked. "See, this is what happens when we don't talk every day."

"He's gone."

"Rye? Where'd he go?"

Sniffling, I swiped my arm under my nose. "Oregon. He's comin' back, but he says he loves me, and he wants me to forget about everything else in my life to be with him."

"Really? He said that?"

"Well, no, but that's what it all boils down to."

"I admit," Roxi said, "I don't know Rye well, but are you sure you aren't blowin' things a little out of proportion? I can't imagine he'd want you to forget about your boys and your store. He did pay five grand so you could keep it."

I felt hysteria creeping up on me. "Of course I'm blowin' things out of proportion! I'm in love with him and I'm scared to death."

Oh God. Here it comes. The heart attack I should've had weeks ago was surely only seconds away. Damn that cowboy. He broke my life. He changed my body, my heart, and my mind.

He made me love him.

The bell on the front door jingled, and Roxi called out, "We're back here."

Daisy's face appeared around the counter, and then she sat in front of me and crisscrossed her legs. "Hi."

To Daisy, I replied, "Hi." But to Roxi, I said, "We really need to have a conversation about privacy. I'm not sure you're gettin' the basic principle."

Daisy laughed. "Roxi called me because I know a thing or two about your situation. José is ten years younger than me, and in case you aren't aware, I have *five* boys who are all pretty macho and who think their mama shouldn't have sex with anyone. They may be a few years older than yours, but they're still little boys in their hearts."

"Oh."

She was right. I'd heard all the gossip around town after she and José had started dating, and when they got married a few years ago, her boys, the five Cade brothers, were all awkward and bristly at Daisy's wedding. Horse ranchers were just as bad as cowboys. Too bad my boys didn't even have the excuse of machismo to fall back on.

But Rye had never acted like that with me. He was as open and positive as the sun shining after a storm.

"Let me catch you up, Daisy," Roxi said. "If I know my best friend, and I *know* my best friend, she's freakin' out 'cause she just realized she loves Rye Graves, and now she doesn't know what to do because she let him walk away."

Daisy smiled softly and sighed, and she held my hand. "Listen, this is the hard part. Deciding to let yourself fall in love isn't easy, not at our age. We're not teenagers anymore, and whether our boys are fifteen or fifty, the choices we make affect them and will be judged by them. They love us, and they want us to be happy; they just don't want to know about what—or who—makes us happy." She squeezed my hand between both of hers. "The question is: can you *let* yourself be happy?"

"I spent so long being a doormat. I don't wanna be that to Rye."

"Are you afraid that if you love him, he'll change?" Roxi asked.

I nodded. "Or I will."

"Why didn't you tell me you've been feelin' this way?" Roxi asked, sounding a little hurt. "Don't you trust me?"

"I'm sorry, Roxi. I do trust you, but it's just that I'm so used to bein' alone. I thought I could figure this out on my own, and I thought if I said what I was feelin' out loud—to you—then it would become real. I wasn't ready for real."

"Aubs, you can tell me anything, okay? You can tell me

when you're afraid. That's the whole point of bein' best friends. We can be scared together."

"Okay," I said, finally ready to lay it all on the line. "Here it is. The second the boys got home, I became Tommy's wife again. My needs didn't matter anymore, and I let them walk all over me. What if… What if that's who I really am inside? What if I'm *not* the woman Rye wants me to be and I let him walk all over me too? I don't wanna be that person anymore."

There was a little steel and ice in Roxi's voice. "My best friend can be whoever she wants to be. Ain't no man gonna control her. She's a goddamn motherfuckin' queen."

I laughed through my sniffles, and I felt awful for keeping this from her.

"Thank you. I love you."

She nodded curtly. "Love you too."

"Are you sure that's not just the fear talking, though?" Daisy asked. "'Cause the man I saw you with worships you. I didn't get the impression he could be controlling or mean."

"No, he's not any of those things. You're right." I sighed. "If that's all it was, maybe I could jump in with both feet, but Rye's mom came to see me last week. I knew she was laying the guilt on thick. I *knew* it, but goddammit, I fell for it."

"What the hell did she say?" Roxi demanded.

"I don't remember word for word, but basically that I was failing as a mom if I stayed with Rye 'cause my boys don't support it. I have no clue how she even knew they were home. What, did she put spy cameras in my house when she found out Rye and I were fake datin'?"

"*Fake* dating?" Daisy asked.

"Oh right. I didn't tell you about that. It's a long story, but it doesn't even matter because pretend turned to real in the blink of an eye. I fell in love with him." I set my coffee on the floor and dropped my head into my hands. "I'm so in love with him. When he's not with me, it's like I can't breathe. I can see it, you know? He said I can't see our future, but I can and it's so good! Why can't I let myself have that? Why can't I have him?"

"Aubrey," Daisy said, "You *can* have that future. You just have to decide to take it."

"Yeah, but then Calla went even further. She said she knew Rye was plannin' to start up his own ranch, which he is. I haven't had a chance to tell y'all about that yet either, but she said it'd be selfish of me to insert myself into Rye's life, and that if I did, he'd fail and end up broke and have to go back to his parents with his tail between his legs."

Daisy scoffed loudly. "That bitch!"

"Don't tell Billie," I said. "I'm afraid she'll sic some crazy malware on Calla Graves's computers or somethin'."

Roxi snorted a laugh. "If she does, don't tell me about it."

"You leave Rye's mama to me," Daisy said in a voice that kind of scared me a little. She was pissed. "It's her own problem if she doesn't have faith in her own kid." Her voice softened, and she leaned forward to swipe tears from my cheek. "But the question remains the same... Can you let yourself be happy? Can you forget about all the gossip and the people who think you and Rye shouldn't be together—or is it only you who thinks that?"

Daisy lifted an eyebrow. "Can you focus on what you want and what you need, and really let yourself love a man who wants to give you everything you've ever dreamed of?"

CHAPTER TWENTY-SIX

RYE

PULLING up at the end of the long drive leading to my dad's barns, I wanted to throw my seat back and wallow in my truck for the next week. When I couldn't see her face anymore, the thought of losing Aubrey made my heart race and put a pit of some nasty feeling in my stomach.

Being the guy stuck carrying hope around all the damn time sucked balls sometimes.

The land sale hadn't gone through yet. I could rescind my offer. I could stay where I was. My dad would take me back, and I could go back to… doing the same shit I'd done my whole fucking life and getting no credit or satisfaction or pride out of it. Whether Aubrey loved me or not, I needed her to be proud of me, like I was a kid again, proving I'd never fall off my horse.

But dammit, I needed to be proud of me too.

With a Thermos of coffee in one hand and some of her homemade banana bread in the other, my mama was waiting for me in front of the barn. I'd smelled the bread baking all the way down the lane at my cabin before I left this morning.

As I approached her, I tried to walk tall. The last thing I

needed was for my mother to know I'd failed again. That I'd fucked up the only thing I'd ever really wanted:

A chance to love Aubrey.

Now, doubt warred with all that hope in my head.

Goddamn. I'm so sick and fucking tired of this feeling!

My parents and their lack of faith in me had worn me thin, and now doubt had infected things with Aubrey. Had I come on too strong?

Mama smiled cautiously. "Thought you might need a pick-me-up."

Shit. She already knew. For the life of me, I couldn't figure out how the fuck she got wise to every single thing I did when I was in town, but I had a feeling she and Uncle Red's girlfriend had made friends, which made zero sense because Liluye was just about the most accepting person I'd ever met. I hoped her kindness would start to rub off on my mama.

She read the frustration on my face. "Yes, Liluye called," she confirmed without me even saying a word. "She said you left the bookstore lookin' defeated. Things didn't go well with Aubrey?"

"No," I said, "didn't go well at all."

"I'm sorry, Ryder. Truly I am. I thought when I went to talk to Aubrey, she understood—"

A red haze washed over my vision. "You did *what*?"

When she saw the anger flashing in my eyes, she fumbled to explain. "Y-yes. I needed to run a few errands in town anyway, so I stopped to see her Monday mornin'. I wanted her to know that it isn't her I don't approve of. It's the situation."

"Dammit, Mama. You wouldn't approve of anyone I love, even if she was the goddamn queen of England! How could you do it? What'd you say to her?"

"Well, I just told her I understood that she needed to be a mother first, and if her boys weren't ready for her to be in a relationship again, then she'd need to figure that out before you two jumped into anything serious, and if you're set on this new business idea of yours, then she—"

Manners be damned this time.

Throwing my head back, I screamed at the sky, "Fuck!" But then I remembered who I was speaking to and *tried* to tamp down my temper. "Mama, I don't give two shits about your approval. My choices and decisions have nothin' to do with you. I need you to hear me right now: Butt the fuck out!"

"Ryder," she breathed. "You've never spoken to me like this." She pursed her lips, and if I had gauged the look on her face correctly, she was trying to hold back tears.

Goddammit! Now I'd made my own mama cry?

"There's your Gemini twin comin' out. Thank God we only see him once or twice a year." She sniffled quietly, collecting herself and looking past me into the morning sun. When she could speak in her normal voice again, she said, "Well, have I made it worse?"

"Yeah, I think you did."

"I'm sorry," she said, guilt filling every syllable. Maybe she'd finally realized she'd crossed a line she shouldn't have. "But she's too old for you, Ryder. You know she is."

Nope. Guess not.

"Damn you, Mama. She is not. Listen to me now. I don't want kids. I never have. Even if Aubrey and I don't make it, I will not be havin' kids with anyone. There's nothin' wrong with me not wantin' children, so it's time you accept it. Process it. Do whatever you gotta do, but stop houndin' me about it. Hear me?"

There were those tears again. But what did she think?

That I'd pop out some toddlers easy peasy just so she'd be happy?

"You have three grandkids already. Maybe you oughta focus on them instead of me for a change. Take a damn vacation and go see 'em."

Her breath hitched in a series of hiccups. "I-I just couldn't stand it if she broke your heart."

"Too late for that," I said, turning to go… somewhere. Anywhere that wasn't the inside of my head. Everything was falling apart. I wanted to rip my hair out. I lifted my hands and gripped it at the roots. "Fuck."

"You really love her?" Mama asked.

I laughed. It was the *only* sure thing I knew.

Looking out at the mountains, I drew in a deep breath and let it ground me, let it slow my racing heart. "Yeah, I love Aubrey, Mama. When I look at her, I see the rest of my life play out in front of me like a movie. She's in every scene. I love her the way you love Dad. The way he loves you. Why can't you accept it?"

There was true sorrow in her voice now. "How can I make it right?"

That stopped me in my tracks. If there was one thing my mama was good at, it was making young men feel guilty and then want to work their fingers to the bone to mend the fences they'd busted.

And I just happened to know of two newly unemployed targets she could set her sights on.

"HEY, COWBOY," a woman slurred when I took a stool at the local bar in the little farm town I found myself in up in Oregon. I ordered a Bud from the bartender as the woman ran her finger over my wrist on the bar top. "You lookin' for a little fun tonight?"

No, I sure wasn't. I wouldn't be having any fun without Aubrey, and I'd spent the last two days up to my elbows in cow shit and crops of clover and, just for the irony, rye. So no. No drunken fun for me.

Scanning the dimly lit, barely occupied bar that looked like someone had thrown up neon and argon all over it, I noticed the woman's purse and keys on the bar five stools away. The bartender caught my eye and nodded. He swiped her keys, pocketed them, and then he called her name.

"Marie, how 'bout we call your daughter to come pick you up?"

"I'm just havin' some fun, talkin' to this cowboy here, Johnny." She turned back my way just as Johnny set my beer in front of me. "You're not from around here, are you?"

"No, ma'am."

"Ma'am?" She scoffed. "I'm not your fucking mother."

"I mean no disrespect, but I got me a woman back home. I'm not lookin' to replace her for the night."

Thankfully, Johnny had already begun to dial his phone to call her ride.

"Whatever," Marie said.

She stumbled away on too-high heels to the back of the room where some other guys sat around a high top, drinking cans of Pabst and playing a game of cards, and I nodded my thanks to the bartender while he spoke to Marie's daughter.

The drive to Oregon had been long and lonely. The whole time, all I could think about was the look on Aubrey's face when she'd tried to set me free. I tried calling her to what... apologize for my mama? Yeah, and for pushing too hard. And for loving her more than she knew what to do with. I knew this wasn't easy for her to navigate.

She didn't answer. I wasn't sure if leaving had been the right thing to do, but I knew if I'd shown up on her doorstep, shit would've gone sideways fast.

She knew how much I wanted her. She knew I loved her. I'd spent the last several weeks drilling home the point. But she needed to figure us out on her own.

And I needed her to choose me.

Yeah, there'd be obstacles. Aubrey's boys' disapproval was one hell of a mountain to climb, but if it were up to me, their discontent wouldn't stop me. I'd lived with Calla Graves far too long to be bothered by a little naysaying.

But that was me. It had always been my style. When I wanted something, I went after it hard, and Aubrey was the only woman I'd wanted for as long as I could remember. But I couldn't force this. As much as I wanted to, I knew this time I had to be patient and wait for Aubrey to decide.

She'd spent the entirety of her adult life letting men, dead and alive, walk all over her.

If Aubrey didn't come to terms on her own, whether she chose me or didn't, she'd never feel secure in the choice.

I wanted that surety for her more than anything. She needed to figure out on her own how to follow her heart again, how to choose something good for her.

With my eyes closed, I held my phone in my hand, trying to will Aubrey to make the right choice. I'd checked my notifications fifty times over the course of the day, hoping to see a missed call or text. I was desperate just to hear her voice, but then, finally, my phone dinged, and when I looked at my screen, relief filled every cell inside my body.

It seemed my Spitfire wanted me too.

SPITFIRE

I miss you.

Goddamn. The way that little text bubble filled me up! Relief flooded my chest and lifted up the hard, empty box my heart had become over the last few days.

SPITFIRE

But the boys have jumbled everything up, and I'm still scared. I don't know how to be your girlfriend.

You're not my girlfriend. You're my everything.

And I'm sorry about my mama. She shouldn't have said that shit to you.

SPITFIRE

You know?

She told me. I'm not proud to say I cussed her out.

SPITFIRE

Was she right though? Am I getting in your way? You lent me that money. Is it affecting your ability to buy Bax's land?

You saw my bank account. What's 5 grand gonna do?

SPITFIRE

Right.

Have you laughed today?

SPITFIRE

What?

> I know this is hard for you. I hate thinking about you alone inside your head again, so I wanna know if you've laughed today.

SPITFIRE

No. I don't think so.

> I'm in Oregon, a couple hours' drive from the coast by a little town called Sweet Hill, and on my way here, I drove by an Italian restaurant, and their outdoor sign said: Why did the tomato blush?

SPITFIRE

What? Why?

> Because it saw the salad dressing! ;)

She started to type out her reply. Three little dots hovered over where her text would appear, but then they disappeared and my phone rang. A picture of Aubrey's beautiful face popped onto my screen, and I answered faster than I ever had before in my life.

In a quiet voice, she said, "I thought you said you didn't want kids?"

"I don't." Confused, I asked, "Why?"

"Because that was a dad joke if I've ever heard one."

I laughed out loud while she chuckled in my ear.

"Miss you, Spitfire."

She sighed. "I miss you, too, but I feel silly missin' you."

"Why silly?"

"Because when you're not here, it feels like the last month didn't happen, like it was all a dream."

It made me sad, thinking that in order for her to feel loved, she would have to be dreaming.

"It's not a dream, baby. I'm real. The love I feel for you is real. Trust in that and do whatever you gotta to feel okay about lovin' me too. I've waited a lifetime for you. A few more days won't kill me, but you can't have one foot in and one foot out the door."

I heard her breathing, but she didn't say anything more.

"Will I see you Sunday?"

"Rye."

No. No maybes today.

"I'll see you Sunday," I said, and I hung up.

CHAPTER TWENTY-SEVEN

AUBREY

STRADDLING A LINE? Worrying my pretty little head?

That was how Rye saw me? Like I was that tired, old woman again, trying to be a mom to my boys, trying to be a perfect wife to my dead husband, a good friend, business owner, community member, and Rye's girlfriend all at the same time.

I knew he was right.

It had come time for me to believe, to be bold, to put my foot down on one side of the line and declare my intentions. I needed to stop worrying about what everyone thought of me. The only opinion that mattered should have been my own.

Before I married Tommy, I *had* been the strong, wild girl Rye kept telling me I could be again, and the world had seemed so much bigger to me back then.

To Micah and Benji, I'd always only been their mom. It felt weird still to think of myself as anything else, but Rye was also right that they could handle us being together if I showed them he was who I wanted.

Who I *needed*.

And it would do them good to see me treated so

preciously. That was a lesson still left they needed to learn. If you loved someone, you didn't walk all over them or possess them like an old trophy in a corner collecting dust; you let them fly and soar and succeed. You cheered them on while they did it, and that was the way to show your love.

"Ma?" Micah said softly, taking the cushion at the opposite end of the couch in the living room, watching me carefully as he stretched his long, skinny legs out in front of him. He'd worn Batman socks, of all things, and seeing them on his big feet brought back so many memories of when those feet were smaller than my hand.

Sipping my coffee, I thought about what I wanted to say to him.

His brother would get over it quickly. That had always been Benji's way—quick to accuse, but also quick to forgive. He was an enigma; he'd always had some innate ability to just accept hard things. Some days I found myself wishing I could be more like him.

Micah was the opposite; he learned quickly, but he took a long time to accept new things or people. Tommy's death hit him the hardest. I'd known losing my husband was a possibility when he enlisted, but I supported him. I always had, no matter the thing he wanted to do. Why couldn't he have done the same for me?

"Yeah?" I said, finally focusing on Micah's handsome face.

It still surprised me when I found Tommy's features in the boys', but the older they got, the easier he was to see in them. It killed me that he couldn't be here to see himself reflected back through them. But I was there, too, in their brown eyes and the way they saw the world, like it was something to be discovered and mastered.

Micah sighed heavily. "Izzy dumped me."

"Oh, honey," I said, setting my mug on the coffee table. "I'm so sorry. Are you okay?"

"No. I think… I think I love her."

Whoa. We're already talking about love? Wait—doesn't that make you a hypocrite? You've only been with Ryder a few weeks, and you're in love with him.

"Did you have a fight?"

"Yeah."

"Wanna tell me about it?"

"Not really, but she says I have to. I told her about your… *boyfriend* and about how sad you've been without him, and she said I was bein' a dick."

"She did? You knew I was sad?"

He nodded miserably. "Yeah. C'mon, Ma. I heard you cryin' in your room last night, and when I told her, Izzy said it's not fair of me to expect you to go the rest of your life alone. And then she looked up that Rye guy online, and she said I was to tell you, and I quote"—Micah groaned and rolled his eyes—"she said, 'you better get you some of that Wyoming cowboy, or I'll come down there and claim him for myself.'"

Pressing my lips together to stop the cackle that wanted to come out of my mouth, I took a deep breath, trying to exude mom energy instead of "ooo, you go, girlfriend" vibes.

"Go ahead," he said. "You can laugh. I'm gonna 'cause if I don't, I'll cry. I've never been so embarrassed in my life."

I chuckled. There, that was an appropriate mom-like reaction.

"Micah, tell Izzy to ease up on you, but tell her thanks for havin' my back. I'm glad she asked you to talk to me because I wanted to talk to you too. She doesn't need to be mad at you, though, 'cause I'm mad enough for the both of us. It's time for you to accept that just 'cause I'm your mom, it doesn't mean there aren't things I want or that I don't have needs."

"Okay, but can we please not talk about sex? I don't ever want that image in my head again."

"I don't really feel like talkin' to you about sex either. Although, as, like, a quarter-life check-in, you're usin' condoms, right?"

"Ma!"

"Well, are you?"

"Yeah! God, Ma."

"I won't apologize for askin'. Babies ain't cheap, and you're broke."

"Yeah, and with my luck, I'd probably end up with two."

Going for another sip of my coffee, I winced and shrugged. "You might."

"Listen." Micah turned toward me, a serious look settling on his face. "If you think this guy, Rye, is okay, then I guess I can allow it. But, Ma, he's not good enough. No one is.

"I love you, and you've been there for me through a lot of sh—stuff. You were strong for me and Benji when Dad died, and then you started your own business? That's pretty badass. I admire you. I hope I can be like you, and I don't want anyone to hurt your heart."

"Come here," I said, and I opened my arms.

Micah scooted into them, and I held my baby close. He still smelled the same way he had when he was nine, like potato chips and fabric softener.

"First, thank you. I love you too, and I don't want anyone to hurt your heart either. And second"—leaning back, I smacked him lightly on his cheek, but then I pulled him into my arms again—"you'll 'allow it'?"

"You know what I mean," he said, hugging me tightly. "I'll get with the program or whatever."

"Thank you."

"Alright, that's enough huggin'. I'm a grown man."

Debatable, but I laughed and kissed his cheek. "So when do I get to meet this Izzy? But just FYI, I already approve."

"If she takes me back, I'll drive up there and bring her down for supper one night before I start my new job. By the way, can I borrow your car? 'Cause Benji's gonna pitch a fit when I tell him I wanna take the truck back up to Montana. It's on its last legs."

"New job?"

"Yeah, Benji didn't tell you?"

"Tell me what?"

"Rye's mama, Mrs. Graves? She came to talk to us at the diner yesterday, and she offered us both jobs at their ranch this summer. The pay's good. Like, *really* good. And Izzy says if I want her to take me seriously, I better accept the offer and learn how to cowboy 'cause her dad won't let me marry her if I don't."

I almost spit out the sip of coffee I'd taken, completely forgetting he'd just said that the judgiest of all moms had hired both my children and now might possibly be a daily influence in their lives. "*Marry* her?"

"Yeah, but don't get all nuts about it. I'm talkin' someday, not next week."

I took a breath and released the panic that the image of my kid standing in front of an altar had created in my mind. "You think Izzy's the one?"

"Yeah," he said, leveling his stare on my face. "I do. Maybe. Do you think this Rye is your one? I mean, I know Dad was, but maybe it's not so weird if you have another 'one'."

"He is," I said, confirming it for Micah, but for me too. "Rye's the *only* one. I love him."

"He treats you well?"

"Better than anyone ever has, and that includes your dad. You know, don't you, that the way your dad belittled me and treated me like a possession and a maid was wrong?"

"I know, Ma. But I guess all this time, I thought if I admitted that to myself, it felt like I was… I dunno, disrespecting his memory, you know?"

"I've felt the same way, but it's the truth, Micah. And there's nothin' wrong with tellin' the truth."

He nodded. "But Rye, he doesn't do that? He's good to you? Does he make you laugh?"

"Yeah," I said, smiling and letting it show on my face that Rye's love made me feel happier than I'd ever been. "He makes me feel important and beautiful and smart. I haven't felt those things in a long time."

"Well," Micah said, "then I'm glad. Alright, I better go call Izzy. She's waitin' for a report."

"Tell her I say hi, and tell her you passed her test with flyin' colors."

He smiled, his little half grin brightening his face like his dad's used to, and I wondered if I would ever stop feeling confused about how much I loved seeing Tommy in the boys' expressions.

As Micah got to his feet, I remembered I'd forgotten to say the most important thing he needed to hear.

"Wait. One last thing. If you think you're gonna get married someday to Izzy or anyone else, it's time you learned to pick up your own dirty laundry. In fact, I remember showin' you how to wash that laundry." I arched an eyebrow and he nodded reluctantly. "And do the damn dishes once in a while. No woman worth her salt will stand for comin' home to a mountain of dirty dishes in the sink while her husband drinks beer and watches NASCAR on TV."

"Yes, ma'am." He saluted me, and I had to hold back a laugh. Time would tell if my message had gotten through.

"And after you pee, put the mother-lovin' toilet seat down. An old woman like me could fall through and bust a hip. Then you'll have to help me shower after my hip-replacement surgery. Nobody wants that, Micah. *Nobody*."

"Aw, God, Ma. Okay."

"Oh yeah, and P.S., now that you've got good jobs, after you two pay off your landlord, if you're gonna live here, y'all are payin' *me* rent. You can buy your own groceries too. You eat enough at every meal to feed a fully grown bear emergin' from his den in spring."

"Yeah"—he shrugged—"that's fair."

"Oh, and one more thing: I like banana pancakes. Learn how to make 'em and then do somethin' nice for me every once in a while, eh?"

He chuckled. "You got it. I can't promise they'll be edible, but I'll try."

"Love you, Emgee," I said, using the nickname I'd given him back in kindergarten when the boys' teacher couldn't tell them apart. She used to check with me every day when I dropped them off to make sure who was who. If she asked them, they lied and traded places, so she separated them to opposite sides of the classroom and then stuck stickers to the backs of their shirts with their initials MG and BG between their shoulder blades, where they couldn't reach to pull them off. It had taken them half the year to figure out they could take each other's stickers off or switch shirts in the bathroom.

"Love you, Momgee. See ya later."

"'Kay. Oh, hey!" I leaned over the back of the couch as he took off down the hall. "Tell Beegee what I said and tell him I wanna talk to him too."

"Yeah, yeah."

When Micah was safe in his bedroom from any more sex talks with his ma, I carried my mug to the now-empty kitchen sink and dumped out what was left.

I turned and leaned against the counter, thinking about what I wanted to do next.

Right.

It was time for me to bag my cowboy, just like Izzy had said.

But first, a little self-care was in order, and when you were planning to spend multiple days holed up and ravishing your man, you needed to shave and pluck and go get your gray hairs dyed.

I pulled my phone from my back pocket and clicked a few times, then held it up to my ear, and when a familiar female voice answered, I pleaded, "Ronnie. It's an emergency. Can you fit me in?"

She laughed. "When can you get here? I'll treat you to the whole shebang: hair, nails, toes, and yeah, I think I'm gonna need to pull out the wax if you've got a hot date with a cowboy."

"Ronnie!"

"What?" she said. "Where is it you think town gossip starts? Everybody knows it's the salon."

CHAPTER TWENTY-EIGHT

RYE

THE FEW DAYS I'd spent near the coast had been eye opening for me. I was right. Regenerative farming was the way of the future.

Meeting those people, seeing their homes and their farms, had been exactly the boost of confidence I needed. They'd all been welcoming, had opened their arms to me and were generous in sharing their knowledge. I left Oregon with my phone full of contacts I could call with questions, and I promised to invite them all out to my place once I got things moving.

I had so many ideas running through my head, about crops to plant, cattle breeds to experiment with, and I'd even visited a farm like the one the Lee brothers and I were planning to start, where people stayed at the farm, helped with the animals and the crops, and then went home with their arms full of the farm's products.

Before I knew it, I'd driven back to the ranch, packed up my shit in my cabin, and Sunday was upon me. I had no clue where I'd stay after the drive since there wasn't a house on the new property yet, but whatever. I could shack up with Bax and Athena or camp until I figured it out.

Like I said, when I wanted something, I went all out.

Sitting in an old Adirondack chair on my little cabin's front porch, I watched the sun rise and felt the familiar low-burning rush of adrenaline coursing through my veins. I felt it before every drive. This time was different, and it was the biggest herd we'd ever driven to range, so the rush of energy was bigger too.

Ten days with nothing to do but ride and think? Great. Just what I needed. If Aubrey didn't show up today, maybe I wouldn't come back.

G&S Ranch would be overrun with friends and their families and more cowboys than I could shake a stick at. There'd be enough food to feed the entire population of Wyoming, more beer than Budweiser would know what to do with, and the air would be full of music. Even the pastor of my parents' church would be here. He shut his doors every time we kicked off a drive with a barbecue. They always started on a Sunday, and he knew better than to expect people to show up for services when Calla and Grady Graves were hosting.

The only question was: would Aubrey be here?

Both her boys had accepted jobs at the ranch with my dad. He seemed cheered up a little to have some fresh blood to boss around since I was "abandoning him," and Benji and Micah both said they'd be here today.

When I talked with him last night, Benji seemed pretty pumped to start his "cowboy lessons," but Presley wouldn't let him come on the drive with the rest of us because the kid was terrified of horses.

Presley had also said Micah was a born rider, but that he didn't seem as interested in our way of life. I had a feeling the only reason he'd taken the job was to impress a girl. I couldn't blame him for that, and he'd still get a thorough education while he was here, nonetheless.

But neither Micah nor Benji could tell me if their mama would show, which was now turning my excitement about the drive into downright anxiety.

I hadn't spoken to my Spitfire in two days. Again, I'd wanted to give her the time she needed to think things through. I wasn't sure if her thinking was a good thing or not, but I wanted so fucking bad for her to see what I saw: our future.

Her kids were on board. All that remained were her own fears and doubts and insecurities.

But no matter the outcome of the day, I still had a job to do, so I dumped the last of my coffee over the side of the porch and left the empty mug on the railing for Presley to wash once he moved in.

I took one last sweeping look at the land I'd spent my entire life on, and then I headed out.

BY TEN IN THE MORNING, Presley had no less than three women suitors. Something about the way he plucked his fiddle strings had them coming from miles away. If he wanted a wife, he could have his pick. He didn't though. He wanted to be out in the hills and mountains, wrangling calves stuck in brush and living free. He always said women were pretty things to look at, but that if I ever caught him settling down, I should turn my shotgun on him and leave him out in the dust for the coyotes.

My dad was enjoying showing off his stock and his land to his usual gang of rancher friends. Roddy Milson had shown up. His ranch closer to Wisper had been G&S's biggest competition for as long as I could remember, but he was a decent guy, and though they'd never admit it, I thought he and my dad had enjoyed their friendly rivalry all these years. There'd been plenty of times we'd traded cowboys or equipment when one of the ranches had been in need, and I was glad now that my dad had that friendship to count on.

Everybody else ooh'ed and ahh'ed at the enormity of my dad's operation, and it caused me more pride than I could describe. Unsurprisingly, he'd given Bax and Brand a wide berth all morning, and he hadn't mentioned my plans for the future to his friends, but no matter. They'd all find out soon enough.

I found myself keeping tabs on Aubrey's boys all morning, hoping for some sign that she might be on her way. Benji had also found himself a young lady to flirt with. He even helped peel enough potatoes to fill a feed trough for my mama just to stay close to Lila Connors. Little did he know, Lila was the heir to a huge cattle processing operation, and the girl would eat that boy for breakfast given the chance. She seemed charmed by his attempts to impress her so far, but if she hadn't crushed him in the palm of her hand by the end of the day, I'd bite my tongue.

People laughed and talked and danced around me. June had arrived quietly and brought with it a mild, warm summer day. The sun shone down on the land and made it seem less harsh than we all knew it could be, but the only thing I could see was Aubrey and me joining in, dancing to Presley's music, eating my mama's food, and enjoying life.

It was almost lunchtime, though, and she was still a no-show.

Finally, after everybody's bellies had been filled with corn on the cob, ribs, fire-roasted potatoes, and strawberry pie, my dad gave his usual speech, and the pastor said a prayer before fifteen of us prepared to head out with our herd and horses.

It devastated me to think about leaving without seeing Aubrey's face one last time, and I wanted to tear down a barn to let loose my frustration, but what good would that do? Inside my chest, defeat began to settle. Defeat and loss.

Loss of love and… loss of hope.

But maybe it was time to let that go. Maybe my parents had a point this whole time.

Screaming at the world wouldn't bring Aubrey back to me anyway.

I'd left Blue out in the pasture so he could run and work himself up. The horse had never needed much direction, and he had more excitement for the drive than I ever had. Once I had him saddled up and packed down with supplies, he chuffed at me, as if to say, "Climb on, man. We got shit to do."

"You're in charge," I told him as the silly horse licked my arm and rubbed his nose over the spit. "I might need to lean on you this time."

Snapping my chaps into place, I looked into the sun. The day grew warmer by the minute, so I pulled off my button-down and the heat felt good on my shoulders. I tucked the shirt into my saddle bag, straightened my undershirt, and mounted my critter, listening to the excited chatter of a few of my outriders while they saddled up too.

Out past the paddock gate, I turned Blue, lining him up with the other fourteen riders and their mounts, so we could all wave and call out goodbyes. Mama waved and tossed me a smile, but I didn't bother waving back. I still hadn't forgiven her. I wasn't so sure I ever would.

My uncle Red and Devo's mama hooted and hollered from the sidelines, and I nodded to them and tipped my hat.

The mountains behind us were calling, and like so many times in the past, I wanted to get lost out there. I wanted to forget the last month had ever happened.

My legs flexed of their own accord, ready to squeeze Blue right into a run. My back tensed, jaw clenched, and I pushed up in my stirrups. Opening my reins to my right, I turned… but something called me back to the crowd. A whisper floating high on the lazy summer breeze.

The cattle bayed and lowed in their pens, waiting for the gates to be opened at last, so hearing much over that ruckus wasn't likely.

The person I wanted to see wasn't there anyhow.

Age and our different experiences, the juxtaposition of Aubrey and me kept her from throwing off her inhibitions and giving herself fully to me. Our families hadn't helped, but it all came down to Aubrey.

She had to let herself need me.

She had to let herself love me, but her absence today made it clear she'd never be mine. Somehow, I'd have to figure out how to get over her.

I'd loved Aubrey my whole life. Would I mourn the loss of her for the rest?

I clicked my tongue twice, ready for Blue to carry me away from all this goddamn heartache.

He nodded, shook out his mane, and took two steps, but I heard that impossible whisper again, and when I looked over my shoulder, I saw a rose-gold halo bobbing through the crowd, weaving in and out between everyone back by the barn.

And I could've sworn I'd heard the angel wearing that halo call my name.

CHAPTER TWENTY-NINE

AUBREY

WHO KNEW a last-minute wardrobe malfunction would almost ruin the rest of my life?

I'd almost missed him! But there Rye sat atop the most beautiful horse I'd ever seen, the blueish-gray color of his coat separating Rye and Blue at the end of a line of cowboys on their horses.

This was it, the last goodbye before their drive. I recognized Grady Sr. at the opposite end of the line, looking stoic and like Kevin Costner in his black felt hat, and I realized then that I had more in common with Calla Graves than I wanted to admit.

God, my man was a vision, his hair curling beneath his tan hat and his strong thighs holding him steady on his steed. His arms were bare; he wasn't wearing his usual denim button down, but I didn't mind one bit. His hands holding his horse's reins, covered by riding gloves, looked strong and sure.

My book-club friends had convinced me to wear the pink dress Rye loved when I told them at our emergency meeting all the beautiful things he'd said to me, and how no matter how much I'd tried, I couldn't stop loving him.

Was it too soon? They'd all agreed, yes.

Did we care? Not a one of us.

And when I tried on the dress in the library's bathroom and couldn't get it zipped up the back, Phil had rushed out to her truck. She returned with a travel sewing kit, ripped that zipper right out, added fabric from a similarly colored pink T-shirt Sam happened to have had in her bag, and then Phil hand sewed inserts on either side of the zipper so I could fit my forty-seven-year-old ass into the dress. Man, that woman had fast fingers.

She said she'd mend it properly later, but for now, it would have to do, and then Roxi drove me to G&S Ranch in her cruiser, lights on and speed limits ignored. Our friends followed in their cars, and as soon as we'd parked, Daisy went on a walkabout to find Rye's mama. She wasn't planning to let Calla ruin things for Rye and me.

As I took off in search of my destiny, I realized the Graveses' property looked like the freaking county fair with all the people, shade tents, and picnic tables. I smelled massive amounts of barbecue sauce and strawberries, but I didn't see any of it because the only thing I could focus on was Rye in the distance.

Somewhere behind me, my friends cheered me on as I weaved in and out of all the people congregating in the pasture next to the biggest rust-red-colored barn.

The other riders' friends and families called out their goodbyes. There were wishes of "good luck," and I heard lots of "I love you"s, but I wasn't going to say it until I knew for sure Rye would hear it.

Raising my hand above my head while I held the dress out of the dirt with the other, I shouted his name.

People had started to notice my desperate sprint toward the man I loved. Women moved out of my path, tugging their little kids out of the way by their shirts and dirty hands. One little boy dropped his popsicle when his mama pulled him out of my way, and he wailed his disappointment. Normally, I would've stopped and found him a new popsicle, but not today.

Today, the title "Mom" was the last thing on my mind.

Today, I was just Aubrey, the wild, "grab the bull by the horns" woman I'd always been, here to claim her cowboy. Maybe it had taken me a few years to find her again, but I had, and I wasn't planning on looking back.

I jumped around the mother and son and raised my other hand in the air, letting the dress drag through the dirt. Jesus. Had I shrunk from menopause too? I didn't remember the dress being this long when I'd worn it twenty years ago. I had on the same boots today I'd worn with the dress back then, but the stupid things were still stiff, and running was causing an unbearable pinch on my toes.

"Ryder Graves! Wait!"

He hadn't heard me. He turned his horse, and I watched as his body tightened in preparation for his ride.

"Rye! Wait for me!"

Calla stood in my direct path. Maybe I should've stopped to talk to her. To promise her I wouldn't hurt *her* little boy's heart, but even she couldn't get in my way today.

As I passed her, her surprise at seeing me running toward her son to tangle him up in an inappropriate love match quickly died when Daisy stepped up to the plate. She wrapped her arm around Calla's shoulder and shook her finger in the woman's face to warn Calla to keep her opinions to herself.

Daisy winked and smiled at me, and loudly she said, "Good girl. Go get your cowboy."

She'd given me the last push of adrenaline I needed. At the top of my lungs, I screamed, "Rye!"

He stopped his forward movement. Looking over his shoulder, his eyes narrowed and he scanned the crowd, but he still hadn't seen me.

Two heavy-set old men were the last obstacles in my way, and I prayed that when I pushed past them, I wouldn't knock them down.

Good grief, has running always been this hard?

The men heard me huffing and puffing behind them. They stepped to the side, and one of them extended his arm with a smile and his hat held out to show me the way.

Rye had given up. I saw the way disappointment lowered his shoulders, and he lifted his reins and began to move.

He was leaving!

"Ryder. Fucking. Graves! Stop. Don't go!"

Finally, he saw me.

His face lit up, changing from a hard mask of defeat to the biggest smile I'd ever seen. He jumped from his horse and walked toward me a few steps, but then he stopped. Another cowboy with black hair under an even darker hat led his horse closer to Rye. Rye handed the man his reins, and then the other guy backed up and Blue went with.

I stopped running and, with my hands on my shaking thighs, tried to catch my breath. I held up a finger, hoping Rye would know I just needed an old-lady minute. Everyone was watching me. I felt their eyes on my back, but I couldn't have cared less.

Some smartass behind me blared "In Your Eyes" from their phone. I couldn't tell who the offender was, but I had my suspicions about Benji, though how he would have any clue who Peter Gabriel was stumped me.

Before they'd left this morning, both my boys told me they supported whatever decision I made. All along I'd known they would, but the fear was real. Who was I if I wasn't Aubrey George, widow and mom?

But I was the same girl from a million years ago, just with a few more miles on her and a lot wiser. I could be all those things at the same time, and it didn't change who I was to the people who loved me.

And if I loved Rye as hard as I knew I could and he loved me back, I'd be a better mom and daughter and friend, because I'd be happy.

As soon as my front door had shut behind the boys, I flipped on my porch light and vowed never to turn it off again, and that was when the mad dash started, which was also when I realized I needed help and called my friends.

I could feel them now behind me, supporting me, and when I could breathe again, I straightened and locked my eyes on Rye's.

At the edge of the fenced pastures, past an open gate at the start of the hills that would lead him away, Rye stood, hands on his hips, smiling and waiting for me to come to him, to let my fears and doubts go and give myself to him.

And that was my plan, just as soon as I took off these godforsaken boots. I yanked my dress above my knees and pulled them off, one at a time, and chucked them into the dirt. Catcalls and whistles sounded around me, and they carried on the wind from the cowboys still mounted on their horses. Even over the incessant mooing of the cows as they moved in increasingly more urgent circles in their pens, I heard them.

Rye laughed, his own age lines crinkling at the edges of

his eyes under the shadow of his hat, and like he couldn't wait one second longer, he took two more steps toward me.

I ran full out, as fast as I could go, my feet hitting the dirt over and over, ruining the pedicure Ronnie had given me and probably the hem of my dress.

When I was close enough to hear him, he said in an easy voice, "Hey, Spitfire. Nice dress. Change your mind about seein' me off?"

"I changed my mind about everything! You're not goin' anywhere without me."

"What about your store?"

"The shop is closed for two weeks while its owner goes through some renovations."

"Oh, I'll renovate you alright," he said, the edges of his smile lifting deviously.

When I was ten feet away, he lifted his hat and pulled his white undershirt over his head by the hem. I couldn't figure out why he'd be stripping in front of literally everyone he knew, but then I noticed the new black and gray ink on the left side of his chest, above his heart.

As he fixed the hat back on his head, I stopped my feet and strands of my hair whipped forward into my open mouth.

Pointing to his new tattoo, I whispered, "Is that… me?"

"You like? Got it up in Oregon. I needed somethin' to remind me of you while we were apart."

"I look—" I stuttered, trying to catch my breath. "I-I'm sexy."

"Fuck yeah, you are."

The pinup portrait of my face and bare shoulders, turned and peeking out from Rye's muscled chest, with thick, waving tresses of my hair curving and wrapping around the image, was so realistic that I had a hard time not looking at it. The only color in the entire design was the rosy, golden hue of my hair. The peonies surrounding the image—my favorites—were black and gray too.

I stepped forward slowly, reaching my hand toward the tattoo. "Can I touch it?"

When I met Rye's gaze, I found a proud smile plastered across his lips. "You don't have to ask to touch me, baby. You own me. You can do whatever you want with me."

Taking the last few steps until I was a breath away from him, I touched my portrait forever inked onto Rye's skin with tentative fingers, softly tracing a line of a peony's leaf and then the ridge of my nose. The lines were still a little raised with irritation.

"You really should have this covered and protected from the sun. It's still healin', but… she's beautiful."

"She's *you*," he said, pulling off his gloves and tossing them down to the dirt, "so yeah, the most beautiful woman in the world."

"But she doesn't look like me now."

"Fair maiden," Rye whispered, wrapping me up in his strong arms. He lifted me, and I wound my legs around his hips, trying not to picture him naked, wearing only his leather chaps. "What have I told you about how you see yourself? The only reference the artist had was the picture I took of you after my birthday dinner. Remember?

"You were on my bed on your knees wrapped up in my sheets. I called your name, and you turned toward me and bit that sweet bottom lip." He touched my lip with one finger. "Your hair was messed from the love we'd made, your face was flushed and bright and happy, and you seduced me again and made me watch you pleasure yourself with your eyes on my body.

"Baby," he said, "she *is* you. Look. Says so right here,"

and he tipped his head, looking at a banner beneath my image where, in swirling script, two words had been etched:

My Spitfire.

My cheeks heated, and I peeked around us to make sure no one had heard what he'd said, but he claimed me in front of everyone, took my mouth roughly with his, and he kissed me like no one else was watching.

As he crowned me with his sweaty hat, the crowd cheered us on. I swore I heard Billie somewhere, hooting like a rabid owl on steroids.

But I paid them no mind. I was lost in Rye.

"I *love* you," I promised him, and I kissed him back, moaning and grasping for handfuls of his hair, wrapping my body tightly around his, letting him know with everything I had inside me that he was it for me. I'd finally found my happy ever after…

And my happy ever after was Rye freaking Graves.

EPILOGUE
RYE

"BABY, hold on a sec. Me and Blue are havin' a moment."

"Yeah, sure," Aubrey said in my ear. "I'll just wait on the phone while you have a heart-to-heart with your horse."

"Great. Thanks," I told her, and I reached through the stall door to pat Blue's shoulder. "Listen, buddy. I know this is weird. You were born at G&S, and this is a new barn, but you're my number one guy. I couldn't do this without you. You're up for it, right? A new farm, new mares to suck up to."

Blue chuffed his displeasure and went back to nosing through his hay.

The new barn had gone up in record time, thanks to the help of Bax, Brand, Aubrey's cousin, Max, and some other local farmers and ranchers. Aubrey's parents had even come out, and once her mama got over the shock of Aubrey dating a younger man, or any man at all, she warmed to me pretty quick. She was impressed by my parents, who'd surprisingly also come to see the new barn, and they'd already made friends.

Fall had arrived with its usual kaleidoscope of colors, and

the nights were growing colder, but Blue and I were still living in the barn. He had a fancy, decked-out stall, and I had a tack room with a mattress on the dirty floor while I waited for my house to be built. I shacked up with Aubrey some nights and stayed out here the rest. If I needed food or a shower, Bax and Athena had opened their house to me anytime. They'd offered me their couch, but I liked being out on the land. She and I needed to get to know each other.

"I think I'm gonna stay here again tonight. He's depressed."

I swore I could hear Aubrey roll her eyes.

I hated leaving Blue, but it was necessary when I wanted a little alone time with my woman. Her boys were both staying out at my dad's place while they worked and learned the ropes. My mama liked having kids to feed and spoil again. I tried telling her twenty-three-year-olds weren't kids, but she doted on them all the same. She even let them stay in my brother's and my old bedrooms in the big house.

Mama had taken on the role of the twins' granny pretty quick, and since Aubrey's parents lived a few hours away, and their dad's parents lived on the East Coast, Benji and Micah ate that shit up.

The things the boys did that drove Aubrey batty seemed to be the things my mama enjoyed about having them around. Although, she had someone on the payroll to clean up their dirty dishes and clothes. But my dad had already started turning them into cattlemen, and no self-respecting cowboy let other people pick up his shit. They'd learned quickly not to need a maid to follow after them with a broom and Lysol.

"If you think that's best," Aubrey said. "But then, I dunno what to do with this delivery that just arrived."

"Delivery? What kinda delivery?"

"It's from this boutique I found online that specializes in leather bras and corsets—"

"I'm comin' right now. Pun intended."

Taunting me, she said, "But maybe I should just put it away for now. You're busy."

"Woman, did you not hear me? I'm leavin' right now."

In addition to Aubrey's and my house, Brand had teams of guys on the property all summer, Monday through Friday every week, finishing Bax's cabins, Abey and Devo's house, and a house for his mama and youngest brother, Dixon. The dude was fast. He'd had all the permits ready to be submitted and the blueprints done before I'd even formally bought the farm. Aubrey was in the process of selling her house, so as soon as Brand and his crews finished building—

"Bax! Watch out!"

Brand screamed at his brother, and I ran out of the barn and right into the problem on the west side of the building when I found Bax pinned between it, the metal fence gate, and my new bull.

Bax roared in pain and slid down the side of the barn as the animal trotted off in a huff.

I chased after him, yelling and threatening to turn him into steak, and herded him into a holding pen. Thankfully, Athena and I had finished fencing it off the day before. That goddamn bull was a menace. If all our bulls acted like this dick, then I'd made the wrong decision in choosing to cross Herefords with Red Angus. They were supposed to have docile temperaments!

My phone was still in my hand, and Aubrey's voice coming through the speaker sounded worried. "Rye! Rye? What's wrong?"

"Sorry, darlin'," I said. "I'm gonna have to take a rain

check. There's a problem at the homestead. Bax just had a run-in with the new bull. Call you later."

I hung up as Brand and I both rushed to Bax, whose ass had landed in a puddle of mud lovingly created by the two straight days of rain we'd just had. His face was drawn from the effort of holding back another wail, and his right leg didn't look exactly straight anymore, but his voice was eerily calm.

Through clenched teeth, he said, "Think y'all may need to call an ambulance."

"Can you move?" I asked.

"Nope. Pretty sure my leg's broken. Heard the bone snap."

Fuck.

Brand got on his phone, and I stayed with Bax. I tried my hardest to occupy his mind, but after two minutes of me reciting a list of did-you-knows about the benefits of cow and sheep shit as cover-crop fertilizer, he let loose his scream at me.

"Shut the fuck up, Rye! Jesus!"

"Sorry, man."

Athena came running from the big balsam poplar tree she'd been playing under with Figaro, my new German shepherd, and the cats I'd picked up from the local shelter to live in the barn and catch mice. She'd named them Factoid, Deltoid, and Altoid.

At nearly fourteen years old, she was so much like her aunt Abey, never afraid to get dirty or work hard. She'd helped me fence in the barn and pastures. The kid could handle an earth auger and a post-hole digger better than Bax, and she'd already driven my new skid steer. She'd been teaching me how to feed and care for the two orphaned lambs I'd picked up at a livestock auction, and I was teaching her how to rope calves on a roping dummy I'd pilfered from my dad.

"Daddy, are you okay?" she said, sliding down next to Bax in the mud.

"Careful!" he yelped. "I'm sorry, Road Trip. I didn't mean to yell. I think my leg is broken. Just don't touch me, okay?"

The nickname Road Trip had made me laugh, but Bax said Athena was so busy, could never sit still longer than a couple minutes. "There she goes again on another road trip," he'd say when she ran off on one of her many adventures.

"I'm sorry, Daddy."

"No, baby. I'm sorry. It hurts, that's all. Just be careful."

"Ambulance is on the way," Brand said, shaking his phone in the air. He came to stand in front of his brother with his hands on his hips. "Well, this sucks a d—" He stopped himself before he said the word "dick" in front of Athena. "I'm gonna have to call Sweetie, ask her to come out here to keep an eye on things for me while I'm gone."

"Sweetie?" Bax looked a little green. He lifted his not-broken leg, bent his knee, and leaned on it, trying to act normal in front of his kid, though, I was pretty sure he was a breath away from another scream. "Not that ball-buster foreman of yours?" He fluttered his hand around his head, like he was caressing imaginary hair. "With the long, dark—"

"Fore*woman*," Brand said. "You don't like her 'cause she beat your ass at poker, but yeah. She's the best, and it doesn't look like you'll be available anymore. We've got multiple builds goin' up. I can't just leave 'em unsupervised while I'm in Sheridan for that ridiculous court case. Where will Mama, Abey, and Devo live this winter if I don't get these houses done?"

"Uh, did you forget somebody?" I asked.

Brand waved me away with a swipe of his hand. "You don't count. We can just keep you in the barn with the horses."

That made Athena giggle, which I hoped had been Brand's intention.

Bax groaned. "Fuck, this hurts. Shit, sorry, Athena. I didn't mean to cuss."

She rolled her eyes. "Please, Daddy. Like I haven't heard worse. Want me to call Granny?"

"God, no."

Brand snorted. "Not unless you want her to pray the pain away. Besides, she's at that retreat with her new church."

Bax glared at his brother. He tried hard to keep Athena sheltered from curse words and her granny's search for the true word of God. Poor kid had been born to the wrong family if he wanted her to escape unscathed.

We heard the sound of tires on the dirt lane leading up to the barn, and we all breathed a little easier. I had just been about to say "that was fast," but then Abey's truck came tearing round the bend, lights flashing.

She parked and jumped out. "What happened? I heard the call on my radio that there was an accident. The ambulance is about five minutes out."

"Yeah," I said. "Bax *accidentally* got caught between a bull and a barn."

"You idiot," Abey said once she'd determined that everyone was alive. Even though she was the youngest of the Lee siblings, she looked down at her oldest brother, her eyes shaded by her brown sheriff's hat, but her exasperation was plain to see. "You know better than that."

Bax leaned his head back against the barn and closed his eyes, still trying to act like he wasn't in a massive amount of pain, but I could see his pulse ticking quickly in the artery on the side of his neck. "That damn bull is sneaky. I swear he was across the pasture when I turned to get the wheelbarrow. I checked."

"Mm-hm," Brand said. "Sure you did."

Bax scoffed. "He's gonna taste good after I roast him on my grill."

"Uh," I said, jumping into their argument, "that bull is a prized breeder. You eat him, you owe me seven grand."

Athena jumped up to hug her aunt. "Where's Devo?"

"She's at the community center today."

Athena frowned. "Oh."

"I'm on duty," Abey said. "I was on this side of town when I heard the call. You're lucky too, 'cause if I hadn't come, it would've been Frank, and he would've thrown your dad over his shoulder and stuffed him in the back of his truck to get him to the hospital."

Bax grimaced at the thought, and Athena sighed and sat by her dad again.

Abey laughed. "If I didn't know any better, I'd think you love Devo more than you love me."

Athena shrugged just as a female voice patched through on Abey's radio.

"Sheriff? You on site? Where the hell is this place?"

Abey rolled her eyes and pulled the transmitter off her shoulder to respond. "I'm here, Sylvia. Did you take the turn I told you to, off old Fish Creek Road?"

"Yep."

"Then just keep drivin' till you see my truck."

"10–4. Got an assessment for me?"

"It's my brother, Bax. Looks like his leg might be broken. He's immobile, in pain, and cranky, but breathin' and talkin'."

"Gotcha. Be there in two. I think."

Abey clipped her radio back onto her shoulder. "Well, who the hell's gonna run this place now?"

"POOR BAX," Aubrey said as she busied herself in front of Bax's kitchen counter, preparing meals for him and Athena. "They said it was a clean break though?"

"Yeah." I leaned back to sneak a peek through the kitchen door to check on Bax in his living room, where he'd passed out on his couch in a pain-medicine haze as soon as we got him home from the hospital, but my hands never left Aubrey's hips.

I held my woman tight. Sometimes, I found it hard to believe she really was mine.

Letting go with one hand, I swiped her hair over her shoulder and whispered my lips over her neck. "He thinks the bull pushed against the gate hard enough so it clipped him at the perfect angle to snap the bone. They had to patch him up with a metal rod inside his leg. He'll probably be cryin' for a few days, but he'll live."

Aubrey loved my hands on her. When I thought she'd had enough and needed space, I'd pull away, but she'd grab me and guide my hands back to her body. She never got enough of my worship, and good thing, 'cause I had a lot of it to give.

"Well, I made them some turkey and veggie soup, and I separated it into containers so Athena can just pop it into the microwave and zap it. Lasagna's next."

Stepping closer, my chest touched her back. Her warmth made me smile, and I had just been about to slip a hand between her thighs when I heard Brand out on the front porch.

"Somebody say lasagna?" he asked when he kicked the kitchen door open with his boot, holding his open laptop.

A female voice sounded from the speaker. "Jeez. Are you ever not thinkin' about food?"

"Can it, Sweetie."

"Don't call me that," Sweetie growled through the computer. "My name is Bea. You know this. Fuckin' use my name, man."

Aubrey whispered, "It won't be ready for dinner tonight, but y'all can bake it tomorrow."

Brand gave her a thumbs-up and whispered back, "Thank you." To Sweetie he said, "Yeah, but if I use your name, you don't get mad, and makin' you mad is the highlight of my day. So when are you gettin' here?"

"Whatever. I'll be there in a few days. I've got some stuff to finish up before I leave, but you don't have to be back in Sheridan till Monday, right?"

"Right, but if everything here is good, I'll probably head back Friday so I've got the weekend to get ready. Maybe Thursday if the lawyers need me early."

Sweetie scoffed. I caught a glimpse of her on Brand's screen just as she rolled her eyes and yanked her hair up, then tied it with an elastic band so it sat atop her head like some kind of black-brown fountain. From the little of her I could see, the woman looked fit. I'd assumed she was more of an "office" forewoman, but it seemed clear she did plenty of the physical labor for Lee Construction.

"They don't think this douche can actually win his case, do they?" she said. "I still can't believe we're in this mess. I literally watched that asshole throw himself off the second floor of our build. He did it hopin' for a payout. You better not let him get one."

"The lawyers are confident," Brand said. "They're pretty

sure they can prove he injured himself on purpose, but we gotta go through the whole rigmarole. Besides, this is why I pay for liability insurance and worker's comp. I feel bad for the guy's wife, though. She seems like a cool lady. I doubt she planned on her husband bein' such a mooch.

"Anyway, one of the cabins is mostly finished, so I'll recruit my niece and we'll get it ready for you, and I'll make sure you have Abey's and Rye's numbers in case anything goes wrong and you can't get ahold of me."

"Good deal," Sweetie said. "I'm pretty stoked I get a free vacation."

Now Brand snorted. "Vacation? You'll work harder here than you ever have in Sheridan."

"Hey! Where's everybody at?" Bax called from the living room in a groggy voice.

"Kitchen," I answered. I couldn't help myself. I turned Aubrey and planted a kiss on her lips.

"Get a room," Brand said, and Aubrey blushed. I felt the heat from her cheeks warm mine, but she didn't stop kissing me. She reached up on her tiptoes to wrap her arms around my neck, careful not to touch me 'cause her hands were covered in tomato sauce.

Bax whined, "Somebody come help me. I gotta take a piss."

Brand laughed. "I'll bring you a bucket."

"I ain't pissin' in a bucket!"

"Empty beer bottle?" I offered between kisses.

"Guys, c'mon!"

Aubrey laughed and moved out of my embrace, and Brand grinned at me.

"Just like old times?" he said.

"Oh yeah."

Aubrey and I followed Brand as he carried his laptop into

the living room and handed it to Athena, who'd just plopped down on the couch next to her dad when she heard him bellyaching.

She studied the little box on the screen with Sweetie's face in it. "Hi."

"Hi," Sweetie said. "Is Bax your dad?"

"Yep."

Bax peered over Athena's shoulder and groaned when he saw his brother's forewoman.

"You look like sh—crap," Sweetie said to Bax.

"You're really pretty," Athena told Sweetie. "Why does Uncle Brand call you Sweetie?"

Sweetie didn't respond to Athena's compliment. There was an awkward pause, but she collected herself. "Because he's dumb. My name is Bea."

"Bee, like buzz buzz?" Athena asked. "That's weirder than Sweetie."

"No, B-E-A as in Beatrice Baker."

"BB," Athena said. "But I still don't get why they call you Sweetie."

"Because I'm *not* sweet, but your uncle thinks it's funny."

"Why aren't you sweet?"

"Because I don't let whiny men off the hook."

"Huh?"

"She's a battle axe," Bax said, "and she's mean."

Sweetie's bark of indignation echoed out of the computer. "Ha!"

Athena rolled her eyes. "Y'all make no sense. I'm more confused now than I was when we started this conversation."

"Never mind," Brand said. "Sweetie, I'll call you tomorrow."

"Fine," she replied, and we heard the little *beep* when she closed out the video call.

Bax's leg had been wrapped groin to ankle in an unbendable brace. The doctors wouldn't cast it until the stitches above his knee came out, so Brand and I converged on Bax. We both held out a hand, he pulled himself up onto one foot, and then we lifted and carried him toward his downstairs bathroom like the time he'd rolled his ankle on the football field and we had to lug his ass to the Wisper High locker room.

"If Sweetie's stayin' here," Bax said, "you better tell that woman I got me a deck of cards with her name on it. I'm gonna whip her ass."

"Yeah, that's the pain pills talkin'," Brand said under his breath, grunting under his brother's weight. "Although, maybe if it's *strip* poker…"

IF YOU LIKED ***Midnight Surrounds Us*, please consider leaving a review—even just a few words would help— wherever you buy your books, Goodreads, or Bookbub.** Self-published indie authors rely heavily upon reviews to get our stories out to the masses. And thank you. I know it takes time to do this. I appreciate the time out of your day and the effort.

DEAR READER,

Thank you for reading *Midnight Surrounds Us*!

If you want to know what happens with Aubrey and Rye a few years down the road, click here to join my newsletter for the password (or go to www.gretarosewest.com/VIPS). There's a super secret page on my website with extra content, and the stuff I wrote for Rye and Aubrey is top-shelf. I think it might be the steamiest thing I've ever written.

I hope you loved this cowboy and his lady as much as I do. It took me a while to write their story. My family and I moved across the country during the crafting and writing of this book, but once I got to Denver and set out to explore the mountains, the story flowed like honey.

And the next book is well on its way.

Bax and Sweetie's story is up next in *Roads Behind Us*, and it's equal parts hot and heartwarming. Coming summer 2025.

xoxo

Greta

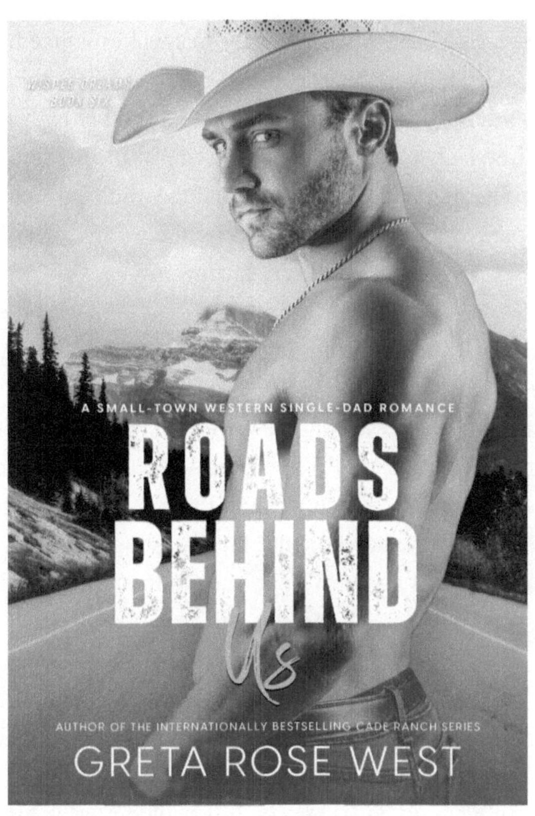

From small-town Western romance author, Greta Rose West, comes a steamy, heartwarming love story, the sixth book in the Wisper Dreams Series, Roads Behind Us. Grab a fan and a hankie, and get ready to fall in love with sexy single dad, Bax Lee, and the grumpy woman who starts his heart again, Sweetie Baker...

Who knew one game of Texas Hold 'Em and a bottle of gin could seal two strangers' fates?

Two years ago, Bea Baker walked away from a dead-end

marriage. She hasn't had a family to speak of since her dad passed, but whether she knew it or not, a family's what she's been searching for. When Brand Lee hired her as his right hand at Lee Construction, she was grateful for his faith in her. To prove it, she takes her job seriously, which earned her the nickname Sweetie, but spoiler alert: she's a hard ass. Screw her southern upbringing.

Bea says what she means, and none of it's sweet.

When she finds herself in her boss's hometown of Wisper, Wyoming, running multiple projects for Lee Construction, Bea's smacked in the face with all the family she could ever want. And at the head of that family is the same guy she decimated in a game of poker one sultry summer night forever ago.

Baxton Lee has his hands full with a teenage daughter and too many memories of the past and all the things he lost. He used to be a farmer; now he's a rancher and a new business owner. He's also a single dad and a widower who guards his heart like Fort Knox.
And when he goes and gets his leg broken by a rowdy bull, he's stuck in a cast, watching the world pass him by and remembering the life he used to have.

Until his brother's forewoman shows up to help build the new Lee Valley rental cabins. Bold and unapologetic Sweetie knocks Bax right back down in the dirt, takes his breath away, and offers him hope for the future.

Too bad she's off limits.

Bax can't afford to love anyone but his daughter anyway. Why go looking for something that could be ripped away at any moment? But when it lands in his lap, he has to figure out whether to continue protecting his heart, or if he should let it grow bigger and give it away.

Join Bax and Bea in the best small town west of the Mississippi, and you might find yourself falling in love too. *Roads Behind Us*, the sixth book in the Wisper Dreams series, is a tale of two lost souls looking for a place to belong again. Throw in a hopeful, meddling teenager, a menagerie of farm animals, and a big ol' found family, and you got yourself a hoedown.

No bison were harmed in the imagining of this story.
COMING SUMMER 2025

ABOUT THE AUTHOR

Greta Rose West was a floundering artsy flake until cowboy Jack Cade showed up, knocking on the door of her brain, pounding on it, and then he just plain kicked it down. She's a boy mom to a grown freakin' man, who has recently gifted her with the title of GRANNY! She comes from the "Region" of NW Indiana, but Greta, her husband, and her two precocious kitties, Geoff Trouble and Sally Mae Midnight, now reside in the Denver, Colorado area, where she often makes her husband drive her out into the mountains so she can look and dream. When she's not writing, she's reading and devouring music. She enjoys indie films no one else likes, and her favorite food is Aver's Veggie Revival pizza.

You can find her on Instagram @gretarosewest, in her Facebook group, Wisperites Unite, or on her website.

gretarosewest.com

facebook.com/gretarosewest

instagram.com/gretarosewest

bookbub.com/authors/greta-rose-west

goodreads.com/gretarosewest